K. A. QUINN

The Demon Within

Modern Chaos Magick Trilogy Book Two

Contents

Chapter One

Eight-year-old Victoria Wight knew she was forbidden from going into the storage shed, and that was what drew her to it the most. When she had asked why, her mother threw her a dark look and sent her to her room before turning back to the tablet screen that captured her frequent attention. Victoria didn't listen.

She slipped past her mother, out the back door and into the backyard. Ahead was the detached garage that had been there long before she was born. The paint was peeling and the structure leaned slightly to the right, but it seemed the perfect playhouse. Dark shapes loomed behind the eight glass panels in the double doors. For a minute she paused, fears of hidden monsters rising in the back of her little girl mind.

Curiosity overcame her, and she moved closer. The splintered edge of the heavy doors pricked her hand as she eased her fingers through the crack. The rusty hinges creaked as she opened the left door just wide enough to slip through, and its weight pushed her in even as she dug her heels into the floor to stop at the entrance.

Everything was covered over with tarpaulins worn dull by heavy dust. She didn't move until her eyes adjusted to the dimness. The large shapes unnerved her, but she firmly reminded herself that treasure hunts required bravery. There was undoubtedly something exciting and forbidden here, and just as a chest of gold lay buried deep in an unstable cave, she would have to root through these wobbly dangerous piles to find it.

The shortest stack nearby was composed of three boxes, which were up to her shoulders. Laboriously, she lowered the top one to the floor and opened the tattered cardboard flaps. They were books, real musty paper books, and she lovingly ran her fingers over the gilded edges of a large antique Bible.

There was a place for a photo in the front, the features too faded to make out in the dimness, so she opened it to see a name in a familiar handwriting. "Olivia." Not a Bible, an old diary. She set it down gently as her eyes focused on a shadow in the far corner of the room.

A piece of the plywood floor was loose on one side. It was undoubtedly the best place to hide treasure, and her heart thrilled with excitement. She dragged a broken rocking chair away and knelt down to pry up the heavy board with her dusty little fingers.

She wrenched it back as far as she could manage, stopping to ease a long splinter from her palm. It revealed a small square dirt hole nearly filled by an old rusty trunk. Reaching down, she found that the latch was already opened, and the lid opened with less force than Victoria expected.

A small, pink knitted blanket covered its contents. It was hard to see in the trunk at first, so Victoria climbed into the hole, which had just enough room for her feet to the right of the trunk. She peered in to see an ugly old doll. As she reached out to lift it up, its skin peeled away, and she began to scream.

Black eyes rimmed in blood stared back at her from a caved-in bluish face that could barely be identified as a baby's corpse. Two rigid hands were stretched towards her. She scrambled back out of the hiding place, dashing away from the terrible sight to see her mother waiting by the back door. She grabbed the woman tightly and sobbed into her waist. But Mother shoved her away with a fury in her eyes that Victoria had never seen before.

"What is it?" Victoria choked, falling to her knees.

"It should have been you," came the soft answer.

"What? Mommy?!"

"You should have been the one to die. I didn't want you." Her mother leaned over, and the girl begged her to take her back inside, but cold hands grasped her neck instead of her arms, and she couldn't breathe. She tried to scream for help, but the world was going black. She struggled to understand what her mother had meant, and a faint memory of a sister, a twin sister, came to her before she lost consciousness.

Twenty-five-year-old Victoria Wight woke up shaking with a raw throat.

"There is no shed," she whispered hoarsely. She struggled to recall the house she'd grown up in and remembered it was half-destroyed now, at the edge of the Accident Zone in southeast Macallister, and it never had a shed at all. Still, unease lingered in her, and the image of the baby's horrible face was burned into her mind. No, she didn't have a sister. That couldn't have happened. And the diary... it was Olivia's. The memory of the smell of burned flesh made her gag.

No, it was just a dream, and she had to get out of bed. In a swift movement, she dashed out of the bed like a little girl terrified of monsters and went to the bathroom for a glass of water. It soothed her parched throat and submerged her panic.

Ever since she found out that she was pregnant, she had disturbing nightmares. Sarintha said it happened sometimes, it was normal, and nothing could be done about it. She knew better. Yesterday she found out she was having twins.

She lingered by the bathroom to peek out the curtains. There it was, the same black car, too expensive for this run-down neighborhood where she and Sarintha lived now. The windows were tinted limousine dark, but she knew someone was inside watching, and she knew she could not go outside for the breath of air she needed.

She and her aunt Sarintha Malik had been under surveillance ever since Michael Esser's killing spree. They had both been cleared of any involvement, the blame pinned unjustly on Ethan Sullivan, but they were still under suspicion of Occult involvement. Victoria felt if she heard any more about the Occult, she'd be sick. Sicker, she corrected, as her stomach lurched in morning sickness that should have been gone by now.

Somewhere, something was very wrong, and she was helpless to stop it.

* * *

"Victoria, I need to tell you something," Sarintha began gently.

The pregnant woman's eyes flashed with fear, as if she already knew. "Just say it."

"Your mother's not coming. She left yesterday, but there's been an accident—"

The laughter came low and harsh. "An accident? Who's responsible this time?"

Would the girl ever trust anyone again? "No one, dear. I've just been speaking with her neighbor, and the train—"

"The train!" Victoria shouted, sounding unhinged. "The train what? It crashed? Am I supposed to be surprised? Nothing fucking works. Let me guess: they don't know why."

"The brakes failed," Sarintha murmured futilely.

"Who did it? You know who did it, don't you?"

She took a deep breath, trying to spread her emotional control to the younger woman. "No one did it. Please don't do this to yourself, not in your condition."

"My condition? I didn't ask for that either!" Victoria clenched her fists tightly, fighting back tears. Softly, she asked, "Couldn't you do something about it?"

"Do what?" This was the first time in eight months that Victoria sounded like she resented her pregnancy.

Victoria's shaking hand clenched her glass hard enough to crack it. A thin trickle of blood dripped onto her sleeve. "Can't you do *anything?*"

"I can't fight your battles for you." Her niece would never know how much she wished she could.

Victoria's face drained of color. "I'll kill them!" she screamed and the glass shattered on the floor. "I didn't ask for this! I just want my life back. Why won't he leave me alone?"

"He's gone, Victoria," Sarintha murmured. "He's already gone."

"No, he's not," she answered, her voice dangerously low. "He's not gone, and he's inside of me, and I won't be a part of it. There's nothing else for him to take. I won't live this way."

4

"Calm down, dear."

"How can you say that? You don't know how it feels! How am I supposed to go on carrying these... these demons?! I won't do it!"

"What do you propose to do then?"

In a flash, she seized a knife from the counter. "It's you or me, now."

Sarintha was baffled. Even at the worst of times, Victoria had never behaved like this, and the older woman detected no outside influences. Naturally, Victoria was under tremendous stress, but this was extreme.

"I know you can do it, Sarintha. I know you can kill me. Go on."

"Stop this nonsense," she said sharply, willing an ounce of reason into the madwoman. "No more talk of this."

"What, you can't? You're a fraud? I'm in pain— *heal me!*"

Sarintha flinched, forcing back the memories of the hospital mercy killings. That wasn't her choice; she'd only followed Richard Aldon's lead. How had Victoria known, when she hadn't said a word about it?

The pregnant woman's voice was growing hoarse. "I can't take this. I'll kill them. You can't stop me."

Sarintha ignored the knife and reached out to her niece.

Victoria dropped it to the floor and began to sob hysterically. "You're all I have left," she gasped.

Sarintha murmured, "I know."

"How am I going to get through this?"

"I'll help you."

Chapter Two

Victoria had never been so close to giving up. She seemed to exist moment to painful moment, and nothing could give her peace. Where were Ethan and her mother? What did her life matter if it was as transient as theirs? What the hell had she contributed to the world? Would it matter more if Ethan were rich or famous or something more than the nothing he'd become? The media would care more.

What had her mother possibly done to deserve this?

She looked at the pungent soup Sarintha had prepared for her, and her stomach turned. There was no point to eating. There wasn't anyone left to care if she died. It was uncomfortably warm on the couch as the memory of the winter chill outside cut through her, and there was no one to keep her warm. Then again, maybe you can get used to anything, even the Accident Zone.

Her aunt's discarded glass of sherry sat across from her, glowing gold in the shaft of winter sunlight from the rear window. Her hands shot out on its own, and in a moment, she had downed the whole glass, the last of the sweetness tingling on her tongue. It did nothing to numb her. She knew the bottle was on the kitchen counter, and she rose stiff-legged towards it, blanket falling to the carpet, light-headed from having stayed still so long.

The knives had been removed. She tried to distract herself with the package of crackers nearby but poured another drink anyway. Soon her nose was burning as if she were about to sneeze, cheeks hot and bottle empty. The pressure was momentarily lifted from Victoria's heart. Then she grew tired, so tired that her legs went limp and darkness brought her to the floor. She didn't move to rise, just let the darkness hold her down until she felt nothing.

She didn't know how long she'd lain there, but Sarintha was back, standing over her, looking furious, voice coming from far away to pierce the fog in her mind.

"You're pregnant, you fool! What were you thinking, drinking that? You didn't eat a bit of the soup, did you?"

Dim shame made her try to stand, but her legs refused. Sarintha hooked her arms under Victoria's with a grunt that made the younger woman wonder if it hurt her. Victoria's voice came out a dry mumble.

"What?" Sarintha had no sympathy.

Victoria started to cry when she realized she couldn't stand on her own. She'd never before felt so stupid and vulnerable. "I can't walk," she tried again, and her aunt hauled her across the tilting room. Sarintha brushed the oily hair out of Victoria's eyes, and guided her to the couch.

"Stay here."

Victoria couldn't do much else while Sarintha vanished, but she dreaded the inevitable confrontation.

Sarintha came back quickly with a glass of water and reheated soup.

Her stomach revolted at the scent.

"Eat it," Sarintha insisted. "Then I'm going to expect a good explanation."

"I can't—"

"Can't what? Eat now, or I'll make you."

She forced down two spoonfuls without choking.

"Now tell me what's going on."

Victoria's mouth moved, but she couldn't will the words to come out. She began to cry, and Sarintha finally softened.

"Tell me."

It all came out at once. "There weren't supposed to be two! Ethan only said one, and now he's gone, and what am I supposed to do?"

"It was lucky that he knew anything, dear. He's not very experienced."

"Luck? I wouldn't expect to hear that from you."

Sarintha just frowned.

Victoria gathered her courage to ask. "What if—what if they're not his children?"

Sarintha stopped breathing for a moment. "What other father could there be?"

She couldn't bring herself to say the name—either name.

Sarintha spared her though, murmuring, "When?"

She could hardly bear to think of it. Swallowing hard, she said, "Before the end, when you were gone. And there was a dream too."

"A dream."

Searching the older woman's eyes, Victoria found that she already understood. Unlike anyone else, Sarintha had spared her an explanation.

"It was too close together to tell."

"There are ways to find out."

She should have guessed Sarintha would find a way, but now that she considered it, she wasn't so certain. How could she reject her own children before they were even born? What if somehow, one was innocent and one was not? How could she choose? Responsibility tempered her hysteria.

"It's too early right now, but after they are a few years older—"

She knew her aunt meant using the Occult. No, she couldn't judge them that way. The children had nothing to do with Richard Aldon or Michael Esser's crimes. She needed to forget about the past and love them for who they would be. "Maybe I don't really want to know. It wouldn't change anything."

Sarintha smiled. "It will be fine. Try not to worry. It will only harm you." She rose suddenly, walking toward the kitchen.

"Where are you going?"

"I'm removing the rest of the sherry. I believe you've had enough."

Shame flooded through her again. "I'm sorry."

"I am not the one who requires an apology, Victoria."

She rested her hand on the swell of her stomach and leaned back on the couch. "Sometimes I think I'll never get through this."

"Write it down," Sarintha commanded, and it made sudden sense.

With an unexpected urgency, Victoria rushed upstairs to her closet to find Olivia's diary, not daring to read the fragile pages with their scrawled handwriting.

Every time she picked up the journal, she heard Ethan's voice mocking her. *"You didn't even read the damn diary..."*

She didn't know why she kept the book. Perhaps she felt it would somehow be useful someday, but just the thought of it made her feel sick. She tried to read it again, to understand what Richard had done to her, but every time she touched the cover, a panic seized her and she'd put it away.

It seemed appropriate to finish Richard's story in this book. Maybe someday, everyone would know the truth. She owed it to Ethan, at least.

Victoria put pen to brittle paper and began to fill up Olivia's journal, writing for hours without rest, then put it away to forget forever.

* * *

"Sarintha, have you ever killed anyone?" Victoria asked suddenly one afternoon.

"Don't worry, dear, I can take care of you," she answered, not meeting the younger woman's eyes.

"That's not what I asked." She wouldn't let Sarintha change the subject so easily. Even if it would change her opinion of her aunt, Victoria had to know.

"Then why would you ask a question like that?"

"You said you wouldn't kill Richard, before."

"Now's not the time to be thinking of that." Why did Sarintha insist on keeping things from her?

"He wasn't the only one you would have killed, was he?" Victoria pressed.

Sarintha sat down and sighed, rubbing her palms together, avoiding her niece's gaze and spoke carefully. "Just because you can do a thing doesn't mean you should. But sometimes you don't know your capabilities until they're tested."

Terribly roundabout, but it was an answer. Victoria didn't know whether to be relieved or nervous. Desperate times, she reminded herself.

"Why did you leave him?" It had taken so much before Victoria learned the truth about Richard.

Anger brightened Sarintha's eyes. "He was *wrong*."

"Well then, why did you join him in the first place?"

"You know what he can do. And when I was all alone, my family gone, who could I turn to?"

Victoria remembered her father's funeral and how Sarintha had walked out without saying goodbye to her half brother. They'd both been so angry, for different reasons. "Maybe you could have talked to me. Or Mother."

"Don't be ridiculous," she replied, but her heart wasn't in it. "You were too young, and your mother was teaching you I was some sort of crackpot." Her aunt tugged at the seam of her shirt, a rare gesture of anxiety. "He gives false hope. He pretends to be kind to take advantage of you."

With a flash, Victoria imagined another funeral: Richard Aldon rubbing Olivia's shoulder, saying, "I'm so sorry about Lawrence. If there's anything you need, just ask."

How had Sarintha turned out differently? Was she a tool more than a toy? "It's hard to believe he's gone," Victoria said, by way of awkward consolation.

"Richard?" She looked up. "He's not gone, not entirely. I just hope they can't call him back."

Victoria choked. No, he was *dead,* she saw him dead, but she'd seen him dead once before: Richard Aldon's body lying on the bloodied rug, after he'd released himself into Michael Esser. No one touched him the second time. Sarintha wouldn't let anyone touch him until she was sure he was gone, until the final bits of fog lifted from their minds as he faded away.

Sarintha had been following her thoughts. "Yes, he's insubstantial, and the more time goes by, the more likely we're safe. But that doesn't mean someone can't channel him if he hasn't completely dissipated."

There was no reasonable way to stop him, no logical possibility of incarcerating a spirit. Any deliberate attempt to manipulate him risked permanent possession. She had to look toward more obscure answers. "Can't we curse him?"

Her aunt seemed disappointed that Victoria had even entertained the possibility. "We could try, but we'd have to pay for it. And he died in a place of power, so it would be a high price."

"It should have been me who died. None of this was Ethan's fault. I should have fought Esser—"

"You can't bring Ethan back," Sarintha said abruptly.

"Can't I?" she asked quietly. "Can't you? Or will you just lie to me again?"

"Listen to me. If you brought him back, you'd bring back Esser and Richard too. Even you can't be foolhardy enough to want that."

"Are you sure?"

"They died together, by each other. They're bound together now. If Ethan's lucky, he's gone to oblivion."

"You mean Richard might still be hurting him somewhere?" Victoria's guilt worsened. "We have to help him."

"I doubt there's anything left to help. He's a shadow of a person now, disintegrating as time goes on. He's given you children. Be happy with what you have."

* * *

Victoria couldn't take it anymore. The confinement was just too long, and whatever might be lurking outside the little townhouse couldn't be worse than this. She could barely breathe in here. It was time to go.

Eight months pregnant wasn't a good time to run off, a sensible voice in the back of her mind told her. She ignored it and slammed the front door.

It was a beautiful day, unseasonably warm for late November. The bright sun still flashed behind her quickly closed eyelids. She opened them again reluctantly, shading her eyes with her hand until they adjusted from her long indoor isolation.

They lived not too far from her childhood neighborhood, but it neighborhood wasn't familiar anymore. It was a wreck. The occupants of the street seemed to have taken their frustration of their computers very seriously. Monitors, their flat screens twisted, lay with their guts exposed to the sky.

Splintered circuit boards shone in the sun, and Victoria recalled the riots during her childhood when the old cell phones were declared obsolete, the fury of people too poor to afford new electronics. Victoria cringed and wondered what the residents would do to people who crossed them.

The first spasms came to her, as if warning her or chastising her for her foolishness. Victoria gasped and slowly made her way home.

* * *

Victoria thought she'd be relieved that her pregnancy was over, but she didn't know the first thing about taking care of children. Rhianna and Sam were more difficult than she could have imagined. They were constantly hungry, and when one cried, the other began to scream in response, and she hadn't slept well in weeks.

Then came the pain. Her body seemed heavier and wearier than during her pregnancy, and her legs felt as if they would barely support her. Climbing down the stairs became difficult enough that she stayed in her bedroom all day.

Sarintha brought up lunch and adjusted the blanket that covered the infants.

"Sarintha, why do I feel this bad? Can't you do something?"

She looked down. "What could I do?"

Victoria sat up with a cracking sound in her back and grasped her aunt's hands. "I know you can help me."

She shook her head. "You just need time to recover."

She wouldn't do anything? Victoria was supposed to stay like this forever, every day getting harder, until she died? She gritted her teeth and squeezed Sarintha's hands.

The older woman flinched and pulled away. "There was no need for that."

She'd sensed the pain; Victoria knew it. "Damn it, I hate this! Sarintha, is someone doing this to me?"

Her aunt looked angry and glanced at the ceiling to hide it. "I don't think so. I think it's stress."

"When's it going to go away?" She cringed at the desperate tone in her voice, and the babies began to cry.

Sarintha went to the crib to fuss over Rhianna and Sam until they quieted, then turned to regard her carefully. "Just how hard did you try to save Ethan?" she asked slowly.

She didn't think she could take hearing his name at a time like this, but then she understood. "You mean this is his pain?" she ventured.

"Not exactly." Sarintha seemed uncomfortable.

"What, do you think I'm crazy?" Victoria burst out, despite herself.

"No. I don't want to hear that nonsense. I think... you've taken away more than his pain. There's a fine line, and maybe you took a little death into you by giving too much."

She had to have misheard. "What! I'm going to die? Why was I fine before?" The room seemed to rotate slightly.

"No, no. It's what killed Esser, but I doubt you will get worse, but you'll... suffer. I don't know how to overturn it. You may have to live with it."

It was too much to process. "Why now? That was back in the spring."

"The children... they were likely helping you. And so was your own body as long as it could. I'm sorry, I don't know enough about this."

Somehow, she felt betrayed. "I don't see how you know *anything* about this. No one has done it to you."

Sarintha raised her chin. "Richard used to take us to hospitals. We'd help people... or so I thought." And that was all she'd say.

Chapter Three

"Don't you hear the ghosts?" eight-year-old Rhianna Wight asked with a superior smirk that overshadowed her feigned concerned glances toward the closet.

"Where?" Sam asked his sister, instantly afraid, despite himself.

She rolled her eyes. "They're everywhere."

His skepticism returned. "Don't tease me." Rhianna always teased.

"It's true, can't you tell? Would I lie?"

"That's not funny," Sam grumbled and crossed his arms.

"I'm not *being* funny. I bet I can talk to one."

"No, you can't." But his interest was piqued, and she knew it.

"Can too."

"Go on. Show me," he demanded.

She tossed her blonde hair, closed her eyes, and stretched her little arms out from sides, palms up. "Oh, spirits, come to me," she moaned.

Sam snorted.

She abandoned her dramatic pose and smacked him. "Shut up! You'll ruin it."

"It won't work. Nothing to ruin."

"Oh, really? Do *you* know how?"

Sam bit his lip. He knew he wasn't supposed to say, but he was sure something good was in the red book hidden in Sarintha's room. He hadn't told Rhianna where to find it, just enough to tease her and lord his secret over her.

She was watching him expectantly. "I didn't think so."

He battled with himself for a minute. He really didn't want to tell, but she was looking at him in that annoying way. "All right. Come on."

Her eyes lit up. "Right."

Sam looked around quickly around the small lower level and climbed the stairs while creeping along the wall, pretending to be a spy, even though his own room was also up there. At the top of the stairs, he paused to listen, and Rhianna shoved him forward.

He shoved her back and ducked his head around the corner. "All clear."

"Just go," she demanded.

"Fine, I'm not going to tell you."

"I already know."

"No, you don't. You've never been in Nanny's—" He hadn't caught himself in time.

She smiled smugly and marched forward.

"You still don't know where in there!" Sam yelled, and caught his breath when his mother came out of her bedroom.

"What's going on out here? What have I told you about fighting, Sam?"

He drew back from her anger. She always thought he was doing something bad.

Rhianna put on her best sweet-little-girl face. "Sam's been in Nanny's room, Mommy. He looked at her books."

Victoria went red and grabbed his shirt. "I told you *never* to go in there by yourself. Did you listen? No."

Sam tried not to twist away, knowing it would get him in more trouble. "I wasn't by myself. Nanny was there—"

Her frown grew darker. "I thought Nanny had more sense than that. But that doesn't matter. You know that what I say is more important than what Nanny says."

Sam glanced over at Rhianna who was smiling angelically. "It's not fair."

"What's not fair?" Victoria asked coldly.

"Rhianna was just going to go in there, and she didn't get in trouble."

"If she was going to go in there, you should have stopped her. Besides, she didn't, did she? Go to your room, right now, and I don't want to see you until tomorrow."

"I'm hungry!" Sam whined.

"I don't care. You should have thought about that before you broke the rules."

Sam knew it was useless. Maybe Nanny would be on his side, but she wasn't home right now. He dragged his feet to his room and slammed the door, hearing his mother mutter, "Little nightmare," and then the loud sound of Rhianna asking for a snack.

He wished there were ghosts. Then he'd have someone who always listened to him.

* * *

"Mommy where's Daddy?" Rhianna asked directly, sounding much younger than her age. She curled up onto her mother's lap, her blonde hair soft against Victoria's arm.

Victoria frowned at her. She had made sure her children didn't feel something was missing in their lives. "You don't have a daddy. You have a nanny instead," was the best she could manage. How could Rhianna always manage to touch sore points so innocently? And seeing the sadness in her daughter's eyes, she asked, "Aren't we good enough?"

Something flickered in Rhianna's face. "Maybe. But I want a daddy." More quickly, she continued, "And maybe Sam wouldn't be so bad if he had a daddy."

Victoria felt the anger flare in her unexpectedly. "You don't want Sam's daddy."

"What do you mean?" she pounced. "Sam's daddy's different from my daddy?"

Once the words were said, she knew Rhianna would never forget them. The girl thrived off of new knowledge. "No, of course not." She didn't want to think about that. There was no way to explain to a child.

Rhianna sniffled. "I'm sorry. I love you, Mommy."

She swept her daughter up in her arms and wiped her tear away. "Oh, baby, what can I do to make you feel better?"

"I don't know," she moaned.

"What about that doll at the store you wanted?"

"They're all gone! You said they'd all be gone! She was so beautiful," she said softly.

"They might still have one. You and Nanny could look."

"I don't want Sam to go!"

"No, he can stay in his room." The boy seemed to like it best there anyhow.

* * *

Sam lay in bed that night, wishing more than ever that he wasn't alone. The summer sunset still glowed sherbet orange through the blinds, casting a thin stripe on the floor. Dust motes danced through it like the butterflies he wasn't allowed to catch outside. He thought about his loneliness while the room darkened. He stared at the same spot, holding the sunlight in his memory. Something billowed, like a sheer curtain in a gust of wind, and a shape coalesced.

It was vaguely human-shaped, roundish at the top then spreading out triangularly at the bottom like a person in a robe. Sam watched the still figure curiously but soon had to blink, which wavered the ghost away. He called out softly, disappointed that his new friend was gone.

He tried not to blink this time, gazing intensely until his head began to ache, and there it was again, and it moved closer. He reached out, and his hand passed into the grayness and began to tingle. He closed his eyes for a moment to wish the headache away, and something came from the ghost, a whiteness that soothed his forehead and eased the ache in his heart.

* * *

"Hello," Rhianna said to the empty air near her bed. "What do you want?"

She wasn't afraid, but she knew someone was there. A soft off-color cloud was affixed in the air.

She had seen ghosts before. She even knew how to make them, or something that looked like them, if she crossed her eyes just right and made the sparkles in the air come together in a sphere. But this was different. She hadn't made him, and she hadn't invited him.

He felt just like a person, with normal feelings and dreams, but he was invisible. Maybe he could teach her how to be invisible too, and then she could go anywhere she wanted. Tentatively, she focused on him with her mind, just as she did when making ghosts, but instead of moving him, she gave a poke to let him know she saw him.

She felt it latch onto her, making a soft fuzziness in her head, the feeling she had when she was about to fall asleep. It was pleasant and relaxing, so she let it grow. It spread from her head down through her fingers and toes. Now she thought she was nearly floating, and it thrilled her.

She thought it was trying to talk to her, but its voice was too quiet or far away to hear. She tried to concentrate on it, to hear better, but she must have accidentally pushed it away, because she was jolted back into her too-hot skin.

"Hello?" she asked again into the darkness.

She couldn't sense him any longer, but a thin connection remained, a reassurance that he'd come again soon, and she'd never be lonely again.

Chapter Four

Sam wasn't supposed to be outside alone, and he was sure he wasn't supposed to talk to strangers. He frowned at the uninvited man in the gray suit. The man leaned down and tried to offer him a piece of chocolate. "I don't know you," Sam declared loudly.

"I don't know you either. Don't you ever go outside to play?"

There was really no room to play, except in the road, and this man had come from the big car that he saw parked on it everyday. He knew he shouldn't answer.

"Who are you?" Sam demanded, close to solving the mystery of the black car.

"Mr. Pulaski. I'm a friend of your mother's."

"No, you're not," he said. He was sure that Mommy wouldn't like this man, not his suit or his false smile or his candy.

Pulaski saw he was losing and broke off a piece of the chocolate. "Guess I'll have to eat it myself, then."

Sam scowled deeper, feeling he was being teased. "Fine. I'll go get Mommy." She would know what to do.

The man grabbed his T-shirt sleeve. "No, why don't we talk for a minute?"

"No. Let me go." He twisted away and wondered where Sarintha and Rhianna were. They were supposed to be out any minute, so he'd come out ahead of them.

"What's your name?" Pulaski tried again, patting Sam's shoulder.

"Go away!" Sam shouted and turned to pound on the front door. "Nanny!

Mommy!"

The man looked angry and turned to leave when Sarintha stepped out, face blazing with fury. "Who are you, and what are you doing to my boy?"

Pulaski's brow furrowed and he said officially, "Nothing, ma'am. I seem to be at the wrong house."

She glared at him hard enough that he stepped back. "I know what you want, and I'd better not see you here again. If I catch you disturbing Victoria, you'll find your answers in the most unpleasant way."

Sam had never seen her so angry, and he was impressed at the way she made Pulaski swallow and back off. He thought in that moment he loved Sarintha more than anything.

She grasped his hand a little too hard, ushered him in and slammed the door. Then she knelt in front of him. "What did he ask you?"

Sam bit his lip, wondering if he was in trouble. "My name, and he had candy, and said he knew Mommy."

"Is that all?"

"I think so." He couldn't remember clearly after all the excitement.

"His name is Officer Pulaski, and Mother does know him, but she doesn't like him."

He felt a thrill about being trusted with the information and finding he was right. "I didn't tell him anything!" he said excitedly. "And he grabbed my arm, right here, and I called for you."

She smiled and patted his head. "Good boy. Tell me right away if he comes again. Let's get you a cookie."

Sam savored the cookie like a trophy and noticed Rhianna peering from on top of the stairs, cookieless and missing her promised walk.

* * *

Andrew Pulaski had been waiting all day for the little girl and her great aunt to come out for their walk, and he was surprised to see the little sullen boy. His records did show that Victoria Wight had twins, but he had begun to wonder if something had happened to the other one.

Why was the child kept inside constantly? It seemed a bit extreme, even for recluses, and Pulaski's suspicion went up a notch. He honestly didn't see how the family could be dangerous subversives, but something odd was going on.

The Indian woman, Sarintha Malik, was the one he really distrusted. He'd faced down gunmen, but somehow she genuinely shook him. And that threat she made was just vague enough that he couldn't incriminate her on it, but it seemed to show she knew what he was after.

When he'd come upon the two women and the dead bodies in the Accident Zone, Sarintha Malik had been too collected. At the time, he had checked to see if she was a veteran from the war, which would be a plausible explanation, but she wasn't. Old ladies just weren't that stolid in the face of murder in a nuclear explosion site. Surely at one point she'd been involved in the Occult, even if he didn't have any proof. Right now, she seemed to be as clean as a whistle, and he was wishing for a more interesting assignment.

Pulaski knew he'd have to be subtler in the future, but he decided to give the little girl a try. She seemed an average, doted-on child and quite talkative, just like his pride and joy, Ellie. It was a shame that Rhianna's guardians wouldn't let friends over. Maybe he'd find a reason to get her to come out of there, and then Rhianna and his daughter could visit.

Now, there was an idea. His wife would kill him if she knew what he was doing, but maybe Ellie could get Rhianna talking. And he could get transferred out of this crappy part of town to play spy on someone actually criminal. Angela hated his long hours, so she'd approve... indirectly. He'd have to hurry back before she got home.

* * *

Rhianna was intensely jealous that Sam had seen the bad guy and she hadn't. Plus she hated being stuck inside when it was so nice. She'd just have to go on her own walk. Sarintha was upstairs telling Sam not to tell Mommy what happened, and they were arguing again. Mommy was in her room as usual, reading those old paper books Rhianna wasn't allowed to touch. She wondered if she'd ever be old enough and why those musty, fragile things were interesting anyway.

It was perfectly warm and bright by the front door. She shaded her eyes and looked for the bad guy, eager for adventure. As many toys as she had, she was still bored. And then, she spotted him, a balding man walking hand-in-hand with a little girl wearing a much nicer dress than Rhianna's used one.

Rhianna knew him instantly by his formal walk, pale skin, and his too-fancy suit, unlike any of the clothes she spied the neighbors wearing. He was new and interesting, so she watched him closely. He didn't look comfortable, actually, and she was proud of herself for noticing. Someone down the road started shouting for no reason, and the man increased his pace.

Rhianna thought she'd see what he wanted from them.

She strode right up to Officer Pulaski and cocked her head. "What do you want?"

His mouth quirked. "I'm just going for a walk."

"Who are you?" she addressed the red-haired girl in the sky blue dress with pretty lace.

"Ellie," she whispered and held the man's hand more tightly.

Rhianna immediately didn't like her. She looked Ellie in the eyes. "You don't belong here." It was a simple statement, and it seemed to bother the man because he put his hand around her waist and drew her in close.

"What do you want?" she tried again. "Mommy doesn't like you. You should go away."

"That's not very polite. Aren't you lonely? Maybe you and Ellie would like to play."

Ellie asked softly, "What's your name?"

"Rhianna," she answered. This new girl didn't seem worth playing with at all, the way she was cowering behind the man. Rhianna bet she was easy to scare. "Do you believe in ghosts? I do. I have one in my room."

The little girl sniffed. "Aren't you scared of it?"

"No. I can call him outside if you want to see him."

"I like dolls," she mumbled.

"You're right, this isn't a good place for ghosts. The best place to find ghosts is in a graveyard. Want to come?"

Despite the warmth and sunshine, Ellie was as frightened as if she were already there. She shook her head quickly.

"You're boring, you know."

"Hey!" Pulaski stepped in. "Be nice to her."

Rhianna looked him steadily in the eyes. "I am being nice. Leave us alone, or you'll find out what not nice is."

He blinked and ushered Ellie away, and Rhianna was sure Ellie was crying. Maybe they wouldn't come back.

* * *

"This can't continue," Sarintha began with her unquestionable authority.

"What can't?" Victoria asked and regretfully put her book on her lap. When Sarintha was in this mood, there was no use ignoring her.

"You have to go outside. The police are suspicious."

"Suspicious of what? I'm not doing anything wrong."

"You need to get a job."

"I—" She cut herself off with a laugh. "I can barely walk. Are we running out of money, is that it?" Sarintha hadn't been clear about how much of her retirement money they had left, but at least it hadn't been seized.

"Frankly, yes, but that's not the point. The police are watching you, Victoria. They've spoken to Sam."

How dare they frighten her children! "What the hell do they want? What do they think they're doing? We haven't done anything wrong!" She struggled to her feet as a wave of fear overtook her.

"You're wasting away, Victoria, and I'll be no part of it anymore."

"Any *part?* What—" Then the guilt hit her, and she remembered that she was living in Sarintha's home, and the woman was virtually a full-time caretaker for her children. Victoria hadn't wanted this to happen, but neither had her aunt. Apologizing didn't seem enough, so she didn't even try. She sighed. "Well then, where will I work? Who wants a disabled ex-librarian?"

Sarintha looked at her so pointedly that she was embarrassed.

"The library? None of the computers work there either."

Sarintha stared down at the book on Victoria's lap.

"Damn it, do you always know everything?" she sputtered stupidly.

She commented, "I've heard they'll be used for fire fuel this winter."

That was it. She couldn't let that happen, and Sarintha had known it. Victoria's legs gave out, and she sank to the bed. "What about the public records?"

"The government's seized the building. They need someone who can take care of these files, organize them, and it seems a good way to ingratiate yourself to them."

She had the whole thing planned out, didn't she? "Ingratiate? I should be so lucky. If they come near the house again, I'll—"

"You'll do what? You can't do anything from this bed, Victoria. You must take care of yourself and your children, or you can't stay here any longer. I'm sorry, but it must be done."

The dark eyes were stern, and Victoria was certain she meant it. Sarintha held out her cane, and she took it reluctantly, afraid of what lay outside the front door.

Chapter Five

The sunlight flashed off the tinted windows of the ever-present black car. Victoria averted her eyes, her heart racing as she heard the window roll down, but then she thought of Sam talking to the policeman. If her child could be that brave, surely she could make a good impression herself.

She relaxed her spine and tried to walk smoothly. "Hello," she offered and couldn't think of anything else.

"Are you Mrs. Wight?" the balding man asked.

With a start, she was reminded of how many months it had been since she spoke to a man. He was a little too plump for his suit, and he didn't remind her at all of Esser. That was little reassurance though. "Miss Wight," she corrected, "and yes. How may I help you?"

"Name's Pulaski. Those twins your kids?" He was trying to sound friendly.

"Yes. I... haven't been well." She gestured with her cane.

"Need a hand?"

Her instinct was to be angry, but she realized he could help. Maybe he could finally see she was just a normal person. It took all of her courage, but she answered, "Yes, I need a ride to the library, if you would."

"Hop in."

She climbed in the back carefully, trying not to strain herself. At least there wasn't a grill separating them, like an official police car. She would have felt caged. The car was spacious and extremely loud, being the gasoline-powered sort that hadn't been made in ages.

She looked up at the house as they pulled off and saw Rhianna staring after her from her upstairs window. She felt a twinge of guilt that wouldn't go away.

"So, you lived here long?" called Pulaski over the sound of the motor.

She bit her tongue. Of course he knew; he'd been spying on them for months, but she just smiled. "Since my children were born." She couldn't resist, suddenly remembering the game that was social interaction. "That was eight years ago. Were you around then too?"

Pulaski scowled. "What do you mean?"

"Are you a police officer or national security? I'd just like to get to know you better. I'm a librarian." She should back down. Suddenly she wondered what danger she was putting herself in and how far she would go to protect her family. There were no door handles or buttons back here; she couldn't get out.

He skirted the question. "Librarian, that's nice. I remember them paper books. Suppose we'll be using them again, hmm?"

"I imagine so. I'm hoping to get back to work, to help out with the transition. Do you know anyone involved with that?"

"Mmm?"

"I heard the federal government's coordinating it. We could have used a government grant before. The local budgets were so low."

"Just why would you be interested in that?" He thought he was clever, that she'd slip up and say something suspicious.

"I told you, I'm a librarian. I'd like to get back to work."

"Hmm…" In the rear view mirror, his expression lit up a little, like it had been his idea.

Victoria realized that if she left the house more, she'd be easier to observe for suspicious activity. Maybe the surveillance at home would stop.

"Come to think of it, I do know somebody. I'll give you his info after I drop you off. He's a little busy, though, so you might have to wait a while."

"Oh, I expected to, dropping in unannounced." She tried to imitate his casual tone to reassure him, but he didn't talk again until they arrived. He handed her a little business card and wished her good luck.

26

"Thanks. And sometime when you're sitting out there in that hot car, maybe come in for some iced tea?"

He smiled, and she saw him put a headset in his ear as he drove off with the sound of a growling motor. She was nearly giddy with relief.

* * *

Stepping into the library filled Victoria with nostalgia, and the thought that she wouldn't see her old sexist boss, Jas, made her smile. But the front desk seat was now filled by a big, dark uniformed guard, whose formal demeanor was surely scaring off most people who would want to visit. He would probably have scared her off too, but she clenched the handle of her cane for reassurance and waited for him to finish his phone call.

His face was the same as on the business card labeled "Jackson," so she started with, "Your friend Mr. Pulaski dropped me off."

He didn't look surprised. Or anything at all, actually.

She tried again. "I used to work here. I'll bet you need some help preserving the paper books."

"I suppose." He barely moved.

"I'd like to help, if you have a position open."

"Victoria Wight, is it?"

She hadn't given him her name, so obviously this had to do with his phone call. "Yes, that's right. I worked here a few years ago."

"Do you have a security clearance?"

"Uh, no. I could get one if you told me how." This wasn't such a good idea after all. She hadn't worked in years; the police were watching her. It would never work.

Jackson touched his earpiece again, pretending she wouldn't notice. "No problem, I can get you one. Would you like a tour of the place?"

She nodded and he rounded the desk. He was bigger than she thought, but his gestures were suddenly friendly.

To her surprise, no one else was there. Piles of papers and useless old discs littered the tables and desks, and most of the servers were still intact. The government's acquisition must have been very recent.

She had heard that at first they'd blamed the malfunctions on the software and hardware companies and had spent years trying to sue them before they realized the problem was too widespread to blame on a single corporation. Microchips just weren't working well anymore.

It looked as if some government office started printing files out a few years ago and threw them in envelopes as best as they could. The thick, jumbled folders were interspersed with little scraps with notes written on them. A torn post-it caught her attention. On it was scrawled, "R. Aldon."

She backed out of the little room into Jackson and struggled to compose herself. His thick eyebrow was raised, and he was watching her too closely. Damn it, she wasn't going to let a name upset her, even if this whole thing was a test. She forced a laugh and mumbled, "You need a miracle."

Jackson seemed appeased and laughed loudly in return. "It's not as bad as you think. See those big drawers? We're just working on alphabetizing this mess, then we'll try to create an index. I don't know how my great grandpa used to do this."

She warmed toward him a little, now that he was out of security mode. "Was he a librarian, then?"

He shook his head. "Some kind of accountant. Can you imagine? People used to do payroll and taxes all by hand, just calculators, and big charts. Took them years to learn how."

Victoria thought for a minute. "Have you seen any books on cataloguing, maybe textbooks? I thought we used to have some in the paper reference section."

He bit his lip. "It's a huge mess, but I think most everything's still there, except for restricted things. Want to check?"

She knew he meant books referencing the Occult, which had long since been destroyed. Still, she nodded and followed him.

She stepped up the stairs and was met by a sense of homecoming. Other than large boxes by the doorway, the room looked nearly the same, except that everything had been misshelved during some untidy search. There under the bookshelf was where she'd found Olivia's journal. No, she didn't want to think about that now. They split up and got to work searching through the antiques.

Victoria made a triumphant sound when she found a filing manual and waved it in the air.

Jackson seemed as pleased as she was. "If you plan on coming back, you can borrow it to look over."

Without hesitation, she agreed. The opportunity seemed so satisfying that she couldn't resist. They went downstairs together, Jackson leading.

"Did you know that down there in the Accident Zone, they found a whole warehouse full of paper files on people? They shipped them all here to the regional office, and they threw away everything on people who had died. Said they didn't have enough space."

She had to agree, looking at the mess the library had become. "And the files still aren't sorted yet?"

"It's a major project. I'd be surprised if it ever got done."

"We can do it. It just requires organization." She'd just volunteered herself again but felt no guilt. Who knew what she could learn, working here?

"You on board then?"

"Certainly, if you'll have me." She didn't go as far as saying she was the best person for the job. He'd see that for himself in time, no matter what his motive.

"You're hired. I'll get to work on that security clearance. It's just me here now, so I'll appreciate the help. See you tomorrow then?"

She nodded and patted the antique book. She felt truly useful again.

* * *

Victoria hung up her coat by the door and turned to see Rhianna sitting glumly at the bottom of the stairs. "Hi, sweetie."

The girl didn't cheer up.

"What's wrong?"

"Where did you go?" Rhianna asked, her voice raised in the pitch that indicated an upcoming tantrum. "Why didn't you tell me you were going?"

Victoria's knees cracked as she sat next to her daughter. "I went out. Nanny should have told you."

"I didn't ask her."

Victoria smiled and teased, "Whose fault is that, then?"

Rhianna's eyes flashed, and she wanted to apologize. The girl never took even gentle criticism well.

"I missed you too. I have good news though. I have a job now."

It astounded her that Rhianna looked confused by this. How much had she sheltered her children? She explained, "I'll be going out for a while each day, but we'll have more money. You might be able to go out more too."

"Will the man in the car go away? I saw you go with him. I was afraid."

She had seen her leave then. "I hope so. He was just giving me a ride today." She might need to rely on him for a while as there was no public transit anymore.

"I don't like him. He's a bad man. I don't like the girl either."

"What girl? Wait, did he speak to you?"

"Yes, I saw him after Sam did. He had a girl with him. Her name was Ellie. She was boring."

Victoria hadn't known Pulaski had a family. It upset her that he had spoken to her children alone, but perhaps bringing his daughter to this part of town was a kind gesture. Or a reckless one. "I don't think he's a bad man. He's only doing his job."

Rhianna stared at her feet sullenly.

An idea came to her. "Would you like it if Ellie came back, even if she is boring?"

Rhianna twisted her mouth in thought, then brightened. "Maybe."

"She'll be more fun once you get to know her. She could keep you company sometimes while I'm at work. If Mr. Pulaski would allow it."

Rhianna was on the edge of tears again, and Victoria's head started to pound. "How long will you be gone? I don't want you to go!"

Her cries carried up the stairs, where Sarintha and Sam had come to the landing. Sarintha smiled and patted Rhianna on the head. "Congratulations, Victoria."

She smiled weakly. "Thank you. It was a good idea."

Sam frowned. "What's going on?"

"I was just telling Rhianna I've gotten a job. It's good news! And she's met someone who wants to be your friend."

Sarintha raised her eyebrows. "We may need to think about that," she disagreed.

Sam looked back and forth between them and guessed, "The bad man has a kid? I don't like him."

Victoria sighed. "If we're nice to him, he'll stop watching us. Besides, the girl may be very friendly."

Sarintha narrowed her eyes but said nothing.

"You're going away?" Sam tried to clarify.

"No, no. Just a few hours a day. We'll have lots of money and get lots of new things."

"I don't care!" Rhianna said passionately and grabbed at her leg like a toddler.

Victoria sighed and stood up, shaking her off. It would be good to get away from the children a bit. "It's the way it has to be. I made the choice, and I'm not going to change it."

The wailing grew louder as Victoria went up to her bedroom. Sarintha would calm them down.

But Sarintha was following her with a determined look on her face. Her aunt ushered her into Victoria's bedroom. "I didn't intend that you should take fraternizing that far."

She set her teeth. "Do you mean Ellie? What harm can a little girl do?"

"More than you know. Little girls don't always tell the truth."

That was ridiculous, she thought. Rhianna never lied.

"What if they have an argument? It could be misconstrued. The situation could get worse."

Suddenly the strain of the day began to break her. "Sarintha, I'm trying everything I can to make our lives normal again. It's a start. They'll play a few times, Rhianna will relax around strangers, and then maybe I can find a way to send her to school."

Sarintha seemed to be too concerned about the situation. There seemed to be something larger troubling her, as always. Victoria knew Sarintha wouldn't explain; she never did.

"I want her to make friends. The other children won't come around our house because of the police. God knows what their parents have said to them. If just one girl comes here, they'll see it's not true. And so will Mr. Pulaski."

"That's oversimplified," the older woman said tightly.

"I'll ask to meet the girl. I don't even know how old she is," she realized. "I am a little suspicious too, but I think it will turn out fine. It's worth a try."

Sarintha's frown grew deeper. "I'll meet her as well."

"That sounds fine. You know I trust your judgment."

Sarintha shook her head and left the room to comfort the still crying Rhianna.

It didn't matter what Victoria did. Someone always thought she was wrong. She picked up her cataloguing book, filled with trepidation about beginning a new life.

* * *

It wasn't so hard. Victoria had to work up the courage to ask Pulaski for a ride again, and he quickly mentioned that he drove past there regularly. She doubted it was true, but if it made him leave her house occasionally, it was worth the anxiety to ride with him every day. The third shift surveillance officer, whose name she didn't know, often didn't come by every night.

The management at the library was different, but the books were the same. And the new information, the classified paperwork, was simply fascinating. She looked for folders with her name, or anyone familiar, but they seemed to be absent, no doubt on purpose. She couldn't even find the note with Richard's name on it again.

Even so, Jackson treated her very well, and he seemed to enjoy working with her. Every day after she fled from Pulaski's car, he greeted her with a smile.

The silence was unusual though. The library had always been quiet, but without public computer terminals, no one entered at all. She was beginning to hope someone would come just to ask directions, but no one new had come to the town for a long time.

Still, it made her more grateful for company when Rhianna welcomed her home each day.

Chapter Six

Deep within the Accident Zone, the remains of Richard Aldon's cult were looking for a way out of their obscurity. Since Esser had died, they had stagnated and begun bickering among themselves until only three were left.

"Who is this girl?" Lori asked uncertainly. They had been involved in many questionable activities before, but never the kidnapping of a child. She couldn't say why it unsettled her; perhaps the mother in her was rebelling. If they had suggested taking the girl's life in an instant, as her own Aubrey had died, that was different, painless and fleeting, but surely abduction and separation from her family would be agony for the girl.

Although she had to admit, she was still angry to have lost Aubrey, and it had colored her every decision since the fusion explosion at Calin Energy Labs.

Wellington drew himself up with the authority he only displayed when he was unsure of himself. "I had a vision. I believe Rhianna Wight is the child of Richard Aldon."

"He died nine years ago. The child would have been born after his death," she pointed out, despite the suspicion growing in her that he was right. A thread of Richard had still been bound to them, and she had been the first to suggest that something earthly was tethering him.

"The mother is one of those who killed him. I believe we can use this girl to bring Aldon back."

Her skepticism rose again. "Surely he would have already returned if it were possible."

Rebecca spoke up. "What if his work is done? He achieved his goals, didn't he? We haven't run out of power yet."

Wellington turned on her like a leopard, spitting, "You know he always had bigger plans. To whom are you loyal, woman? He is our leader. We have accomplished nothing since his death. Do you want his death to be the death of us?"

Fighting among themselves would surely be the death of them, Lori felt. She said, "Perhaps she is only wondering why we waited so long." Rebecca shot her a relieved glance. "Where did this new information come from?"

"The mother's come out of seclusion recently."

"Have you approached the girl? Perhaps she would be receptive to friendly curiosity."

Wellington's look clearly said this was not their way, but she bore the weight of it easily until he relented. He sighed and explained, as if to a child right now, "She's not alone. Sarintha Malik is with her. We'd be recognized."

Lori's stomach lurched when she heard the name. "You know where she is?" she asked carefully.

"She's a traitor. What does it matter?"

The words sucked her breath from her throat. She hadn't dared to believe that Sarintha had survived Richard's wrath. She always suspected that since Sarintha hadn't moved against them, she had been punished for her disloyalty. Lori had never been able to forgive Richard for entrusting the children to her, when Sarintha had abandoned them. They could have been led to safety with more help.

Her eyes began to burn and she shut down the thoughts that were about to reveal her. She had to stay on task. "What if Rebecca went to gather the child? Sarintha doesn't know her."

Wellington's condescending tone remained. "The family is very suspicious. The government is also after them. They won't trust anyone." He lowered his tone. "And I don't believe a younger person could protect herself from Sarintha. She'd know in an instant."

It was likely he was correct, but now Lori wanted to go herself to steal the child as hers was stolen from her. It was such a foolish approach that Wellington might even allow it.

No, it was too much a risk. She was beginning to think like the rest of them. She was tired of their ways. Why choose subtlety when outright chaos would suffice? Soon, it would lead them to capture. Another way may be as effective. "What if we were to lure her from a distance?" She was speaking of the child, but perhaps the woman would also follow.

Rebecca looked up. "Just call her, and she'd wander off to meet us?"

"She couldn't get far on her own, but we could call her outside. She would follow us. Children are naive. All we need to provide is incentive."

"What do little girls want?" Wellington asked.

Lori flushed with pride to see him admit he didn't know. "They want presents. Toys, candy, pretty things."

"It sounds too simple," Rebecca said, but it wasn't a protest.

"Where will we find children's toys?" the man asked derisively.

It pained her to think of that precious box she had hidden after their flight, but it was the obvious answer. Aubrey was gone, her soul long ago blown to bits and consumed. Perhaps her loss could be avenged. Swallowing hard, she offered, "I have a few of my daughter's things still. Some of them may be appropriate."

"Do it then."

She turned to leave immediately, knowing the hate in her eyes might shine through in that moment. She hated Wellington, she hated Richard, Sarintha, the entire world. She'd wanted to leave so many times, and she had disobeyed silently in the past, but really, she had nowhere to go.

* * *

After Lori had said goodbye to her little apartment when they first went into hiding, she brought only two boxes of her belongings with her. One contained the most necessary of clothes and papers and the other, with which she couldn't bear to be parted, was entirely Aubrey's, as if the girl were still here.

She knew it would sentimentality would seem weak, so she shut away the pain from the start, hiding Aubrey's box in one of the previously cleared, abandoned offices.

Richard had said the children were far enough away to be safe. He said that she needn't worry about leaving them in the park by the old homes. Sarintha was supposed to care for them, but the woman had never come. Had Richard known? Was it also Lori's punishment to lose her child?

With a pang, she realized Aubrey would now be seventeen if she had survived, nearly a grown woman. The girl had been the same age as this Rhianna when she was taken from Lori. An eye for an eye, a daughter for a daughter was a primal comfort. Still, she wanted to look in Sarintha's eyes to see her pain.

Lori couldn't let grief overtake her, not even in private. When she returned, it would split open her face and heart, and they would fall on her like wolves. If she didn't do this errand properly, they would cast her out, and she would starve in these barren streets alone.

What a shame it would be for a murderer such as herself to be added among the numbers of the dead in this place. For she had undoubtedly contributed to the death of her own child and the orphaning of all the children of those who had worked here.

The least she could do was face the box of memories.

With shaking hands, she removed the plastic lid, reminding herself she was looking for a suitable treat for a living girl. She removed a small, shiny photo disc and tossed it aside. It was completely useless now, with no way to view the files. Her only pictures were forced deep away in her mind where they couldn't hurt her.

Out she pulled a tiny lace-trimmed dress that Aubrey had worn shortly after her birth. The labor had been painful, but the loss of the girl's father had been worse. He had hoped that the child would be stillborn like their last, and then he had finally left them alone at the hospital. She had no home to return to, desperate and unable to pay her bills, until Richard had offered to help her. She didn't know then that he preyed on desperation.

She threw it aside. It had been a symbol of what she had overcome, but she had overcome nothing. She was merely manipulated in more subtle ways by an even stronger man.

Here was a teddy bear, soft as cashmere, that Lori had bought the first time she had become pregnant. She had hidden it carefully, imagining the happiness her life would finally have when she had a child. Here were the stitches from when her husband had ripped the arms from it when she found she was with child, along with the memory of stitches in her own head from the wine bottle he had thrown. No, it wasn't perfect; it wouldn't do.

Here it was: a flawless porcelain doll, with elaborate blonde curls and sky blue eyes, wearing a velvet frock of complementary deep blue. Aubrey had displayed it on her dresser, gazing upon it affectionately but unwilling to test its fragility with play. It was still virgin after all these years, and no girl could resist its beauty.

Lori smiled down on it, kissed its forehead and carefully put it in her bag. She was ready for Rhianna Wight.

Chapter Seven

Lori was surprised to see that Sarintha had settled so close to the Accident Zone, in the run-down side of town. Even among Richard's people, the older woman had maintained an aloof grace and immaculate appearance. It must have nearly killed her to move into this dingy, ill-maintained townhouse.

The family lived in the left unit of four. There was no garage and only one exit, the front door. They didn't own a vehicle. Lori had waited across the street for over an hour for the policeman in the black car to move. He only left when a blonde woman who walked with a cane came out and got into his car. That must be Victoria, Sarintha's niece, if she recalled correctly.

Surely the family wasn't on bad terms with the Security Department if they had a police escort to protect them. Was Sarintha planning to turn in Wellington and the others? Wouldn't she would have done it already if that were her plan?

Lori wanted to scan the place in closer detail, but she feared Sarintha would notice her presence. From this distance, unannounced, Lori was secure. But how would she know when to summon the girl?

Her only choice was to search for signs of Richard in the house. Sarintha's mind would feel very different: serene, organized, and very controlled. Lori looked inside herself for the faded old link she had with the man and followed it outward.

There it was: a conniving, cold-blooded power, diluted among the easily attainable ambitions of a little girl. Feeling it again made Lori feel sick.

Maybe this wasn't right at all. Richard was a great leader, but he was also a manipulative, hateful man. He had fooled her until the end. She believed in his mission at first. She even participated in his great destruction, but she hadn't thought he would sacrifice their own innocent children. The man loved no one but himself and his power. They could have changed the world, but to him, the cult was a violent means to a dangerous end.

Sarintha could have stopped him. Lori knew the woman had opposed the plan. The two had once shared a secret honesty in the group. Only Sarintha had the strength to urge the others to turn against Richard, but she had run away in the end. Turning the women wouldn't have been hard. Those who had lost their children went mad with sorrow and vanished. Thinking about it now, Richard surely had something to do with that. Turning the men, however… They were all drunk on power.

It should have shocked Lori to think such revolutionary things, but she realized she had believed them all along but hadn't had the freedom to think about them clearly. She couldn't let the situation worsen.

Perhaps Rhianna's youth and innocence would improve Richard. Perhaps this incarnation could be taught compassion. The child was young enough that Lori could mold her with the sort of ideals Richard Aldon should have had. Together they could end all the violence perpetrated by this ignorant government and its ignorant sheep, as Richard had promised her when he took her under his wing years ago.

She abruptly wondered if Richard had promised everyone something different.

This was a very dangerous line of thought. She sank back into the shadows on the side of the brown apartment building that hid her and checked Sarintha's townhouse again with her mind. The girl was not alone. Someone young, impatient, and sullen was with her, and they were beginning to argue.

Lori would have to keep waiting. She reached in her bag, brushing the cool cheek of the doll for good luck and gingerly removed her tattered book to occupy herself. She made herself as comfortable as possible on the concrete slab. She should get a head start on understanding the ritual they would perform soon.

A small hand closed around her shoulder, and she looked up with a gasp. A blonde girl, clearly the miniature of the woman with the cane, was watching her expectantly. "Hello, child," Lori murmured.

"You wanted to see me," the girl said plainly.

Lori hid her shock. "Are you Rhianna, then? I hadn't called you yet."

"I felt you watching me. Who are you?"

Aubrey had been very perceptive at that age, but this girl was an extreme case. Lori doubted that she could detect observation as well herself. "My name is Lori. I wanted to meet you."

"Why?" There wasn't a hint of fear in Rhianna's voice.

Lori unzipped her bag to hide the book, instinctively covering the title with her fingers.

"What's that?" the girl asked excitedly.

Lori smiled to herself. Rhianna had caught sight of the doll. "This is for you."

"No, no, that red book."

What sort of eight-year-old girl was more interested in books than toys? Rhianna's feminine outfit seemed to indicate an interest in girlish things, but many children didn't choose their own clothes.

"I think you'd find it boring," Lori said firmly.

The girl's face creased in the beginning of a tantrum. She was the type who was rarely denied something she wanted. "Show me, or I'll tell Nanny you're here."

This was unexpected as well. Aubrey would never have tried to threaten an adult. "What makes you believe she doesn't know I'm here?"

"No one ever comes to see Nanny," Rhianna said firmly. "I'll do it. She'll notice I'm gone soon."

For a moment, she wanted to tell the child to call Sarintha, so she could face the older woman, after these long years. But she knew revealing herself would be a terrible mistake, and Lori couldn't win against Sarintha.

It couldn't hurt to show Rhianna the book. The girl wouldn't understand the content enough to know that it was banned material. Lori flipped to an unillustrated page with particularly large words. "Dull, see?"

Rhianna seized it away from her with a carelessness that made Lori flinch. That book was irreplaceable. The girl's eyes widened as she traced the gilded letters on the cover. Had she seen it before?

Lori watched her closely, then gazed out at Sarintha's house. Of course. Sarintha might have a copy of the necromancy book as well. Was Sarintha training the girl to plot against them? Lori should use extra caution. "Does your Nanny let you read books like this?"

"Oh, no," said the girl before she could help herself.

Lori smiled to herself. So the appeal was that it was forbidden. It would be easy to enthrall the girl if what she wanted was knowledge.

Rhianna tossed her hair and closed the book quickly. "Mom has lots of books, but she won't let me touch them. She says they're valuable."

Lori saw through the half-truth. "I have many books. Come with me, and I'll show them to you."

Rhianna glanced back at her house nervously.

"Is your home really more interesting?" Lori asked casually.

Rhianna's eyes flared with something like anger as her desires battled each other.

"What do you want most, Rhianna?" Lori chilled as she heard herself echoing Richard's words from long ago.

It took only a moment. "I know magic is real," the girl whispered. "I know you can show me."

Lori reached out her hand. Rhianna's slipped into it naturally as they walked down the road together, looking for all the world like mother and daughter.

* * *

Now that they were touching, Lori detected more oddities in Rhianna. Her hand tingled with electricity, and they were being followed by a well-defined shadow that prickled against Lori's mind. It was Richard; she knew it. The man's spirit had already found the girl. Even tied together by blood, Lori wouldn't have thought Richard would aim to corrupt someone so young.

Perhaps they shouldn't go back to the Accident Zone.

How long would it be before Sarintha found her grand niece missing? How long would it be before Wellington found Lori missing? Longingly, she thought of the office where she kept Aubrey's box. It always seemed a safe shelter.

No, the area was too tightly patrolled. It wasn't hard to escape the police, but no one could enter the Accident Zone without the cult noticing. And where else could she go?

Rhianna was watching Lori intently, probably sensing her conflict. It was several minutes before she asked where they were going.

"A secret place," Lori said conspiratorially, knowing how it would thrill the girl.

"Are there ghosts there?" she asked.

It was a relief to hear her sound her age. Lori hadn't even realized how unnerved she had been. The question was a painful one, though. Tears threatened to well up as she thought of Aubrey. No, she must not show weakness. "It's the most haunted place there is," she answered, with only a slight crack in her voice.

Rhianna didn't seem to notice. "I have a ghost."

"Yes, he's following us." Lori realized for the first time what a risk her thoughts had been. She didn't think that in this state, Richard could attach himself to anyone who didn't share his blood, but she didn't care to be proven wrong. She kept her thoughts fast and buried deep.

"You can see him then?" Rhianna sounded disappointed that her secret was no longer private.

"Yes, I can. I know him too."

"You do?"

Lori quickly debated revealing Richard's identity to her, deciding against it. If the girl didn't know who her father was, it would be a blow to find out he was dead. Not that it would matter if they planned to saddle Rhianna with resurrecting the man.

The more she thought about it, the more she resisted the idea. But what would she say to Wellington? Surely they wouldn't use the girl immediately.

They needed to build trust first.

Here they were. Wellington's car came in sight, and there was no turning back. Reluctantly, she led Rhianna down the alley. It was too late to return the girl and too far to continue on foot in daylight without being caught. With luck, the recently stolen car would work long enough to return them to their headquarters.

Wellington had a particularly deep scowl on his face when the two entered the back seat. Rhianna gave Lori a disapproving look. Lori shrugged slightly.

"Who are you?" Rhianna demanded.

Wellington shot a fierce glare at her, but the girl stood up against it nicely. Lori found herself admiring Rhianna, but the girl had best not speak her mind too much.

Lori half-expected Wellington to shoot back a childish, "None of your business," but he ignored their captive entirely.

Captive. Locked in the car, heading toward the safe entrance of the Accident Zone, Lori realized fully what she had done. She had kidnapped the girl from her home, and Rhianna didn't yet realize she was trapped. What should Lori tell her? Perhaps she'd leave it to Wellington and pretend that it wasn't her doing.

"Don't you think you should introduce yourself?" Lori asked him, taking pleasure in irritating the man.

"I'm Wellington," he said. She could tell he wanted to proclaim that Rhianna was his hostage, but somehow he had the good sense to refrain.

"I don't like you much," Rhianna said outright.

Lori stifled a laugh, unwilling to defend the man. She got far too much enjoyment from hearing him criticized. The girl was more pleasant company than the dour group which was restless with boredom.

"What's that?" Rhianna gasped, pointing toward the windshield.

Lori noted that they were approaching the edge of the Accident. How could she be unaware of it, living so close by? Sarintha must have taken particular effort to shelter her. Lori found her hate of the woman temporarily dwindling. A woman with such obvious love for the little girl couldn't hate other children. On the other hand, Sarintha had let Rhianna be whisked away so close to home.

To fend off Wellington's probable speech about glory and revolution, Lori explained, "A laboratory's power generator blew up here before you were born. Many people died."

In the rear view mirror, Wellington's frown tightened.

"This is the haunted place?"

"Yes."

Rhianna's eyes and mouth were wide open. Obviously she sensed the location's uniqueness. Lori cast Wellington a meaningful look that he ignored.

Rhianna pressed her face to the window, concentrating silently on her new surroundings. Lori wondered why she didn't ask more questions. Perhaps she was too young to understand. It disturbed Lori to think that the girl could have such deep fascination for the destruction, much like Richard. She looked on it again from a child's perspective.

The shimmering fire long put out, intact bodies removed, and the worst of the wreckage cleared away, it seemed more a geographical oddity than a site of horror. The center was littered with interesting concrete formations among shining pools of glass. The standing buildings were windowless and worn smooth in parts, reaching up high like the ruins of ancient castles.

The sunset turned the dull blocks bright orange, lighting all the dark crevices Lori dared not explore. For a child, it was a fascinating ancient city. Perhaps in her long acquaintance with the place, even Lori had begun to find a beauty in it.

Wellington slowed and shifted to climb over the high pile of rubble that served as the boundary of their haven. He turned sharply and drove directly into the doorless hole that served as an entrance to the abandoned microchip factory that was optimistically called their headquarters. The car shuddered, and Lori doubted it would start again.

In the winter, it was bone-numbingly cold. In the summer, it was sweltering. Today, however, it was just comfortable enough to support Rhianna's spell of enchantment.

The girl followed quietly as they headed to the enclosed offices. Rebecca looked up quickly to greet them before turning back to poke the makeshift fireplace with a wooden chair leg. Here was where the allure would vanish to reveal them as pitiful homeless people.

She couldn't let it end yet. Smiling brightly, Lori guided Rhianna to her own "office." She'd fought hard for the choice of this barren building so that they wouldn't all have to live in one room again. The children would have appreciated the space to play.

The inflatable bed on the floor wasn't impressive, but it was better than some had. What drew Rhianna's attention though, were the books. They were stacked in six high piles along the opposite wall under the warped tip-out window that was already letting in too much cold air. Lori deftly wired it shut to block most of the draft.

The girl looked imploringly, and Lori nodded her approval. This was Richard's collection, scavenged from his various hiding places and reverently guarded by Lori. Whatever else the man had done, he deplored the destruction of knowledge and had dedicated much of his life to protecting banned books.

They weren't especially useful to someone with years of practice, but to a novice, the Occult books would serve as an excellent start. Lori gently guided her to a thinner book that Aubrey had found interesting, about communication with ghosts.

Rhianna's expression was nothing short of rapture, until she flipped to a blurry photograph of a woman's face in a window. "That's not a real ghost."

She closed the book and considered it critically. "Why are there lies in this book?"

Lori sensed that her answer was pivotal. How could she explain that the concept could be real, despite false examples? "That is only a mistake. This book has some useful information and some speculation. Nothing is perfect."

Rhianna's haughty expression showed that she disagreed. "Why keep it if it's not right? Throw it away."

"Surely you can see *some* of the information is right, from your own experience. It's only a tool—"

She had opened it again, scowling. "This thing, this board with the letters, it's not useful either."

"It was useful at the time," Lori said tensely. "It was the best way back then, before things changed."

"So people used to be stupid?"

It had been many years since she had dealt with a child. Lori knew she'd lost much of her patience. Gently, she closed the book and took it from the girl. "We also keep it to teach you to learn about correctness. There are no absolutes. If you discount other people's ideas completely, you may miss a valuable lesson." Lori sighed. This problem would not be resolved quickly. Children were very stubborn. She tapped the girl's shoulder and pointed at the corner of the room. "Take a look at these."

Rhianna leaned forward in interest at the large, brightly colored cards on the floor. "Is this a game?"

It's another archaic means to an end, Lori thought. "Yes, it is. It's a game that tells the future."

"Can we play?" she asked, her temper swept away by this newest fascination.

Lori took a quick glance at the doorway. "We have time for a quick game. Take these cards and mix them up. Think of a question about your future."

She frowned in disappointment. "Just one question? I want to know my whole future."

Lori smiled and handed her the cards. "No one can know the whole future. It's always changing."

"Then what good is the game?" she asked, but she was shuffling the cards with a furrowed brow.

"It tells you things you might not know about yourself. Sometimes we don't know how we will react to a situation ahead of time. This tells you early, so you can plan ahead."

The idea intrigued the girl. As Rhianna continued to handle the cards, Lori nudged them with her mind, asking, *Will this child be significant to us?*

"Is that enough?" Rhianna asked, placing the cards on the floor.

Lori nodded, and laid out the five cards in a short line. She pointed at the center card. "This is the present. We'll start here."

Rhianna leaned eagerly close as Lori turned it over. She frowned and turned over the rest of the cards, thinking better of explaining too much to the girl.

"What does it say?" Rhianna demanded, pointing at the sword card.

"That says someone misses you, Rhianna," she answered softly.

"Oh," Rhianna said with the air that that was obvious. "What's that?" she asked, pointing to the inverted King of Pentacles on the right.

Lori bit her lip. This had been a poor idea. "That's ambition in your past," she said half-truthfully, leaving out the negative connotations.

Rhianna seemed to think that was boring. "I want to hear about the future." She pressed her finger on the Sun.

"That's good luck," Lori said brightly. "You'll be very happy in your childhood." Somehow, it didn't seem quite right, and she thought of a great power burning bright, consuming all that dared oppose it. She shivered.

"Hmm." She pointed to the first card. "What's this one?"

The Eight of Wands concerned Lori as well. "It says you'll have a lot of decisions to make soon. Take time to make sure you choose carefully."

Lori was certain now that the girl knew Richard. How could they burden her with this at such a young age? Rhianna had to have a normal chance to grow up.

"It's time, Lori," Wellington announced, stepping in without knocking. "Bring the girl."

Chapter Eight

Rhianna flinched away from Wellington and looked worriedly at Lori for reassurance, and the woman's heart opened to her. "Don't worry, Rhianna. We have a few questions, and then we're going to tell you a secret." A secret that may end her life as she knew it.

They walked back to the common area, where Rebecca's fire was at least maintaining the fading warmth. Rhianna seemed interested in the crackling flames, which confirmed Lori's information that electricity was still functioning in most of the city.

"Rhianna," Lori began kindly, "what do you know about your father?"

The girl looked surprised at the direct question. "Nothing, really. Mom didn't tell me. I think Sam might have a different dad."

Wellington's head shot up. "Sam? Who is that?"

Rhianna reddened. "My brother."

Lori rubbed the girl's back soothingly. "You didn't mention him." She was annoyed at the lack of information as well, but the girl wouldn't cooperate under interrogation from Wellington. "How old is he?"

"Eight."

"Like you?" Lori asked. They had been misinformed, but she should have studied the other presence in the house more carefully.

"Twins?" Wellington burst out. "Why didn't you say, girl? Richard would prefer—"

Lori shot him a painfully intense look. "We're confused, Rhianna. If you and Sam were born at the same time, how could you have different fathers?"

The girl shrugged so honestly that it was clear she didn't understand such things. "He's not like me."

"What sorts of things does he like?" Rebecca asked.

Lori was relieved to have the chance to think this over.

"He likes drawing. I don't know. He's always by himself."

Lori said, "Does Sam like ghosts?"

"No, he's scared. Or he says I'm lying. I don't like him."

Lori considered. Based on her observations of the girl and the impression that Richard was still near, they had the right child. She communicated the idea to Wellington silently, but his irritation wasn't quelled.

"Why do you care?" Rhianna asked.

"Your father was our friend. We want to know all about you."

Rhianna frowned and twisted the hem of her shirt with a quiet ripping sound. "Why didn't you come sooner, then?"

The three looked at each other for an answer.

"You weren't old enough," Rebecca decided.

"But now you are," Lori put in quickly. "We miss your father and want to talk to him. For that, we need your help."

"Enough!" Wellington shouted. "You'll do as we say, and stop asking questions."

"No. If you want my help, you have to be nice," Rhianna said petulantly.

Lori and Rebecca drew closer instinctively to protect her.

"I don't need your help," Wellington spat, unsheathing his knife.

Rhianna squirmed and ducked behind the two women, clenching Lori's hand tightly.

"This isn't the way, Wellington," Lori said sharply. "We have more questions."

"She'll live."

"That's not the point. Ignore him, Rhianna. He won't hurt you."

The little hand squeezed tighter. "I want to go home."

There it was. They had lost their chance to question the girl naturally.

"Must you make everything difficult?" Lori spat at the man.

"I'm in charge," Wellington reminded her. "This was my idea."

"Yes, it was," Lori agreed, hoping the girl would catch on and forgive her. "A ludicrous one at that. She's only a child."

Suddenly she questioned why Wellington would want to give up his informal position as leader. Surely he hadn't realized his own ineptitude so easily. Did he think he couldn't keep them in line on his own?

Richard would have never tolerated this dissent, Lori realized with a chill. Wellington rarely went beyond threats, but Richard would have killed Lori by now. She no longer wanted Richard back. She couldn't do it. It went against everything she held dear.

Rhianna had begun to cry, while Rebecca awkwardly tried to calm her.

Lori stepped close to Wellington and gritted out, "You've upset the girl. Richard wouldn't want that. Let me take her for a walk so she can calm down. Then we can try again."

Wellington stared hard at her, trying to pierce her thoughts, but she resisted easily. He surrendered when he saw she wasn't going to back down. "Take her then."

Lori wiped Rhianna's eyes with her sleeve and led the girl outside a bit too quickly. "Come. Let's get some fresh air."

Rhianna let out a little sob as soon as they left the building. "What does that man want? Why does he hate me?"

"He doesn't hate you. He's just bad with children. He's a very impatient man."

"You won't let him hurt me, will you?"

"Of course not."

Lori lifted Rhianna as they walked around the pile of rubble and set her down near the clearing to the west, not far from the residential area. "This used to be a park," she explained. She knew Richard had chosen this location to remind her of where her loyalty should lie. She hadn't let herself venture in this direction for a long time.

Rhianna kicked at the dirt. "Where are all the trees?"

"They burned… with the people." Lori couldn't stop herself.

"If you think this is a bad place, why do you stay here?"

"Do you think this is a bad place, Rhianna?"

"No, I guess not." She fidgeted and shaded her eyes from the sunset. "What's that tree?"

She was pointing at the pomegranate tree on the other side of the park.

"It grows food," Lori lied. The fruit wasn't yet ripe, and Richard had forbidden them to touch it.

"Is it good? I'm hungry."

That had been the wrong tactic. Lori considered the decision heavily. Richard wouldn't mind if she touched his tree. In fact, it might give them the answers they wanted. Before she could finish decide, Rhianna had begun walking toward it.

The girl paused, cocking her head as if listening hard. Lori watched with bated breath to see what the girl could sense. "Are there people inside?" Rhianna asked reverently.

Lori pressed her lips together. "There are ghosts," she said, figuring the girl had surmised as much.

The girl reached to pick a piece of fruit from a low branch. Lori's heart skipped a beat, fearful that they would be caught. Lori hadn't dared to see what would happen if she touched the energy pillar herself. She should probably stop the girl, but curiosity overcame her.

"This tree is special," the girl said aloud, digging her fingernails into the leathery rind. She put the fruit to her mouth, squeezing out the juice.

"It's sour," she announced, screwing up her face.

"It's not ripe," Lori explained. Still the girl sucked at it thirstily, spitting out the seeds.

Behind them, Richard's bodiless form grew nearly opaque.

Lori sensed a shifting in the energy with nervousness. "I could get you a better treat," she offered.

The girl squeezed the fruit and dropped it on the ground. Lori surreptitiously kicked it out of sight. She ushered the girl away before someone saw.

"I'm cold," Rhianna complained.

Lori knelt down before her. "Do you want to go home?"

"WIth Mommy and Nanny?" she asked hopefully.

The shine in her eyes broke Lori's heart. She had to let the girl go. She could convince Wellington that Rhianna was too young. He couldn't handle a child this age properly, and he knew it. They could always come for her again when she was old enough.

"Do you remember the way home?"

Rhianna looked around with overwhelmed eyes.

"No, of course not. I'll take you. But it's a secret that you were here, okay? Tell them you were lost."

"Will I see you again?"

It hurt Lori to manipulate the girl. "Only if you keep the secret."

She didn't answer.

"Hurry, let's go. There's a nice path over here."

They walked along a trail that had once been cleared by an bulldozer. Lori tried hard to avoid thinking about the consequences of her actions. She could leave the girl by the edge of the Accident Zone, and one of the policemen would pick her up.

As they reached the edge, she knew that would be heartless. It was becoming very dark, and the welcoming streetlights in the far distance weren't enough to comfort a child. Lori shouldn't abandon her here.

She hadn't realized she'd stopped, but Rhianna tugged on her hand to urge her on. There were only a few blocks between here and the girl's house, and Lori remembered Sarintha with trepidation. All her anger against the older woman couldn't hold up in her formidable presence.

"We're almost there," Lori said shakily.

Rhianna had a burst of energy, and Lori nearly had to run to keep up with her. She feared they'd draw attention, but the neighborhood seemed unusually quiet. Perhaps it was inadvisable to be out after dark.

Shortly, they were in front of the little townhouse, and the door opened before Rhianna banged on it.

Before Lori could slip away, she was faced with the furious face of Sarintha Malik.

The woman looked just as she remembered her, her long black hair with few strands of gray neatly brushed and tucked back behind her shoulders.

She was wearing the lavender outfit with an intricate pattern embroidered in gold that Lori had envied years ago. Given her love of new things, Sarintha's financial situation must be bad indeed.

Just then, Lori realized that she must look quite bad herself.

Sarintha didn't say a word, just ushered the girl in the door, before closing it to face Lori on the porch. "What do you want?" she finally asked clearly.

Staring into those dark eyes, it all burst out of Lori in a minute. Years of hate and hurt and loss turned on her old friend. "How could you let them all die? Where were you?"

Sarintha frowned deeply. "I don't understand."

"Aubrey's dead. They're all dead. You were supposed to watch them, and every one of them died."

Her hand shot out to hit the older woman, but Sarintha caught it with a painful grip. "Explain yourself."

Her breath was coming in burning gasps now. "The ritual. You were to watch the children. They waited in the park, but they were too close."

Sarintha's eyes flashed. "Look at me. I was not there because I did not know I should be there."

"Richard said—"

Sarintha glanced down the street and whispered, "I was never told. I had already left. You know I would not leave those children to die. Richard lied, as he always did."

Lori began to sob, forgetting why she was here and that she was in danger. Sarintha wouldn't lie. She never had. Richard had used Lori again, and she had nearly helped bring him back.

"All of them died?" she asked quietly.

"Yes."

"And the other women?" Sarintha sounded as if she already knew.

"Gone," was all Lori could say. "I'm so sorry. I thought it was your fault."

The sympathy abruptly fled from Sarintha's face. "It was not. I still expect an explanation."

Lori's face flared. "Rhianna."

"Yes. I am pleased to see she's seemingly unharmed. What have you done?"

"You didn't call the police?" Lori realized.

"We couldn't, of course. They don't trust us."

"What about the black car?"

"The man is a fool. He would never help us. He monitors us. Sometimes we watch over his child."

She didn't know why the man would allow that. A sudden kinship welled up in her heart for the woman, and she embraced her.

Sarintha placed her hands against Lori's back stiffly.

"I'm so sorry. I was so wrong. Wellington wanted her."

"Wellington?" Sarintha pulled back quickly. "That imbecile thinks he's in charge?"

She should explain, but terror gripped her. She had betrayed everyone now, and if she continued, there would be nowhere to go. She was nothing. Before this woman, or before Wellington, she was as good as dead.

Sarintha watched her quietly, even though she could force Lori to answer. She couldn't trust anyone, but as a mother, Lori owed the woman the truth.

"Wellington wants her. He wants to bring back Richard. I did return her to you."

Her eyes narrowed. "What does Rhianna have to do with Richard?"

Then she didn't know! Was the woman suppressing her abilities, or was she just too blinded by maternal love to see the truth? Cautiously, she said, "He believes Rhianna shares Richard's blood."

"His blood!" Sarintha laughed unexpectedly. "The man as good as shed his own blood. He was already in another form by then."

Lori's brief association with Esser had chilled her. The man was unhinged, and she hadn't been surprised at all to hear when he had met a violent end. "Do I have you to thank for killing him again then?"

"Not I," Sarintha answered sadly. "The girl's father did, and he died as well."

"So Richard is not the father?" It was almost a relief and a good justification to give to Wellington.

"It's not certain, but Richard's body was already dead by that time. Esser, however, is a possibility." Quickly, she added, "I do not see him in her."

But Lori had recognized the ghost with Rhianna. Was there another way? "I fear Richard is after her."

"That's nonsense," Sarintha said firmly.

"Please consider—"

"Thank you for returning her. Do not come here again, or I will kill you. Tell Wellington to stay far away, or worse will come to him."

Shame overcame Lori. A small part of her had hoped to gain Sarintha's trust, even her friendship again. "I can't go back," she murmured.

"They'll deal with you as they see appropriate, I'm sure."

"I can't!"

Sarintha cast her full fury on Lori. The younger woman shook under the knife-sharp scrutiny, realizing fearfully what Sarintha meant to do. It would be best not to resist. Sarintha would have more mercy than the others. Lori lowered her defenses, reducing the pain in her head to strong pressure. She closed her eyes and opened herself to her enemy, hoping she would be swift.

"Stupid child," Sarintha spat. "I'm not going to kill you."

Lori blinked up at Sarintha blankly.

"I believe you."

"Will you help me?" Lori blurted out in disbelief.

"I fail to see what I can do. At least you have not led all of them directly to me."

"What will I do?"

Sarintha sighed. "You will lie. And if your convictions are strong, you will stop their destructive plans."

"I don't see how—"

Patiently, Sarintha explained, "You are of more use to me if you know what Wellington is planning. Come to me to report if you dare, but you must go back immediately."

She wanted to protect Rhianna. Sarintha was probably right. How could she do that if Wellington's long term plans were not shared? She closed her eyes and swallowed hard. She'd find a way.

"Thank you," Lori said shakily.

As Sarintha clasped her hand, Lori caught sight of a furious blonde face peering through the glass behind Sarintha. She owed it to the woman to meet the eyes of the woman whose child she had stolen, but Lori found herself turning and running.

Chapter Nine

"Oh my god, Rhianna, where were you?" Victoria was sobbing as Sam came down the stairs.

His sister had been gone over three hours. Sam had spent the first two being shouted at, even though he didn't even know exactly what time she left.

Victoria had wanted to tell Mr. Pulaski, but Sarintha said no. Then there was another fight. Victoria wanted to go looking for her but was afraid she couldn't walk far enough to search for long. Nanny said no again and said she thought she knew where Rhianna was. They couldn't go there.

Mother didn't even feel better when Nanny said Rhianna was coming home, and all they had to do was wait. Sam had never seen her so upset.

Then Sam went to hide upstairs, wishing someone would apologize to him and secretly hoping at first that his sister wouldn't come back. But soon he did start to miss her, and that was when he heard the front door slam.

His mother was so upset that all she could do at first was check Rhianna up and down for injuries. She didn't notice Rhianna's expression, which was really not very frightened. Sam thought if she ran away, she should be punished at least as much as he had been for doing nothing at all.

When Victoria saw Rhianna was fine, she began to ask where she had been. Rhianna took time to think, before explaining that a nice lady had offered her a doll, then had taken her to a different house. They had read books and played a game, and then the woman had brought her back. Victoria glanced at the door nervously, where Sarintha still had not come back inside.

Sam knew it was not true, but Victoria was too relieved to question Rhianna's childishness. Maybe Nanny would explain better.

After a few more questions and a repeat of "don't talk to strangers," Victoria brought them both cookies and milk, and Sam knew she was sorry she blamed him. Mother didn't sit down while they ate, instead pacing back and forth, and finally she went back to the door to check on Sarintha.

"That woman is still out there!" she shouted and forced back the stiff lock.

Just then, Rhianna stood up with her empty plate, and it fell to the floor, shattering in a thousand pieces of pink glass on the floor. It was Sarintha's favorite plate, and she would be angry.

Victoria ran to Rhianna, scolding her for not asking for help. Rhianna was unusually quiet, and so was Victoria, when she looked at the floor. Sam didn't understand why, but they were both staring at the broken glass.

"Did you try to clean this up, honey?" Victoria asked.

"No."

Sarintha came back in, with a tired sigh, and Victoria called her to the dining room. "Could you take a look at this?"

Sarintha frowned when she saw her plate was broken, but Victoria pointed at it significantly. "It looks like a star. See how evenly it shattered?"

Sam didn't think it looked interesting at all.

Sarintha's eyebrows raised. "That is unusual." She leaned down, counting to herself, and Sam tried to see better.

Victoria put her arm around him. "See?"

The shape was arranged around the small circular center of the plate, and twice as wide around it, evenly spaced spikes of different lengths jutted out.

He tipped his head. "I think it looks like the sun."

Sarintha looked up at that and began to sweep it up.

Rhianna's face was blank and unblinking until the glass clinked into the dustpan. Sam didn't understand why everyone was acting so odd. He'd broken cups and plates lots of times, and it wasn't interesting. "Isn't she in trouble?" he blurted out.

"No, no, she was just nervous. Weren't you, Rhianna?"

"That's not fair!" he shouted.

"If you think so, you can just help Nanny clean it up."

Sam couldn't see how that made sense at all. He would have gone back upstairs out of the way, but he wanted to hear more about Rhianna's adventure. Finally he asked, "Were you scared, Rhianna?"

She debated for a moment. "Yes, at first! I missed you, Sam."

Sam scowled. Sure she had. He began to regret the brief moment he missed his sister. Maybe it wasn't even a whole moment. "Where's your doll? What game did you play?" Maybe he could catch her in a lie.

Rhianna tossed her hair. "The woman has it. I didn't take it. And we played cards."

"You don't know cards!" he accused.

"Be polite, Sam," his mother said.

"She taught me, stupid. They had neat pictures on them, swords and stuff. You'd like it."

Sarintha shot her a warning look, but evidently, Victoria didn't think anything was wrong with that answer.

"You can show me," Sam said.

"We don't have those cards," Rhianna said archly.

Victoria's eyes narrowed. "Sam, leave your sister alone. Rhianna, are you okay? Would you mind if I talk to your nanny?

"I'm fine," Rhianna replied archly as the two adults went upstairs together. To Sam, she said, "I should have just stayed there."

* * *

"What the hell happened?" Victoria burst out. "What did that woman say? Who was she?

Sarintha's face was creased in concern, but it wasn't the parental kind. She looked as if something was deeply personal was wrong, and she was trying to work out how to fix it.

"Are you ready to tell me, or am I going to have to give up?"

"You're as stubborn as Sam is," Sarintha murmured as she began to fold her clothes neatly.

"That's not funny."

"Rhianna's quite stubborn as well."

Victoria pursed her lips. She would have to wait for Sarintha to work out her answer, as usual. Why couldn't the woman just tell her? She knew her aunt had many secrets, and it wasn't hard to guess this was connected. "You knew her, didn't you?"

Sarintha raised her eyebrows over the shirt she held up. "I didn't say that."

"You do, though. Will you just tell me what happened? I don't want to be afraid for Rhianna anymore."

"You won't like what I have to say, at all."

"Does that give you the right to hold it from me?" she exclaimed. She held her forehead. "I know you've done a lot to protect us, and I know what a burden it is. If you tell me, I can understand better. How can I help if you won't tell me?"

Sarintha sat down on the bed heavily, crumpling the shirt in her lap. "Yes, I knew the woman."

"So, who was she?" she asked impatiently. "What did she want with my daughter?"

"What she wanted and what she was asked to do were very different things. As is was what she thought was the truth."

Victoria closed her eyes in frustration. Sarintha's cryptic answers never made sense at first, but the woman was still considering her words.

"She thought that Rhianna was someone else other than who she is. I still can't say she's completely wrong. She was asked to take Rhianna to determine her identity."

"Her identity? She's my daughter, that's all." Victoria stopped short. "This is about…"

"Her father," Sarintha nodded.

"Esser?" Victoria asked hysterically. "Is that it?"

"Richard Aldon," Sarintha corrected.

"It was Richard's people? They know where we live?"

"Not exactly. One does."

How could Sarintha be so calm about it? "We have to leave!"

61

"I don't believe so."

"Why not! Will you just answer me?"

"Be still," Sarintha commanded.

Victoria should have been offended, but she found herself complying quickly. Sarintha was considering what to do, and hysteria wouldn't help her decide faster. She always made the right decision.

Sarintha sighed and looked at her directly. She looked very tired and suddenly quite old. "This particular woman held a mistaken grudge against me. She was the only one who knew our location. The mistake has been resolved."

"Won't she tell them?" How many people were involved in this?

"No, I don't believe so. She's promised to keep me appraised of any changes in the situation."

"Will they come back?"

"If so, we will know in advance. As you see, I have done what I could. I now suggest you impress upon Rhianna the importance of staying at home."

"I thought I already had," Victoria sighed, feeling useless. "I shouldn't go to work and leave them here. I feel like this is my fault."

"It isn't. If anything, it's mine, but we cannot change that now. What's done is done. I also suggest that Rhianna not share her little adventure with anyone."

"Who? Ellie?" If word got back to Andrew Pulaski of a new connection to the Occult, they would be in serious trouble. "I'll tell her." She didn't know if Rhianna was old enough to understand, but she could try. It was always possible to deny her stories as childhood fantasy if Victoria were confronted.

Sarintha rose, her expression renewed. "I'll be keeping a closer eye on Rhianna, at any rate."

"Yes, we can't let this happen again."

But Sarintha looked as if they weren't talking about the same thing.

* * *

Lori spent the entire walk home preparing her defense. As she grew closer, she began to run, teary-eyed from the wind and flushed with guilt. She was relieved to find Rebecca first, calling out, "Have you seen the girl?"

Rebecca's serious look eased. "I've been looking for you, not her."

Had Wellington decided so soon that Lori had defected? How long had she been gone? "She got away from me." Lori stopped abruptly, clutching her chest and wheezing. She didn't have to feign the fact that she couldn't keep up with a young child. "I can't find her."

"I'm glad to see you. He's furious."

"I expect so. He will only be more furious when I tell him she's lost."

"Do you think she has gone back home? We could simply recapture her later."

Of course they would expect Lori to try again. When the time came, she'd worry about dissuading them. She couldn't make so many plans ahead. She had one goal right now, and that was immediate survival. "That's true," she agreed. "The police may find her quickly."

"Would she tell them where she was?"

"I doubt she could remember well enough. Besides, would they believe someone her age?" It was a weak argument, she knew, yet it seemed to satisfy Rebecca, who had little experience with children. Wellington was the same, so it might suffice.

"I've been looking for an hour," Lori sighed. "I don't think I can find her."

"Did you try to track her?"

Lori glared at her. "Of course. She's such a little thing, there's nothing to her to find." Fortunately the others had too little exposure to Rhianna to know how much of a lie it was. She took a deep breath and marched toward the headquarters. It was best to get it over with soon.

She kept herself carefully closed when she faced Wellington's rage. Rather than asking directly, he grabbed her to his chest, pinning her arms to her side. Lori didn't resist. Fiercely, she held the image in her mind, investing all her strength into believing it as truth, under his heavy scrutiny.

Rhianna had run from her at the park, screaming that she hated the bad man. Her gold curls had trailed behind her in the breeze, and Lori had begun to chase after her. The girl ducked around the barricade of debris, and Lori had fallen, giving Rhianna a clear lead.

Lori leaped to her feet, calling Rhianna's name, but the girl was silent. Lori reached out with her mind, searching for fear and confusion, but the girl's thread was too weak to follow in the strength of the place. Lori assumed this meant she headed into the epicenter rather than the frightening skeletal buildings, but she searched and searched and found nothing.

She headed back to the cult's usual entrance, knowing Rhianna would find it familiar, and still she found nothing. The girl had hidden or eluded her, and after an hour, Lori was risking being noticed herself by the patrolling police. Lori ran back and found Rebecca, explaining what happened.

Lori held this story in her mind, as she had since she left Sarintha's house. She had given it image and emotion and depth enough to fool even herself for a time.

She wrenched free of Wellington's grasp and shouted, "What do you think you're doing?"

"Testing you," he growled.

"And you found nothing, did you?"

"Nothing," he admitted.

She channeled her fear into indignation. "I've had about enough of this. If you have an accusation to make, make it."

Rebecca watched closely, ready to side with the winner.

"No accusation." He looked bitterly disappointed.

"Why do you wish to get rid of me?" Lori spat, as she knew Sarintha would have said. She had enough, and only a show of force could protect her now. All the things she had always wanted to say boiled to the surface.

"Why do you suddenly question everything? Why do you fail at the simplest tasks?"

"It was so simple," Lori said tersely, "that you could not plan it without my help. The girl was worthless. It doesn't matter."

"You say she's worthless?"

"Yes, I do! How long did you spend with her before you frightened her off?" She took a deep breath, preparing herself. "It was your fault!"

"That's ridiculous! I would have had it over with immediately, not coddled the girl."

Lori faced Rebecca squarely. "He frightened her, didn't he?"

Rebecca nodded.

"Did she look as if she were about to run when she was with me?"

Rebecca shot a look at Wellington before answering, "No."

"It's clear," Lori continued, feeling like a woman possessed as her rage burst out, "that you are a poor leader. That's why you wanted to resurrect Richard. He would never have chosen you."

Rebecca gasped, and her eyes lit up in sudden agreement. Lori knew just how pliable she was.

"Who would he have chosen, then?" Wellington shouted.

"If you had watched over him properly, there would have been no need to choose anyone. Esser, at least, would still be alive."

"He didn't ask for help!" A tremor was coming into Wellington's voice. His decisions had never been dissected before, and he wasn't holding up against it. He had relied on their weakness and gullibility to support him.

"You were afraid of him," Lori asserted.

"I was not."

"Esser was mad. We would have been fools not to be afraid of him."

"Do you claim to lead then, woman?"

She stared at him coldly. "Lead what? There's nothing left." And with that, she walked inside, a little thrill buried in her heart that she would have made Sarintha proud. It was time to start living again.

Chapter Ten

After five years, Rhianna and Ellie had become close friends. Rhianna relied on her for news of the outside world, unable to convince her mother to let her attend the public school far out in the center of the city.

"You were right, Rhianna," Ellie exclaimed with shining eyes. "I told Mallory to mind her own business, and she went away. I was so sick of her telling me what I should wear and who I should talk to."

"What did she say?" Rhianna asked evenly, trying not to sound too curious.

"She said she was just worried about me, then she called me a you-know-what. You were so right about her."

"I told you she wasn't a true friend," Rhianna agreed.

Ellie smiled and hugged her, soft and fragile.

Rhianna's hand brushed a chain around the other girl's neck. "Who gave you this?" she asked accusingly.

Ellie smiled. "Daddy did. It's a real diamond, see?" She untucked a heart-shaped necklace with a small stone in the center.

Rhianna felt her stomach go cold at the waste. Ellie always had so many more clothes and treasures than Rhianna did. "You took it? He's just buying you, you know."

Ellie pulled away. "You know that's not true. You're jealous because you don't have a father."

Rage flooded through her. How dare Ellie stoop to petty insults? "I do have a father," she said between clenched teeth.

"Don't start this again. He's dead, Rhianna. You can't bring him back."

"You'll see. I can do anything I want to do. Someday your father will leave you, but mine will be a part of me forever."

Ellie looked disturbed but managed, "Fine, tell me when you see him, then I'll believe you."

"You shut up. You don't know what you're saying. I'm not like you."

"That's for sure," Ellie muttered.

"What did you say?"

Ellie swallowed hard. "I said you're not like me."

"And what's that supposed to mean?"

"That— that we're not the same. You believe things I don't." She was visibly fidgeting, clearly wishing she hadn't pursued this conversation. Rhianna would make her wish she hadn't.

"That's right. How does that make *me* wrong?"

"Father says…"

"Go on. What does he say?"

"Father says it's criminal."

"Damn him. Don't you ever think for yourself? Do I look like a criminal?"

Ellie stared down at her hands.

Rhianna lifted her chin. "Do I?"

"No," she said softly.

"Did it ever occur to you that if there was something to be afraid of, that it means I'm right?"

"What?" she asked vaguely.

"Something that isn't real can't be criminal."

Ellie shivered and drew her arms to her chest. "Father says it's illegal to talk about those things. They arrested a girl at school—"

"They can't arrest teenagers," Rhianna insisted. "Besides, what did she do?"

"They can," Ellie insisted. "I haven't heard anything about her for weeks. She just disappeared. Just because she had some necklace on with a symbol on it."

Rhianna glared at Ellie's own necklace. "There's no such thing as evil jewelry," she muttered, but if she knew a way, she'd curse Ellie's gold heart.

"That doesn't matter. I'm scared. I don't want you to get in trouble."

Rhianna knew she was mostly concerned about herself but charged on. "I've seen it, Ellie. I've seen the dead. I know what's going to happen. He's just ignorant if he's afraid of that. People like me can help him. We can save the world."

Ellie bit her lip but faced her again. "You really think so?"

"I know it. You could be like me too, Ellie, if you only tried. You're different from the rest of them." She held the other girl's chin, forcing her to look Rhianna in the eyes. "People like your father and Mallory already know it. Take a look at yourself, and you'll see."

Rhianna could see Ellie's warring emotions: the desire to be obedient to both her father and friends and the desire to be special and powerful. She'd never truly be powerful, Rhianna knew. Ellie was too much of an indecisive follower, but she was easily enticed.

"Can we talk about something else?"

"This is my house. We talk about what I want to talk about."

Ellie stepped toward the door like she was going to leave, but Rhianna knew she wouldn't go. The other girls had left her since she spent so much time away from her own neighborhood, and her parents were always fighting at home.

"Can't you show me what you mean though?" she asked with a sigh.

"Do I have to prove everything to you?"

"No, I just want to see. I want to learn."

Rhianna smiled slightly. Finally, the girl had come around. "Close your eyes, and sit right here." She gestured to the carpet in front of her.

The other girl repressed a nervous laugh that would have infuriated Rhianna, but at least she didn't have to repeat herself. Ellie swept her red hair behind her shoulders and closed her eyes. Rhianna could do anything to her in that moment, and Ellie wouldn't be fast enough to stop her.

She tried to stay focused. "Think of what you're most afraid of, and I'll tell you what it is."

Ellie began to breathe faster, and Rhianna could feel the resistance as the girl's mind began to race. Ellie was wondering the meaning of this, if she should just go home now, was her father right, no, she had to concentrate…

"Pay attention," Rhianna spat. "You're wasting my time."

Ellie's eyes shot open in shock.

"You said you wanted to do this. Think of what you're afraid of. Now."

Ellie closed her eyes tightly and bit her lip.

"Dogs? I know that's not it." This was going to take all night. Rhianna followed the tendril that connected them deeper, past Ellie's random self-justifications and worries into a darker place. Rhianna hadn't expected that Ellie had so much anger inside her, but there it was, and Rhianna sipped at it like a cool spring. It wasn't strong enough to be what she was looking for, however, and she slid to the side, a little deeper.

Ellie's brow furrowed, and she gasped as if in pain.

Rhianna felt it too and brushed it aside. There it was, *a flash of pain and sobbing, and even worse, alone with the blood dripping from her nose because she must never, never tell. Even now, years later, she was filling with terror, because somehow she had told, even though she promised.*

"Never tell," Rhianna murmured aloud, despite herself, and Ellie jerked away.

"How could you know? How could you do this? I didn't tell you! I didn't think of it until now."

Rhianna nearly laughed. Something so fleeting, inconsequential and scarless as being struck once by her father would never have damaged Rhianna. This wasn't the time to say that though, and Ellie was looking so upset, so upset that she might tell her father what just happened, no doubt an edited story to avoid his fury.

It annoyed her, but Rhianna had to be supportive now, to save herself. She reached out to touch Ellie's hand. "I'm so sorry. I didn't know. Has he ever hurt you again?"

Ellie twisted away half-heartedly with a moan. "No."

Right now was the moment where reassurance and trust could be bought, and Rhianna let Ellie lay her head close and sob.

The mood was quite an improvement from when Ellie arrived that day.

* * *

The air was cool and musty and thick dust floated in the thin beams of sunlight in the haze of her dream. Rhianna was in a dimly lit great hall that stretched out into eternity, with pillars on each side reaching high above her head. The right was adorned with dark velvet curtains shading floor-length windows. Gilt-framed paintings obscured every free inch of the paisley-papered walls.

The left was bare and pale, but the nearest stone pillar was ornately carved with hundreds of shapes. It was ancient and worn, but well preserved. She leaned closer to see a rose carved so perfectly she could almost smell its scent. Her fingertips explored the surface. The petals were burnished soft as silk, and next to it, a hummingbird's carved feathers seemed to pulse beneath her hand. A butterfly inched closer, kissed her with its antennae and fluttered round the pole. She pressed her face to the strangely warm stone and felt something hum deep within it, regular and familiar as a heartbeat.

With each beat, comforting heat spread through her. She breathed out a tightly held sigh and let herself sink into the sensation. Her eyes fluttered open as a soft touch brushed her cheek. An image of a rabbit licked her face, a wolf had come closer, bowing its head low to her, and the butterfly had fluttered into her hair.

The desire to explore the grandiose pillars called to her, and she straightened quickly, scattering the animals away and crushing a bed of flowers as she removed her hand. With a last gaze, she realized she must have dreamed the images. The pillar was like all the others, plain and bare, as rough as concrete. She trailed her fingertips over it a last time, and it left them scraped and raw.

She approached the marble pillars and stopped to examine the crimson drapes over the windows and found they were iridescent. Yellow, blue, and green flickered like oil over the red velvet, entwining and reflecting each other. She leaned in close, looking for a pattern. The oil spread away, leaving an irregular pool of liquid crimson shimmering out at her.

A shape coalesced, and she recognized it as her own reflection, taller, older, with a gold crown in her upswept hair. A powerful, unfamiliar emotion swept over her, and she grew unsteady. Reaching out, her fingers fit exactly into the channels of the nearest pillar, as if it was made to fit them, and the dizziness vanished. Its marble was icy, sharp, and reflective, as if no one had ever touched it before. The coldness reassured and numbed her.

She pulled her hand away. The grooves had cut three even, bloody streaks down her palm. She tried to wipe the blood on the drapes, but it flowed faster. She pressed her hand hard against her heart and turned to the paintings.

The paintings shared the same quality as the velvet. Colors swirled, shone, and reformed, turning a lavishly furnished room into a starlit cityscape into a mountain lake. The pictures were never the same twice, but something was missing. As different as they were, as many shapes as they created, there was never a person in them, looking from any window, lounging in any Victorian sofa, picnicking in any spring park.

It filled her with a chill, yet still she watched, running from painting to painting, desperate for a portrait of a smiling face. What kind of person would paint these empty, mocking pictures? She ran down the unending corridors until she couldn't find where she'd come from. She clawed at a painting angrily, as if she could peel the canvas off to reveal a new image below. It wouldn't rip, but the image stopped changing and rested on an enormous black lake at night.

Moving away, she pulled back a pair of velvet curtains and pressed her face to the dark windows. She could see nothing. No stars, no hills, just a complete void that left her clutching the drapes in vertigo. She was absolutely alone.

* * *

Rhianna awoke in her bed to a room as dark as the void in her dream. As she thrashed about, her eyes focused and she recognized her ordinary floral curtains and the bluish lamplight that illuminated them. She turned to the closer window behind her and jolted as the daisies seemed to writhe in the darkness. She shook her head clear and peered between the blinds. The leaf-strewn street was normal and quiet. She laughed at her nerves and lay back down to sleep.

Chapter Eleven

Ellie had never seen her father so proud as when he announced to her mother that he'd gotten promoted. He said his new security job paid more money and had real responsibility. Ellie didn't particularly care until he took her aside.

"I don't want you going to the Wight house anymore."

"Why?" she asked, confused. He had seemed so eager at first for her to make friends with Rhianna.

Pulaski looked up as if checking to see if her mother could hear. "I don't want you around that family."

"What are you talking about? They're nice."

"Because I'm your father. Just listen to me. They're dangerous."

"Are you sure?" she asked with skepticism. "Nothing bad ever happens."

"Not lately. I don't want anything to happen to *you*."

"I don't know what you mean. Besides, why can you go there if I can't?"

He grabbed her wrist too hard. "It's for work. I was investigating them. I won't be going back either."

She stared at him for a moment and let her wrist go limp. Why wouldn't he listen to her? If he *were* right, why would he put her in harm's way? "Why did you let me go at all, then?" she murmured.

He gave her his none-of-your-business look but burst out, "They wouldn't cooperate before."

She was too stunned to reply as his expression turned to rage. She knew he hadn't meant to admit that and braced herself. The powerful blow knocked her to the floor. She knew she should be quiet as he hauled her up, but she thought of Rhianna's courage and cried, "I'm telling Mom!"

The pounding of footsteps sealed her feeling of doom, as her mother burst out, "You've been taking her *where?*"

* * *

"Sam, I read it," Rhianna whispered.

"Read what?" he grumbled, annoyed to having his drawing interrupted, even if it was little more than bored scribblings.

"The red book, the forbidden one."

"So?"

"Don't you want to know who our father is?"

"Does it matter?" He wasn't going to fall for her excitement. She was a liar and always would be, and it wasn't worth him getting into trouble too.

"Of course it does!"

He put down his pencil. "Mother says I don't have a father. I don't think she wants us to know."

"She told me."

He snorted and asked flatly, "What did she tell you?"

"She told me he died. He saved her life."

How romantic. "Really. Was he also a handsome prince?"

"Don't joke!"

"If he was so great, he wouldn't have gotten himself killed."

"You're just angry because I found out first."

"No, because Mother likes you better, for some unknown reason. I hate it here, and I'm not staying." His secret had slipped out, as they always did when dealing with her.

She laughed her ugly laugh. "Where will you go?"

"Does it matter? Anywhere but here."

She tipped her head back, watching him with narrowed eyes. "You're not going anywhere."

"Who's going to stop me, you?"

"Why would I bother? You're going to stop yourself, talk yourself out of it, like you always do."

"Not this time," he said, but his resolve was already faltering now that she knew.

She held her fingernails up to the light to inspect their cleanliness. "You might want to stick around, see who our father is."

"Let me guess. You can't do it without me." The statement twinged in his heart. She might actually need him for once.

"You're my brother. We're connected. Of course I need you."

He crossed his arms. "You need me so you don't get in trouble yourself. I'm not helping you. Ever."

She smirked. "You will. You're curious, and you know it."

"Let me guess again: you need my blood."

"A little."

He flung his arms down into fists. He'd only been joking, and there she was, straight-faced enough that he knew it was true. He reluctantly supposed it made sense to need blood to locate a dead relative. "No way are you getting my blood. You're crazy, you know that? Completely crazy, and I'm not going to be a part of this. You go have fun with your demons or whatever by yourself." Maybe they would kill her or something, and he would get some peace. No, undoubtedly Mother would blame him.

She seized his arm and implored, "Sam, I *need* you. I'll make it up to you."

"No you won't, and I don't want you to." The idea of her being indebted to him for once tugged at him, but he pushed it back. "No, no, no."

"I'll do anything you want."

I want you to go away. She'd said "anything." He frowned at her. Her face was sincere, and her eyes were pleading. She almost looked human. He expected her to notice he was cracking, expected her expression to flicker to cold satisfaction, but it held steady. Her motives were never honest, but she truly needed him right now. It was tempting to string her along. He wondered how long she could wait. "How did you get the book?"

"You know they trust me." It was merely a comment on her superiority; she was beyond bragging in this mood.

"Couldn't you have found it sooner, then?"

"Well, I did, sort of. I've been going in to read it whenever I get the chance."

It would figure that she'd been breaking the rules repeatedly, while he couldn't manage to get away with anything once. "I suppose you've tried some things, then." If he procrastinated long enough, he could find out more.

Her eyes brightened. "Yeah, look at this." She reached over to plug in his old black radio.

"That doesn't work," he reminded her.

"Doesn't matter, look at this." She closed her eyes and held the cord. The hot smell of melting plastic began to rise into the air, and a large blue spark flew out from the outlet.

He pulled her hand away. "Damn it, what are you doing!"

She shrugged. "It was already broken."

"That's not the point," he sputtered and noticed she was rubbing her right hand. "Did you get hurt?" She would have deserved it.

"Not exactly." She displayed it, and he could see a sort of whitish distortion around it, like a ghost.

"What the hell is that?"

"I shocked myself once, and it went all over me. It felt… really good."

He shook his head. "You *would* think so. Probably fried the sense in your brain."

"Come here." She pulled on his shirt with her left hand then grabbed his with the glowing one. He recoiled, expecting pain but met with tingling warmth instead. His hand was distorted now, and hers was back to normal.

She was watching him with amusement. "Isn't that amazing?"

He was enthralled by it, flexing his fingertips to enlarge the glow before he compressed it into a tight ball and threw it at her head. It smacked through it and seemed to be absorbed within her. She looked angry.

"Just fixing your brain damage," he said.

"That's not comfortable," she muttered, and he figured it probably hurt her. Good.

"Will you help me now?"

"Because you let me throw something at your head? Not good enough."

She leaned close. "I said anything."

He didn't want to know what ideas her twisted mind held. "How does this work, anyway?"

She grinned like she'd already won and ticked off a list on her fingers. "We need a candle, blood from both of us, something he used to own, and meditation."

"What did he used to own?"

"Well, there's a tarot deck in Mother's room that I think was his. And there's a locket I think he gave Mother."

"What if it's not his? What happens then?"

She shrugged. "Probably nothing. Or someone else comes."

"Someone more interesting than you, I hope."

She scowled. "Are you helping or not?"

"You still haven't said what I get out of it."

"If you still want to run away, I won't tell. Anytime you want to leave, I won't stop you."

He knew he had nowhere to go, but somehow it seemed a satisfying agreement. "When do you want to do it?"

"Oh, right now!" She stood up.

"Don't you need a while to get the supplies?"

"No, I took them ages ago, for after I convinced you. I'll be back in just a minute." She rushed out the door.

He flexed his thumb repeatedly while he waited. It was still glowing slightly.

* * *

It wasn't long before Rhianna came back with a battered black duffel bag and a book of matches. "Aren't you excited?" she asked, as if he were about to receive a present.

Sam grunted. They settled into the far corner of the room, backs to the door in case someone were to check up on them.

She unzipped the bag and dumped the contents on the floor. There was the tarot deck, an old coat, a locket, and—

He jumped to his feet. "Jesus, is that a gun?!"

She shrugged. "So?"

"Where did you get this stuff?"

"Mother's closet, way in the back. It was all dusty in there." She wrinkled her nose in distaste, continuing to rummage, and pulled out an open silver-handled knife. "Here it is."

"Oh no," he moaned. It was covered in flaking dried blood.

"It's rust," she said firmly.

"No, it's not." He rubbed a bit off and examined it. "You're insane. There's no way I'm doing this." Where had these things come from? They seemed to reinforce his mother's continuous paranoia that someone was after them. Sam figured he'd be paranoid too if he'd known there were bloody knives lying around.

"Whose blood is this?" he asked, and she took advantage of his lapsed attention to slice his upper arm. He yanked it back, but she had already put his blood on the tarot deck box before lighting a yellowed taper. "Couldn't you have cleaned it first?" he panicked.

She responded by wiping the blade clean on the gray coat before cutting herself.

"No, no, no, I don't care if this is real or not, you put some dead person's blood all over me."

"Oh, fine," she grumbled, and wiped the bloody sleeve on her own cut. "Now I did it too, is that what you wanted?"

"No, I *didn't* want that. Do you have any idea what you're doing at all?"

She scoffed. "Look, it's probably Father's blood anyway. He was stabbed."

He stopped breathing. Was she completely heartless? "Did Mother tell you that?"

"No, it was Nanny. Just shut up and concentrate." She lit the candle and began to stare at it.

Sam didn't want to help, but he might as well make sure she didn't cause something awful to happen. Then he fully realized all this incriminating evidence had been moved to *his* room, no doubt deliberately. Best to get this over as soon as possible. "What am I supposed to be doing?"

She sighed in annoyance, and said sharply, "Just meditate and think of Father. Think about how you want to talk to him, and look at the candle. It's not that hard. Stop asking questions."

"All right," he grumbled and tried not to think of the weapons. He'd never really considered the man before, assuming he was just like Mother, but maybe it wasn't true. *Father, if you're out there, come here and stop her. You can't possibly want her to be this selfish. She thinks she deserves everything in the world.* Sam wished, not for the first time, that their situations had been switched, that he'd been doted on and Rhianna rejected, just to see real pain in her eyes. Damn, she deserved some pain for once.

Resentment peaked into anger, and he shot a fierce glance at her seeming composure. If she saw it, she ignored it. *Someone punish her,* he wished, before chiding himself for his immaturity. Her shallowness craved attention, and here he was, giving it to her. She should be ignored, be given no response at all, and her power would diminish.

He forced himself to concentrate again. He really did want to meet his father, to find out what he'd think of Sam, who so rarely did anything wrong and just tried to stay out of the way. He tried to imagine the man's face, someone kindly with dark hair like his own. Rhianna had begun to murmur some words. Sam felt that words couldn't possibly matter more than intention. He'd have to help her though, for her intention was perennially selfish.

It seemed like nothing was happening at all, and perhaps Rhianna agreed, for she'd grown silent. He realized she'd gone absolutely still, her chest unmoving and her face paling more with each moment.

"Rhianna!" he called and she began to shake jerkily and without rhythm. A jolt threw her to the floor, and he rushed to her side. He grabbed her wrist to feel her pulse and it was fast, much too fast. What had she done to herself? He shook her shoulders and shouted her name again.

Her eyes opened and met his with a look of absolute fury that made him recoil. He'd never seen that intensity in her before, and it scared him. "Why did you do that? You ruined it," she spat and gripped his wrist, digging her fingernails into his skin.

"But what— you were—" he sputtered. She didn't seem to realize what had happened. Should he still call Mother?

Her face broke into a smile, and she tossed his arm away, smacking it into the wall. "You're so gullible."

He wanted with all of his soul to hit her. This whole damn thing was a joke, and she had enjoyed freaking him out. "You didn't read the book, did you?" he guessed.

She smirked. "Maybe."

"Why do you always do this to me? I'll never believe you again." He did his best to convince himself he shouldn't be embarrassed, that it was her fault as always. And who would he tell? No, it was bad enough that she had strung him along and laughed.

"You always say that, Sam. I know it's not true. You'll always be my darling brother." She reached over to kiss his cheek and he pulled away.

"Damn it, I'm not talking to you anymore."

"Don't you think Mother will notice that? I know you can't bear to get in trouble."

He glared at her. "Then I'll just have to tell her why I'm angry at you, won't I?" She'd deserve it. She'd earned the most severe punishment, but he knew nothing would ever happen to Mommy's little girl.

Rhianna tossed her hair. "She won't believe you."

"Nanny might." It was his only leverage, he knew.

"Please, you're not a child. Call her by her name." Suddenly she was so much more mature than he was? But a flicker of fear creased her face.

"I bet she'll notice right away that you touched the book. She always knows." The flicker returned, and he relished it. Someday he would tell Sarintha everything Rhianna had done, absolutely everything, and Mother would finally realize what a good person he was. "I hate you." The words came out before he realized it.

"I know," she answered and smiled a perfect smile.

It wouldn't work forever; he knew it. Some day she'd push too far, get in over her head, and he wouldn't help her.

He rubbed his head tiredly to ease his temper and turned to face her again. He stifled a scream.

The dark muzzle of the revolver was pointed straight at his forehead. He flailed backwards, twisting his wrist painfully, and tried to kick away from her. Her finger twitched, and his vision darkened, and he registered a quiet click.

Rhianna smirked at him and tossed the empty gun back in the bag. "You're pathetic."

He swore he could have killed her at that moment.

Chapter Twelve

Something didn't seem right to Rhianna. The presence she had summoned was no different than the ghost who was always with her. "Tell me your name," Rhianna demanded in the quiet of her empty room.

"My name is Richard," he answered, and a flood of clarity washed away her concerns.

Hearing the words so close and clear after years of vague impressions made her feel stronger than she could have imagined. Maybe the ritual had worked after all. "Are you my father?"

"If I were there," Richard's pleasant tenor voice said to her, *"I'd give you the world, princess."*

Rhianna's heart filled with pleasure. She only wished she could gloat to Sam about it. The ghost must have picked up on the thought.

"Tell me about your brother."

"Sam? He's an idiot?"

"What does he want most in life?"

She had wanted him to ask all about *her.* Was he kidding? "Who cares?"

"I might care," he answered, with an edge to his tone that grated on her nerves.

She supposed he had a good reason to be interested, as Sam was her brother. He'd find out she was more interesting anyway. "He wants to leave. He wants…" She pondered for a moment. Sam mostly wanted to get her in trouble, but maybe there was another reason. She knew he was very jealous of her relationship with their mother. "He wants people to like him."

"*Good,*" Richard said approvingly. "*You understand.*"

She wasn't sure she did. What was he getting at?

"What do you think of Sam?"

She was beginning to get annoyed. "He's boring and useless. All he does is whine."

"Do you ever fight?"

"All the time. I always win."

"Of course. What does he say?"

"Stupid things about how he'll tell Mother. What does it matter?"

"Does he ever threaten you?"

"No, he's such a baby." This was not at all what she'd hoped for. She'd expected to learn secrets, about death, or her family, and this was as dull as her aunt's school lessons.

"*Patience is a virtue,*" he recited tritely. "*You'll need it.*"

"Fine, but I have better things to do."

"*Like what?*" he asked coldly. "*You called me for a reason, and I'm not going to leave.*"

A chill went through her. Something told her playing this game wasn't very wise. His sudden silence made it worse. He was searching her, as she had searched Ellie. Her heart unexpectedly leaped into her throat so that she could barely breathe. She forced the air out of her lungs hard, and it skipped a beat and returned to normal. She was being toyed with.

She wasn't going to put up with this. "Tell me what you want or go away. If you want to talk to Sam, go bother him instead."

She sensed a passing anger. "*Do you know what I could do to you?*"

"No," Rhianna answered pointedly. "You won't tell me anything interesting."

She found herself on her feet, striding toward her closet with too-wide steps that didn't match her height. Her hands began to toss aside the pile of unwanted clothing on the floor, and her curiosity died with a shock.

She was reaching into her mother's black duffel bag. Her hand clenched around a reddish wooden handle, worn smooth and familiar by many years of use. She squeezed her eyes shut, willing him to stop, but he pulled out the old revolver.

Surely it isn't still loaded, she thought. She'd just played with it earlier. Her hand expertly flipped open the chamber to see two bullets.

"Shall we see if you're as lucky as Sam was?" he asked.

He was just trying to frighten her. He wasn't crazy. "You wouldn't shoot me. You'd die too."

"I'm already dead twice over."

A small explosion in her gut doubled her over with the memory of severe pain, but he didn't lose grip of the gun in her hand. She was aware that this jolt was the least he could do to her.

"You can't be my father."

"I can be anything I want to be," he said.

Her mind began to swim. "Mother wouldn't like you."

"Your mother had no choice, and neither do you. It's too late to turn back now." Her thumb flipped back the hammer. *"Will you answer my questions, or will I have to pull this trigger?"*

"Yes, I'll answer."

He didn't let her lower the gun. *"How is your mother? Is she still pining for her dear Ethan?"*

"Who's that?" The name wasn't familiar.

"It's not important. I killed him; he killed me. It's all in the past." Richard laughed, amusing himself.

For the first time in her life, she didn't care to ask more. She hoped he was joking, trying to frighten her, but her finger tightened against the trigger.

"She never found another man?"

"No, she lives with my Great Aunt Sarintha. It's just the four of us."

At the sound of the name, she felt her chest tighten, and she was afraid her heart would go out of control again. Her hand slackened, and the revolver fell to the floor. Richard had gone quiet, but Rhianna had begun to tremble. She was frightened enough now in the spring sunshine. She couldn't spend this night alone.

* * *

Sam didn't say anything at dinner, but Rhianna caught him giving Sarintha dark, meaningful looks. It didn't matter. No one would believe him anyway. She gave him her most polite smile before turning to her mother.

"May I invite Ellie over tonight for a slumber party?"

Sarintha frowned, and Victoria paused in consideration. Rhianna took advantage of the lull to charge forward. "She's upset because her parents are getting a divorce. I'm worried about her. Can she come over?"

Her mother seemed interested. "A divorce? Mr. Pulaski didn't say anything about that."

Rhianna was again disgusted that her mother associated with that man, but she hid it properly. "Yes, I think it's because he works so much. I think it's stupid. He doesn't have to. I don't want him to come here anyway."

"Now, Rhianna, he drives me to work. He's not here all the time like he used to be, and we should be grateful for that. Poor Ellie, though. You say she's not taking it well?"

Rhianna brightened. "No, not at all. She's been crying all the time. She thinks they don't love her."

"I hope you told her that's not true."

"Of course." She plastered on her good-little-girl smile again.

"You're a good friend then. You can tell her she can stay if it's all right with her father."

"I'll call her right after dinner," Rhianna said and leveled a subtle smirk at her brother before watching Sarintha again.

Sarintha was scowling into her corn as if she knew something was wrong. Rhianna pushed down the emotions rising in her to block them from the woman. It wouldn't do to be exposed so soon. They finished their dinner quietly, and Sarintha murmured to Victoria, "I would like to speak with you for a moment."

Pretending she hadn't heard, Rhianna asked, "Mother, do you think you could talk to Ellie when she comes? I'm not sure about the right thing to say."

Victoria was a little flustered by the question. "I suppose. What has she been saying?"

"She feels like she's losing her family. She's acting like they're *dying,* and I can't calm her down. I'd hate… I'm worried something will happen to her."

Victoria gave her a little hug. "She'll be just fine. Lots of girls go through this. It just takes time."

She nuzzled closer to her mother's warmth, noting out of the corner of her eye that Sarintha had gone away.

"I should call her then."

Victoria nodded and went to the kitchen.

* * *

Ellie was a right mess when she arrived. She'd put makeup on one watery eye and forgotten the other, and her shirt wasn't even buttoned properly. She looked ridiculous, like she'd narrowly escaped an assault, and no doubt she had drawn the attention of the neighbors.

Rhianna saw the girl as if for the first time and knew that Richard had returned. Ellie was scrawny and nervous-looking, with garish red hair. Her clothes were expensive and flattering, but she didn't seem comfortable in them. The girl was pathetic.

Rhianna had to force herself to be nice.

"Thank you so much, Ms. Wight," the girl mumbled.

Rhianna's mother reflexively tucked Ellie's bright hair behind her ear but stepped back awkwardly. "It'll be okay."

"Thanks," Ellie whispered and rubbed at her eyes.

"You're a mess. Let's fix you up. Do you want to try on my new clothes?" Rhianna distracted her.

Victoria patted her daughter and hung back to give them their space as they went upstairs. Rhianna closed her door carefully as Ellie sat down on her bed. "How are you, Ellie?"

As expected, the girl burst into tears and began to babble. "Mom's leaving! She's packing right now. I don't know what to do."

"She knows you're here?" Ellie had said that her mother wasn't happy about their association. Rhianna was glad she'd changed her mind.

"Yes. She said it might make me feel better. I'm so glad you called. But now Daddy says I can't come anymore."

The man seemed to find it hard to stay away from Victoria, so Rhianna doubted that decision was permanent. "He'll change his mind, you'll see." It would be easy enough to force him to reconsider.

"I hope so." The girl drew her knees to her chest, with her shoes on, Rhianna noted in annoyance, and began to rumple the blanket with her hands. If Rhianna didn't distract her, this would be a very dull evening of whining.

"Here's something interesting," Rhianna crawled into the bottom of her closet and dug in the black duffel bag. Her heart skipped a beat as her fingers brushed the metal barrel of the gun, but she pulled out the old battered tarot deck instead.

"Let's play a game, Ellie."

* * *

Sarintha Malik awoke with a chill, feeling as if she'd been chased all night long. Her heart was hammering in her chest, and she was sure she wasn't alone. She couldn't remember the dream clearly, but she knew it was about Richard.

She shook her head and put it from her mind. She tossed off the upper blanket, rolled over and let out a small scream. Richard's silvery hair and cold smile were facing her, and she jumped out of bed. No, it wasn't possible.

The fear was broken by a feminine giggle. "Nanny, it's just me," Rhianna said, sitting up, and Sarintha gathered her in her arms like a baby

"What were you doing in here?" She was too relieved to properly chastise her.

She whispered, "I know I'm too old, but I had a bad dream, and I couldn't get back to sleep. I'm sorry I scared you."

Sarintha smoothed the blonde hair. "It's okay. I'll walk you back to your room, if you like."

"I'd like that." Rhianna took her hand, just as when she was a child, and Sarintha marveled at how fast she'd grown. It wouldn't be long before she was an adult. Soon she'd want to see the world, and how could Sarintha protect her then?

"Oh, did you forget your friend was here?" The other girl was sleeping soundly in Rhianna's bed.

"I must have," Rhianna murmured. "I'm fine now. Good night."

"Good night, dear." Sarintha walked back to her room, extra careful not to wake Sam, who was a light sleeper.

Chapter Thirteen

The moonlight wasn't bright enough to illuminate the closet, so Sam held a dim, battered red flashlight to see the back. He had spent many days in this closet, seeking solitude, playing with the little plastic cars that his mother forbade him to break, because they couldn't afford more.

Shouldn't it be his decision to break or care for his belongings? He set the cars back into their box neatly and turned away.

It wasn't hard to pack, since he'd done it many times before. The secondhand navy blue backpack that never held his schoolbooks was too small and shoddy to hold much, but it didn't need to. He gathered two sets of heavy clothing, and another for warmer weather. After he added a few pairs of neatly folded socks and underwear, he stood back for a second look around his room. Once again, there was nothing personal he wanted, even from his private shoebox. His hand lingered over a curled photo of himself and Sarintha, but he didn't take it. No sense being sentimental.

He crawled under his bed to take out his bag of pre-packaged food that he'd saved carefully each week. To his disgust, ants had invaded it. He dumped the whole bag in his wastebasket. He considered taking food from downstairs, but right now it felt like stealing, which was wrong. But how could he be wrong? Rhianna was the one that was wrong, and his mother was too for always believing her so readily.

He turned the flashlight off and stowed it in the backpack, sitting down on the floor tiredly. This was where the routine usually ended, when his conscience began to battle him. He tried to convince himself that his family needed him, but he knew it was a lie. This time he didn't bother. He rested his head against the closet door and looked up to say goodbye to his room. He couldn't stay trapped here any longer. His resolution was calm, not angry or anguished as in the past. He was simply too tired of it, of Rhianna, and it was time to go.

He found himself standing over her bed, her gold hair tucked neatly under her head and her breath low and steady. Why was he here? He didn't care to say goodbye to her.

He leaned closer, smelling her strawberry shampoo. He imagined how a good brother might kiss her cheek, and then he found the silver-handled knife in his hand. He wondered if she had ever known pain, if it would wake her or if she would float along in her self-important delusions, too busy to notice her life draining away.

How might his life be different if she hadn't been born? Would Nanny and Mother love him twice as much or more, never knowing what they'd never had? Would he have had a normal life out in the sun, without Rhianna's fussing about how much she needed Mother and how Mother could never ever go?

Was it too late? How might his life become, even now? He would sob over Rhianna's bloody body, and Nanny would rush in to comfort him, to tell him she loved him and for once it wasn't his fault. The only time it ever *would* be his fault...

He would say someone came in, and he fought the intruder off. Sam would finally be a hero, and Mother would hold him and pat his head and say she was proud.

Maybe they would move away from here.

He clenched the knife in his hand, squeezing the blade with the other to test its sharpness. He couldn't feel it slit his skin, but his blood flowed freely.

A truck rumbled by outside, shining its headlights against Rhianna's window, and he saw her illuminated so clearly. She was the one who was destroying his life beyond repair, and he couldn't live as long as she was here.

He swept the knife over to her throat and covered her mouth. His arm began to shake as he gathered his strength, preparing himself to do it, do it right for once… It was right; it was time. It was a vicious, swift movement that released all his fury in a wild catharsis of joy. He was shaking with his own power and took his wet hand away from her to touch his own whole throat. He was free.

Then a strange sound came from her. Her eyes had shot open, and she was mouthing something, dark blood flowing faster as she moved her jaw. The sound grew louder, and he recognized it as laughter. Enraged, he beat her face, pounding against her to stop, but it rang in his ears again and again. He hated her so much, it had been almost over, and now she was mocking him.

* * *

Sam's eyes shot open, and he was trembling all over. He didn't recognize where he was at first, expecting to see Rhianna's horrible laughing face again, but he was in his own silent room, sitting on the floor with his head tipped back against his closet door.

His heart was fluttering out of his chest, and a huge lump obstructed his throat. There was no blood, no knife, but he was too terrified to move.

He could still feel the electric power in his hands, the life seeping from Rhianna still. Panic swept through him again, and he jumped to his feet. Should he check on her? Maybe something had happened, maybe he really had… No, he couldn't have. She was fine, safe in her soft bed with her many toys and expensive clothes. And besides—he remembered with a burst of relief—Ellie was here tonight. She was missing in the dream. It had to have been a dream.

He stood unmoving for another moment until he heard a shuffling noise and ducked back down to the floor. It wouldn't do to be seen out of bed. The noise quieted and he reached for his backpack to close it. Something was out of place. Glinting brightly on the top of the clothing was the silver pocketknife.

Panic cut through him. He knew it hadn't been there before. Was he still asleep? He didn't dare touch it. In a single movement, he zipped the bag, threw it on his shoulder and ran down the hall.

His feet stopped of their own accord, and he found himself looking into Rhianna's room. He shivered as a truck rumbled by, brightening the room, and saw Rhianna sleeping peacefully together with Ellie in the bed.

The bitch wouldn't haunt him anymore. He descended the stairs with his back touching the rail, turned the corner, seized his coat from its hook, and unlocked the stiff latch. Shutting the door brought him dizzying relief. He stepped out into the cool lamplit night and began to run east down the road.

* * *

Sam stopped to look back at the dead end near a very run-down house. His house was far out of sight, but which way to go now? He turned his face to the sky. The gibbous moon was high, calling him back home. He resolutely headed in the opposite direction, down the nearby alley, determined to walk until dawn.

It was still pitch-black when he sensed he was approaching something. His breath hung long in the oppressively silent air. He gazed to the right, and then he saw it—or the absence of it.

On the edge of a normal city rose a pile of wreckage against than the distant mountains. Nearby, the skeletons of buildings loomed higher than Sam could have imagined. Further to the south was a crushed and melted void. His mind couldn't comprehend the destruction of it all, rejecting it with such a severe shock.

He was as drawn to it as he was horrified. It seemed like some ancient graveyard, yet surely it was related to the Accident his mother sometimes spoke of in a hushed voice. He'd been so close to this disaster all along and never known it, but now he knew it bore a special significance.

Coils of rusting barbed wire fencing lay long abandoned, either never to be erected or never repaired. He imagined the workers couldn't stay a minute longer in this cursed place and assumed no one else could either. Many of the buildings had long since fallen; the workers had gone away to more tenable projects. Not a sound rose in the still air.

Farther out, not a light shone, yet it wasn't dark. No, in his mind's eye there was a sort of soft luminescence that radiated from the flattened center, as if the place had its own moon, which had exploded along with it but left its ghostly light dissipated throughout.

He was walking closer without knowing it, navigating the partially cleared wreckage instinctively, as if he knew his destination. He closed his eyes briefly and stopped over a dark spot in the concrete. He watched it intently. It seemed to flutter and twist before regaining its original human shape: a shadow of a dead soul burned into the pavement.

Sickened, he hurried away.

The power here was enormous, alluring and dangerous, and he could feel it sucking him in. His alarm was fading, and he was growing numb. He became so tired and distant that he let it in. He felt someone was watching him, but it was more like the entire place was watching him, filling him and emptying him at the same time.

His feet led him to a clearing near a mound of fertile dirt that sharply contrasted with the concrete bits around it. It was a bushy tree not a lot taller than he was, with a single fruit near the top. It must have been planted as a memorial. It was the only living thing in this place besides himself.

The pomegranate was sunset-colored, the only spot of brightness in this bleakness, and he longed to reach for it. The more he looked at it, the hungrier he became, until he found himself stretching his arm up toward it, the lower branches jabbing his legs, and as he touched its rough flesh, something round and cold pressed into the back of his head.

Chapter Fourteen

"Don't move," came an authoritative shout. At the same time, someone else ordered Sam to turn around slowly. He stood where he was but let his hand fall back from the fruit. How could he have not noticed someone so close by?

"Put down the bag, and turn around," someone said again.

Sam moved slowly, as not to alarm them, unhooking the strap from his shoulder, and saw a gray-haired, light skinned policeman pointing a gun at his head and two others standing backup.

"This is a restricted area. Why did you come here?"

He couldn't think of a plausible explanation. "I'm lost," he tried, and his voice came out much weaker than he would have liked. He found himself unreasonably terrified, but the fact that these policemen were pointing weapons at him justified it. He'd only gone somewhere not allowed. Why should they shoot him for that? But they looked just as serious when they saw how young he was.

"Signs are posted. Why did you enter?"

In fact, he hadn't noticed any signs at all, but he wasn't paying careful attention during his flight from the townhouse.

"I'm just lost. I'll leave right now." He wanted to add an apology, but he doubted it would put him in better standing with these trigger-happy men. "It was an accident."

The face of the Asian man twitched alarmingly. "Cute. You'll come with us now."

"Can't I just go home?" he tried desperately. "I won't come back."

"You're not going home again, kid," spat the gray haired man.

The third man, who had darker skin and was the tallest, stepped up to roughly handcuff his hands in front of his chest, jerking his shoulder so hard he cried out. "You're being held as a terrorist and enemy of the state. You have no legal rights until proven innocent. Since you are a minor, I'll give you one phone call. Make it count."

Sam sat silently, completely stunned as the two police cars drove out of the disaster, past his house, and into the city. They couldn't do this, could they? He thought people were supposed to get lawyers and trials. He fiddled with the handcuffs until the Asian man in the passenger seat gave him a threatening look.

"What's going to happen?" he asked softly.

"That depends."

Wasn't there some procedure? Maybe they weren't taking him to a police station at all. "On what?" he asked carefully, trying not to sound flippant.

"It depends on what you were doing there. It depends on your past record and on your family's records."

Sam's stomach lurched, recalling Pulaski's long surveillance. Wasn't that a misunderstanding though? What about Ellie? She wouldn't be allowed to sleep over if his family were suspected of being terrorists. Sam decided things couldn't get much worse, so he mentioned, "I know Officer Pulaski."

The man jerked unexpectedly and made a significant gesture to the gray-haired driver. "Oh really?"

The driver cleared his throat. "Then you'd know he's *Agent* Pulaski now, wouldn't you?"

Sam nearly smiled, wondering if this burst of adrenaline was why Rhianna enjoyed trouble so much. "He's not that formal with us." The exaggeration sent a thrill through him, and he was tempted to lie about Pulaski's relationship with his family. Maybe he should ask to see the officer. No, it might get Sarintha and his mother in even worse trouble. What would they think? Would Victoria even take him back?

When had he decided he was going back home? He supposed it was natural instinct to want one's family when in deep trouble, despite the consequences. Nothing they could do to punish him could be worse than being arrested.

"We'll see if he knows you," answered the driver skeptically.

Sam leaned back and closed his eyes. There might be hope. He rode in silence, trying to quiet his racing mind. Panicking wouldn't help at all. He'd get there, call his mother, and she'd come bring him home.

But she didn't have a car. She always said she couldn't keep them running.

Damn, damn. Maybe the men would bring him back home. They'd see it was just a misunderstanding and stop this whole bad cop pretense. Recalling the guns with a shudder, he doubted it was a pretense.

They stopped at a tall barbed wire fence, where a guard buzzed them in. They entered an empty parking lot and drove up to an enormous three-story brick building. This didn't look like a police department, more like a converted hospital. The bars on the windows, the size of the place meant this was some sort of jail or institution. That couldn't possibly be right. Maybe there was something wrong with the police station and they couldn't use it.

The driver slammed his breaks unnecessarily hard to park. Sam realized he had no door handle near his seat. He tried to smile innocently when they slammed their doors and opened his, but the passenger cop had his gun out again. What did they think Sam was going to do to them?

He avoided looking at it closely. They helped him out of the car much more carefully than when they'd shoved him into it. He hoped that was a good sign. He walked between the two men into the building through a side door, down a bright corridor into a concrete interrogation room.

"Identification," demanded a heavy-set guard.

Sam fumbled at his pockets, even though he knew he had no card.

"Hurry up."

"I don't have any,"

"Everyone has to have ID."

The passenger cop, whose name tag said Liang, said, "He had a bag with him. It's in the trunk."

Then Sam remembered the silver knife. There was no way he was allowed to carry a weapon, and the old blood stains looked really bad. "I've never needed it," he tried to explain. "I don't go out much. I think my mother might have the card."

"How old are you?"

"Thirteen." Sam resisted the urge to say he was younger.

"Clark, he's just a kid!" exclaimed Liang, to Sam's relief.

"He's big for his age," acknowledged the guard.

Clark frowned. "It doesn't matter. Where do you live, kid? What's your name?"

"I'm Sam Wight, and I live at 5243-A East Meridian."

"Wight with a 'g?'" asked Clark, and Sam's heart sank further. "Victoria Wight's kid?"

"You'd better call Pulaski. That's his case."

"Wait, I'm not a case at all. He drives my mother to work. His daughter is friends with my sister. Ellie's staying over there right now."

The sudden quiet bothered him more than anything else so far. Had he made a mistake?

"Maybe we shouldn't bother Pulaski tonight," Liang suggested.

"We'll keep the kid overnight if we have to."

Only one night? Then there was a chance Sam could get out of this. He had to stay calm, not say too much. The guard waved his hand in agreement, and Liang left with him, leaving Sam alone with the disagreeable Clark.

The man gestured for him to sit down, straddling his own chair backwards to rest his hands on the back. The position didn't look comfortable, so maybe this wouldn't take long, Sam hoped.

"What were you doing in the restricted area?" Clark began.

Sam chewed his fingernail, clinking the chains on his wrist together, as he decided how to begin. If he was being sent home eventually, he might as well tell the truth. It would make it easier to face his mother. "I ran away."

"Why would you do that?"

"I don't like my sister."

The man stared at him stupidly, then laughed.

Sam's ears burned with anger, but he knew he couldn't express it. "It's true," he said quickly.

"We all hate our families, kid. It doesn't mean you can break the law."

"I don't *hate* her. Well, sometimes."

"Never mind. Why did you go into the restricted area? Couldn't you go to a friend's house?"

"I don't have any friends," he answered quietly.

"Why not?" Clark asked suspiciously, jabbing his pen toward Sam.

Even if they knew Pulaski had scared away the neighbors, he couldn't say the truth. "I'm home schooled. Like I said before, I don't go out much."

"Does your sister?"

What did that matter? "Not really. Ellie comes over to visit a lot."

"Agent Pulaski's daughter," Clark said and bit the end of his pen.

"Yes." What was wrong with that? To prove he was telling the truth, he said, "She said her parents are getting a divorce."

The policeman raised his eyebrows. "That's true." He seemed to relax a little, standing to turn his chair around properly. "But I still need to know why you went to the restricted area. Were you meeting someone there?"

"No, I told you, I don't know anybody. I just got lost."

"Lost? You could have turned back."

Sam gritted his teeth, his eyes burning with tears. Damn it, he was too old to cry. "I hadn't seen it before. I didn't know I wasn't supposed to go there, and it looked interesting. I don't even know why it's restricted."

Clark stared him down in disbelief.

The door opened with a bang, and Liang came in carrying Sam's blue backpack over his shoulder.

"Sam here was telling me that he was running away."

"I've got his bag, Clark. Just some clothes. Might be the truth."

Sam breathed a sigh of relief. They hadn't found the knife. Were they going to give his bag back? Liang tossed it on the table between them.

For a wild moment, Sam considered reaching in for the knife to fight his way out. Their guns weren't drawn, and the door wasn't that far away. No, that was crazy. He was handcuffed, the guard would stop him before he got outside, and he didn't even know the way home.

He lost his chance right away. They both left the room to converse with each other on the other side of the windowed door. Clark didn't take his eye off Sam.

He was stuck here. On the other hand, this was finally a chance to find out why the police hated his family. No one would ever tell him, even though Rhianna pretended she knew. There had to be a good way to ask, if he were patient.

He stared at the two of them as they spoke to each other, wishing he could hear what they had to say. He didn't know how to get out of this situation, and they weren't giving him many clues. Surely they didn't usually give people his age such a hard time. What was so different about Sam and his family?

The gray-haired cop waved his hand in frustration, and Liang came in the room, smiling pleasantly. Phony or not, he was less frightening than Clark. He stood in front of the door, blocking the way out.

"Sam, I want you to understand that if you were anyone else, this wouldn't be so difficult."

"What do you mean? What's wrong with… who I am?" Would they just answer him? Frustration knotted his chest and made it hard to swallow. If only he could make them tell him, he would.

"Your family has had problems with us in the past."

Well, that was obvious. "What kind of problems? No one told me."

The man fiddled with the papers in his pocket as he thought. "They were in the restricted area when a murder occurred."

"When?" Sam didn't know anything about that.

"It was before you were born."

"That long ago? But nothing's happened since then! Why won't you people leave us alone?" He regretted the impassioned plea as soon as it came from his lips. It was both weak sounding and rude under the circumstances.

Fortunately, Liang only gave a thin-lipped smile. "That's not for me to say. But you understand now that what you did was very suspicious?"

Not particularly, but he nodded. "I didn't know, honestly."

"I believe you."

He hadn't realized he was holding his breath until the air flooded back into him. He had done it. He was going to be okay. Maybe they wouldn't even tell his mother. "Can I go?" he dared to ask.

"Not quite yet." Liang turned to leave.

"Wait!"

He crossed his hands. "Yes?"

"Can you tell me who it was? Was it my father who died?"

Liang frowned sadly. "What was your father's name?"

"I… don't know," Sam murmured.

"I'm sorry, I don't have that information, then. Two men were involved and both died. Your mother and great-aunt were at the scene. That's all I know."

Sam covered his face as Liang shut the door. That had to mean that someone in his family was a murderer.

What happened next was a blur. They came back to get him, with some sort of lecture about probation and official warnings, then they brought him back out to the police car.

All he could think about was how he would tell his mother and how he could find out who killed his father. And who was the other man, then? Whose blood was on the silver knife? Rhianna said it was hidden in the back of his mother's closet.

No, Mother couldn't do such a thing. She was afraid of violence. Sarintha wasn't, though.

He shivered at the thought. Nanny was too old to hurt people, wasn't she? But she always seemed to have the position of guarding them all these years. What if neither of them had done it, and that's why she always looked after the family? Would the killer come back? Exonerating Sarintha gave him an uneasy peace.

Too quickly, they were at the townhouse. He thought maybe they'd let him out and leave, but they abruptly turned on their sirens and lights to announce their arrival. Victoria ran out, looking horrified, and Sam tried to sink down into the seat.

"We've got your son here, ma'am," Liang said, getting out of the car. He opened the door for Sam, who didn't move. Maybe he was better off with the police after all.

Sarintha came out next, and Sam prayed Rhianna would stay asleep. He'd never hear the end of it if she saw this. "What's the meaning of this?" Sarintha burst out, apparently unafraid of the police officers. He felt a small burst of pride.

"Your boy was caught in the restricted area," Clark said from the front seat. "You're lucky we let him come home at all."

"He's under official probation now," Liang explained. "One more offense, and he'll be jailed."

They decided he was innocent? Sam jumped out of the car, grabbing his backpack. He wished they would shut up and leave.

"What?" Victoria shouted and pulled Sam toward her.

Sarintha glared at her. "Please be quiet, Victoria."

"We're watching you, Malik," said the older man. "Don't forget that. We didn't have to bring him back."

"Thank you," Victoria muttered. "Is that all?"

"For now," Clark spat. "We're serious. I'll be sending you the guidelines tomorrow. You'd better not let him out of the house."

"Fine," Sam said and ran to the front door with the same fervor he felt running away from it earlier. Sarintha and Victoria followed, but the police car stayed outside for a long time, its flashing lights serving as a warning to the neighbors that the law must be obeyed.

Chapter Fifteen

Sam wanted to hide in his room, but Rhianna was smirking at the top of the stairs with Ellie peering curiously behind her. He might as well get the confrontation over with.

Sarintha told the girls firmly to go back to bed before looking him over closely. "Would you care to explain?"

He could lie. He could say he was kidnapped, just like Rhianna when she was little. As if she knew his thoughts, Sarintha's eyes fell on his dirty backpack.

Sam's mouth opened uselessly.

"Tell me," Sarintha demanded, moving uncomfortably close.

He met her eyes and forced down a sob. "I couldn't stay here. I can't stand it. Everyone hates me, and no one believes me, and I didn't do anything wrong."

"Nothing wrong!" Victoria exclaimed hatefully.

Sarintha turned a fierce look on her. "Leave."

"What?" She sounded shocked.

"I am talking to the boy. If you won't be quiet, then leave. He is obviously very upset, and I won't have you make it worse."

"I won't—"

"He needs someone to listen. Clearly, we have not been listening enough. We'll discuss punishments later."

Victoria looked hurt, looking at him as if for reassurance before going upstairs slowly. Sam couldn't bring himself to care.

"What were you saying?" Sarintha asked gently.

"Nothing."

"That's not true," she reminded him, as if he were a young child.

"Nothing!" he screamed. "Don't pretend you care! I wish I hadn't come home!"

"The police brought you home," she pointed out.

"They told me! They told me the truth!"

Her brow creased. "What truth?"

"They told me about my father!"

"What?" She sounded genuinely confused.

"One of you killed him! There were two dead men—"

She took his hand, and he jerked it back. "I think you misunderstand, Sam."

"I understand perfectly," he said coldly. "Two men were dead, and you and mother were the only people there. How else could they *both* die?"

Sarintha was shaking with something close to rage. He had never seen that expression on her before, and he drew back, even in his own anger.

"They killed each other," she shouted. "I couldn't stop it. Both men are long dead!"

He wouldn't stand for her stupid explanations. "That's not what the police said! Why would they watch us if that was true? My whole life I've been trapped in here, and I want out! I almost got out!"

Sarintha took a deep breath, but her eyes flashed. Her fingers were clenched so tightly together that the ends were white. "Do you think I wanted this? I've been hiding longer than you! Alive or dead, he still won't let me be free!"

It didn't make sense, and he didn't feel a bit sorry for her. "That's not my problem!"

"You ungrateful child, I've been saving your life since before you were born." Once the words were out, she clapped her hand over her mouth, eyes wide.

"I don't need you. I don't need any of you." It felt so good to say the words, but his hands were trembling. The room looked oddly darker.

Sarintha was shaking too. "It wasn't your burden, Sam. I'm sorry."

"It's too late," Sam said with a hoarse voice. "You always try to fix things. They hate me, and it's too late. You can't even see the truth?"

"What truth?" She tried to make her voice even but failed.

Sam shook his head. "It doesn't matter. Don't bother."

She drew herself up and resumed her proper lecture tone shakily. "Regardless, you've made it so that you can't ever leave now. They're watching you too."

"I don't even care." Deep in his heart, he knew he was always trapped, but at least he had said what he meant to say. "I'm finished," he announced, going upstairs.

Sarintha didn't say a word.

* * *

Sam dropped his backpack on the floor and threw his shoes against the wall as hard as he could. He ripped the sheets off the bed, threw some clothes on the ground, and turned, looking for something else to wreck.

He didn't even have enough belongings to continue.

He curled up on the bed, clenching his pillow in a stranglehold. His whole body began to shake. He squeezed his eyes shut so tight that brightness danced behind them.

He had been so close to freedom, and now his life was over. Rhianna must have heard everything. He could never face her again. Mother would never understand, and now Sarintha hated him too. More than anything, he hated himself for his lack of control. He was completely humiliated and desperate.

What was he going to do now?

Someone knocked at the door quietly. "Go away!" he screamed. He was capable of anything right now, and he didn't know what he would do.

* * *

Outside the door, Victoria hesitated.

Sarintha came up to clasp her arm. "No, leave him."

"He has to be punished! I didn't expect you to be on his side about this."

Sarintha refused to let go.

"At least let me see if he's all right," she entreated. "What's wrong with him?"

"I've failed," Sarintha murmured and would say no more.

Chapter Sixteen

It was two years before Sam's harsh probation was lifted, not that it really changed much for him, but during that time the situation grew even worse in Macallister. His mother wouldn't tell him anything, only spoke to Sarintha in hushed tones, but Rhianna could be persuaded to share what she learned from Ellie, if he deigned to beg for it.

One fall day, Sarintha came home from the grocery store in a rage, an unusually large amount of items dragging behind her. "I bought all I could carry," she said, sighing heavily. "I suggest we go back for more immediately." She cast a glance at Sam to needlessly remind him he was not included.

"What happened?" Rhianna said, careful not to sound too eager.

"There were military guards!" Sarintha burst out. "They said a group of people had tried to break into the store last night and that we were lucky to be allowed in the shop today."

"They can't close the stores, can they?" Sam asked cautiously. "Where would they get food?"

"Apparently, they can do as they please!" she raged. "One pointed his gun at me, and it was all I could do not to—"

Victoria came downstairs, and Sarintha silenced herself.

"Do you need help putting those away?" Rhianna asked, as if on cue.

Sam scowled and grabbed a can before she could get to it first.

"They've gone too far," Sarintha continued. "Arresting children, pointing guns at old women, and they sit in their air-conditioned bunkers eating anything they want! This is exactly what—" she cut herself off, "*we were*

106

trying to stop."

Victoria cast Sam a glare at the mention of "arresting children," but then she looked as puzzled as he felt.

"They're only doing their jobs," Victoria offered. She cringed as Sarintha turned on her.

"They're taking advantage of us to convince themselves they're making progress, and it's only going to get worse. They aren't capable of doing what must be done. You of all people should know that."

"Who is?" Rhianna put in, as if she understood all this.

Sarintha looked about to shout again, but then she sighed. "No single person. We need change—"

Victoria cut her off deliberately. "You would like to get more groceries in case the stores are shut down?"

Sarintha nodded, dropping her tirade. "It was very difficult to find what I've already bought."

"I can help you carry things," Sam offered, knowing he'd be turned down.

Sarintha considered carefully, but Victoria said quickly, "No, you're on the list."

"What list?" Sam asked distrustfully. He hadn't heard anything about that before.

Victoria looked upset with herself that she'd mentioned it. "I don't want any trouble."

"You didn't answer," he pressed.

"There's a list of suspected criminals posted around town, and people are... encouraged to report suspicious behavior."

"Suspicious!" he exclaimed. "I didn't do anything wrong!"

Even Rhianna was signaling him to stop talking.

Sarintha slammed a can down on the kitchen counter. "Paranoia! Turning us against each other!"

"Calm down, Sarintha," Victoria muttered.

"No," Sam shouted, furious that Victoria kept stopping Sarintha from speaking her mind. "Someone explain this to me. They put me on some list?"

"I don't want you to get hurt," Victoria said with great control.

"Who's going to hurt me? Aren't the police supposed to stop people from hurting each other?"

"Not anymore," Sarintha grumbled.

"You mean I did what they wanted for two years, and it didn't make any difference?"

"I was lucky Ellie could still come here," Rhianna said bitterly. "You almost ruined everything."

It was all he could do to ignore her. "If I'm some kind of criminal, I should at least have gotten to do something wrong!"

Victoria paled and crushed a package of ramen noodles. "Don't say that. You did do something wrong."

"Whatever," Sam said between his teeth. "That's just because they can change the rules whenever they want. Rhianna, didn't Ellie say that some girl got arrested for wearing a pentacle or something?"

Rhianna nodded behind a box of cereal. "A long time ago." She was only sticking around to see him get in trouble. Sam knew this time would be serious, but he couldn't stop now.

"There are gangs that need to be arrested," Sarintha said, "so the police put armed guards at the grocery stores instead of going after them."

"So if you say they're wrong, they put you on the list?" Sam guessed.

Victoria pursed her lips. "Now you know why I don't want you in school."

"We're supposed to hide and hope it goes away? How's that going to help?" That was her solution to everything.

"That's enough," Victoria finally said. "I'll allow this much, but I don't want to hear you talking about this again." She glared at the three of them. "Any of you."

Sarintha was an adult. She should be able to say anything she wanted. Sam knew it wasn't worth mentioning. He'd gotten lucky so far. He tried not to throw the canned beans as he jammed them in the cabinet. Someday he'd be old enough to say anything he wanted too.

к к к

"How dare they send the military here!" Wellington spat, pacing furiously. "What caused this?"

Lori shrugged. "It's not much more difficult to get around." They rarely ventured outside of the Accident Zone, with no vehicles able to function long within its borders. The soldiers traveled by foot on predetermined paths and schedules.

"Yes, but they're trying to trap us here!" Rebecca exclaimed. As the youngest, she had always been the least pleased to live in such a derelict area. No doubt she'd meant to commandeer an empty mansion.

Lori knew she should point out that the rest of the city wasn't much better, with its frequent power outages, but what Rebecca really wanted were fine linens and jewelry. She'd already stolen more than her share from the citizens who had the better sense to evacuate.

"We have to take action," Wellington declared. He seemed insecure, as if he realized his position was nearly ornamental and that Lori would succeed again in stopping him.

"What sort of action?" Lori asked tiredly.

"We have to stop this interference. How can we make ourselves known in the midst of this paranoia?"

"Should we make ourselves known? Do we need to invite our own destruction?"

"Without conflict, we'll stagnate."

"We've already stagnated. What do you think we're capable of doing without Richard's direction?"

"We won't know unless we try." Rebecca's boredom had driven her to wish for action. Young women didn't adapt well to isolation.

"What do you propose?" Lori asked, knowing he was skirting the issue by not announcing his idea immediately. It would be poorly formed and impractical, as usual.

"We'll destroy the guards' source of power."

Yes, it was unoriginal. Leave it to Wellington to have to copy Richard's plans. But at the same time, she knew that an attack might be effective. Unable to communicate with the outside world, the soldiers might give up and leave.

Most likely, it would get them all killed. She paused. "Wouldn't it be better to distract them elsewhere if we want them to leave? Open antagonism will only make them send more people here."

Rebecca looked skeptical as well. "I don't think three of us can do it anyway." It was practically blasphemous to admit, but it was true.

There was Lori's opening. "She's right."

Wellington had tried to track down Rhianna Wight on his own, but he hadn't been successful. Lori wondered at first if he was too frightened to face Sarintha in person. Now she suspected that the power of the Accident Zone was waning. Their last ritual had failed completely, and as Lori's disrespect for their ways grew, it seemed less noticed by the others.

It was all the more reason to create more energy, but Lori shouldn't encourage him. "We need more people first."

There were too few people left in the town as a whole, so perhaps this would distract him for a while.

Wellington scowled, but he would accept that they were right. Without Richard, they'd certainly fail. Lori wondered how much longer she could keep him from going after Richard's daughter again and how long it might be before Rhianna would come of her own accord.

* * *

"Ellie, I told you to go away and never come back." In the tiny front yard of the townhouse, Rhianna smirked, knowing no one could see it. Ellie's red hair had fallen over her tear-dampened eyes and stuck to her cheeks, and she was still catching her breath from pedaling to the townhouse. Rhianna was reminded of her old doll, whose hair always lost its style after being dragged upside down. Eventually its head had fallen off, and she had thrown it away.

"I can't," Ellie whispered and looked up at her with that pitifully endearing pout. The wind blew an orange lock onto her mouth. "I miss you. I don't care what Dad says, and you shouldn't either."

Rhianna reached out to brush the hair away with her thumb, lingering on the other girl's red glossy lip. Her fingernail trailed over to the corner of Ellie's bow-shaped mouth and pulled away tauntingly.

Ellie's lips remained slightly open and her eyes slightly shut. Her breath fell light and warm over Rhianna's poised hand as Richard took hold of her.

No, not yet, not while they were outside. She let her hand drop. "I've told you I'm too busy for you."

Ellie swallowed rapidly, and Rhianna felt a rush of power at using Pulaski's own words against her.

"I thought you were my friend. You said you cared about me. You can't just leave me."

Rhianna's eyes narrowed. The girl was overstepping her bounds again, even now. "I can do anything I want."

"No!" she cried and reached for Rhianna's shoulder.

Rhianna glanced around to see if anyone could hear them. It would be terrible if Mother ruined this. "If you're going to make a scene, we're going to go inside."

Her eyes widened. "Yes, please. I need to talk to you."

"Damn it, you're such an embarrassment." She grabbed Ellie's hot forearm, digging her fingernails into her smooth freckled skin. She pulled her willingly around the back of the building. "Now, you will be quiet, and you will listen to me."

Ellie was trembling and pale, showing the sort of desperation on her face that Rhianna lived for. She'd do anything for Rhianna, anything she asked, but Rhianna would relish drawing it out as long as possible.

"You care for me?" Rhianna prompted.

"I love you," Ellie whispered. "Why don't you love me? We could be sisters."

Rhianna swallowed a laugh and made her voice as sincere as possible. "But we are."

"Then why do you hurt me? I need you."

Because I can. She almost said it aloud. "You have to learn. You have to do what I say, or I'll leave you forever."

"What?" she whispered. "What do I do? I'll do anything."

Rhianna took the same auburn curl between her fingers again. "Such an angel. You'd be a beautiful angel."

Ellie smiled and some of the ugly redness faded from her eyes.

"You want to be mine forever?"

She nodded, tears shining again in her blue eyes, as she drew nearer.

Rhianna shoved her away. "Nothing's forever," she finished bitterly. "Go along. Your father will be expecting you."

Her lips twitched. "No, he's not. He's going to be late again today." Ellie only came over when she was sure her father wouldn't find out.

"He doesn't make time for you, does he? Sometimes I wonder if he cares at all."

Ellie choked back a sob and fumbled for a tissue.

Rhianna drew back to soak in the beauty of it. Ellie was always crying, but this time was just for Rhianna. She'd created the pain and owned the one who felt it. "You hate him, don't you?"

Her hand froze over her pocket, tissue forgotten.

Casually she continued, "Well, he must hate you. He left your mother, and now he's leaving you. Don't you deserve better than that?"

A sort of shock was coming over Ellie's face, the beginning of the look that means someone's life is crashing down before her. Part of her was seizing up inside, burning in her throat and then freezing in the pit of her stomach. Rhianna could sense it from a distance, a distance padded by her own disgust and pleasure.

Ellie's usefulness was ending.

Ellie pulled back as if she were about to run away. She crossed her arms tightly and swayed slightly.

"Where will you go, Ellie?" Rhianna whispered. "Who will take you now?"

"I… Mom?"

"When was the last time she asked about you? Do you even know where she is now? She wants no part of you, you know that." Ellie didn't know that that was also her father's doing.

Ellie shook harder, but Rhianna hung back a moment longer. "Who loves you, Ellie?"

"You," she murmured.

"Are you sure about that?"

A loud wail came from deep in her chest.

Rhianna no longer worried about being caught. Her full attention was on the other girl, working its way into her fears. "No one loves you, Ellie."

Ellie's head shot around in a last attempt to find a place to hide from her own emotions, then she ran toward Rhianna.

Rhianna tucked her arms around the girl's thin waist, pressing her close and smoothing her hair down, just as a mother would have done. "I'm sorry it had to be this way."

Ellie was beyond listening to her, but she understood the words Rhianna whispered nonetheless. They sank into her brain as she dried her tears, clasped Rhianna's hand a final time, and walked to her bike to go home. The words would be the last thought on her mind.

Chapter Seventeen

That night someone was banging on the front door so hard that the window behind Victoria's bed rattled. An upstairs door banged, and someone charged down the hall as the shouting began. She had barely managed to get up when the front door burst open with a resounding crack. She hurried downstairs, slipping jarringly on the last step, to see Andrew Pulaski pointing a gun at Sarintha.

Victoria tried to shout, but words failed her, so she did the only thing she could. She shoved herself between Sarintha and the flushed, heaving man.

"Get away," he spat. "Let me in."

"What do you want?" Sarintha intoned from behind her.

"Get out of the way," he repeated to Victoria.

She found her voice. "Put the gun down now. What do you think you're doing?"

A strange low wail came from his chest, and he seemed unaware of it. "She's gone," he screamed. "She's gone!"

Victoria's heart trembled. He was clearly insane with rage, and no one could defend them against a vengeful federal agent.

"What are you talking about?" Sarintha asked.

Victoria tried to draw strength from her.

"What's going on?" came Sam's voice from behind her, making her jump.

"Go upstairs now!" she managed.

"Why?" He stepped closer so he could see.

"You did this, didn't you? You and that witch!"

Sarintha uncharacteristically rolled her eyes as she pushed Sam away from the livid man. "Stay with your sister," she whispered.

"His sister! Where is she?"

"I'm right here," Rhianna said firmly, terrifying her mother. Now the entire family was at risk. "What do you want, Mr. Pulaski?"

He grew even redder and raised the gun to aim it. Sarintha lunged forward and smacked it to the tile entryway floor. He seized her and shoved her head against the wall.

"Don't touch her," both children said at once.

Victoria was filled with pride and fear for them. Pulaski raised his fist, and Victoria made her move, surprising even herself. She grasped his arm and tried to force it down, but twisted her wrist painfully until she had to let go. Freed, Sarintha let out a gasp.

Pulaski went on frantically, "They killed her! Ellie's dead, and they killed her!"

Sarintha had gathered herself. "I can assure you everyone has been here all night. No one has killed anyone yet."

He ignored her. "She slit her wrists! I know it was your fault, you goddamned demons! She would never do that, and she was here today."

Ellie? Victoria hadn't even seen the girl.

"No one can make someone do that," Rhianna said. "It's impossible." Her mother wished she'd just be quiet.

"I know it's your fault!" Pulaski shoved Victoria away and reached for the gun on the tile floor.

Sarintha's face grew closed and icy. "Think about what you are doing, sir."

He stopped in his tracks, looking blank. The sudden change frightened Victoria, and Sarintha's fierce expression frightened her more. For the first time in years, she wondered what the older woman was capable of.

The color faded from the man's face and he held forehead as if in pain. His eyes began to bulge disgustingly. Rhianna was watching quietly. Victoria wished desperately that they would go upstairs where it was safe.

Pulaski's mouth opened, and his lungs were heaving uselessly, like a fish on land. Victoria began to panic, considering the man's status. "Just make him leave!" she cried.

Sarintha's gaze froze her. The mother didn't notice that Rhianna's expression was identical.

Sirens interrupted their concentration, and Pulaski gasped and clutched the doorframe. Two policemen came around him and grabbed Rhianna, who had stepped to the front.

"You're under arrest as a suspected terrorist." The officer nodded to his partner, who handcuffed Sam also.

Victoria gave out a cry. This couldn't be happening. She had to stop them, but there was nothing to do against three armed men, and she didn't even have her cane. Her breath caught in her throat as five soldiers ran up to her porch and pointed rifles at her head.

Sarintha seemed drained. She did not speak a word, and it probably saved her from being arrested as well. Pulaski had recovered and gained an official demeanor, telling them where her children were being taken. Victoria was too shocked to understand. The front door slammed, and the two women were left alone, their children in the hands of the enemy.

* * *

"The army?" Victoria finally gasped. "He called the army?"

"Perhaps this is related to his new position," Sarintha suggested. "But it's not the first we've heard of such a thing."

Victoria frowned at the memory of the grocery store fight.

"They've begun guarding the Accident Zone as well."

That, she didn't mind. Normally the extra protection from the Occult would have reassured Victoria, but these same men had just taken away her children to god knew where. "What can we do?"

"I don't know," Sarintha said softly. "It will be difficult to ask for help with so many soldiers around. We may need to wait."

"Wait!" Victoria burst out. "Wait for what? We can't even afford a lawyer."

Sarintha gazed at her pointedly.

"No lawyers? They can hold them with no trial?" This couldn't be

116

happening.

"There has been much precedent in the past."

"But it's not legal!"

"It is now."

"But they're children!"

"Not anymore, Victoria," said Sarintha. "They're nearly grown."

"My children are not terrorists!" Victoria screamed. "They didn't even do anything wrong!"

But Pulaski didn't care, if he was searching for a scapegoat. No doubt he had the power to get away with it, but there had to something they could do.

"I'll think of something," Sarintha promised, but her heart wasn't in it.

* * *

Victoria didn't want to answer the door when she heard the authoritative knock, but she hoped irrationally that someone was coming to bring back Rhianna and Sam or at least give him more information.

She didn't expect that Andrew Pulaski would possibly have the gall to come back to her house.

He bore a falsely sympathetic look that made her almost slam the door in his face. Unfortunately, he was probably the only one who could do something about this.

"Look, I'm sorry, Victoria." Pulaski put his hand on her shoulder, and she pulled away. How dare he touch her!

"You're *sorry?*" she exploded. "What the hell were you thinking? You get them back right now!"

"They have to be stopped. Society's falling apart because of people like them."

"People like—" Victoria sputtered. It was all she could do not to hit him, to pound her fists until that false apologetic look vanished from his face forever. They were her only children, and she should never have trusted him, even for a minute. "People like whom," she asked dully. "Like me?"

"No, no. Not like you. It's not your fault."

"Then whose fault is it?" she demanded

He sighed. "Why did you have to live with that old witch? I told you it would be trouble."

"Sarintha? She's my family! God damn it, you've harassed them their whole lives until you found something insubstantial to pounce on, you bastard."

He raised his hands, and his eyes grew hateful. "I lost my daughter! I could have put you away too, but I didn't. Someone has to pay. If you keep this up, it'll be you too."

She swore he looked darkly pleased about the whole thing, as if this were solely revenge. Victoria's eyes burned with furious tears. "They didn't do anything to her, and you know it. It was very sad, but it was Ellie's choice. No one can make someone kill herself."

A flash of Richard holding the gun to Olivia's head made bile rise in her throat. Her head went light, and her legs shook. Her hand slipped on the cane's handle, but she caught it in time, easing herself to sit on the cold concrete before she could faint. Damn her weakness; this was not the time.

Sitting there on her porch, looking up at Pulaski's hot glare through the haze in her eyes, she felt weak and dominated and hated him all the more. But fighting with him wouldn't help. She had to try to control herself to find out where her children had been taken. "What's going to happen to them?" She hardly recognized her own voice.

"I imagine they'll be interrogated and tested. If the results come out clean, they'll be let go. So you have nothing to worry about, right?"

She didn't believe it for a second. Sarintha said no one ever came out of the facilities. People arrested for crimes against the state could be held indefinitely, so they were never heard from again. Victoria gripped the cane with both hands and pulled herself up with all her strength. She needed to face him on her feet. "If there's any justice left at all, they'd be freed, but I think we can already see there isn't."

Pulaski's eyes narrowed with his sneer. She didn't have time to step back before he kicked the cane from her side.

Victoria blacked out before she hit the pavement.

Chapter Eighteen

Rhianna didn't know what to expect as she was led in to the institution's interrogation room. For the first time in her life, she was truly terrified, and her mind was starting to shut down. There was no way to talk her way out of this situation. The edges of her vision had gone dark with fear, but she could see she was in a small concrete block room with one steel chair bolted to the ground. A single light bulb hung from the ceiling, casting long shadows into each corner. Rhianna was used to being in control, and this place was far different from what she was accustomed to.

The heavy metal door slammed shut behind her. She stood on her toes, but she still couldn't see through the little one-way window. She listened intently, but the door was too thick to for sound to pass through. Richard seemed to have vanished. She was completely alone.

Rhianna bounced on her feet uncertainly for a moment. She'd expected screaming or even beatings. She wasn't comfortable with pain, but she believed she could handle it. She stood by the door for several moments. No one was coming back.

She felt an irrational urge to cry, to call for her mother and tried to force it down with indignation. She didn't have to put up with this treatment. She began to circle the room, peering into each dark corner. The paint was peeling off the concrete, and a large translucent-brown spider crept out from inside a deep crack in the wall. She kicked the wall with her foot, knocking the spider to the smooth floor before stomping on its twitching body.

She knelt down and peered in the small crack. No light shown out. Gingerly, she poked her fingers inside, trying to widen the hole enough to see something on the other side. A few small rocks crumbled away, but the wall was very thick. The hairs on the back of her neck rose, and she jerked away. Someone was watching her; she knew it.

Well, she shouldn't be too suspicious, nor would she give them the pleasure of looking like a frightened child. She gazed up at the ceiling but saw no electronic cameras that she could break and decided the little window in the door was where the watcher was. She stared right back at the blank glass, wanting to frighten the person, but she couldn't think of any ideas at all. After a moment, the sensation subsided, and she sensed the man had gone.

The room being excessively boring, she sat down in the metal chair. The cold was burning into her legs, so she neatly adjusted her skirt, fingering a seam for a moment. She was getting older, but she could still play the good girl. Deep down, she knew she could do whatever was necessary, however unpleasant, but something in her objected that this wasn't supposed to happen, that she wasn't ready yet. She felt childish and hopeless for the first time.

She sat primly and silently. The moments passed, and still no one came. She found herself wondering about Sam. Was he in the same impotent state? What was he thinking right now? She spoke softly to herself, calling Richard's name imploringly. He had been submerged since the arrest, and now he felt completely gone.

The buried panic in her burst to the surface. Why wouldn't it work? She tried again and failed and let out a soft sob. Something was wrong, she wanted to go home, why wouldn't someone just come to do whatever they were going to do to her? What had she really done wrong anyway? Ellie made her own decision, right? Ellie could have fought back, but she was too weak and stupid to try. Rhianna clenched her fists and began to cry. Who cared if they could see her? When she got her control back, she'd show them they couldn't get away with this.

The door creaked open, and her head shot up, tears instantly stopped. Her heart was beating hard. She saw Andrew Pulaski enter. Despite herself, her stomach began to twist, and her head swam. She thought she could handle him by herself, but he looked furious. She hadn't realized how large he was, and here she was, a thin fifteen-year-old girl trapped in the cell with him. She flew to her feet and charged towards the still-open door, colliding heavily with his left side.

The door slammed on her fingers, shooting brilliant pain up her arm all the way into her teeth. She wrenched her hand out and held her whimpering breath against the throbbing. He took her by the shoulders and shoved her against the wall. She could barely feel the crack of her skull over the confusing buzzing in her head. "What'd I do?" she muttered and rubbed her eyes with her stiff, bleeding fingers.

"If you didn't do something wrong, why are you trying to get out?" he hissed.

His hands tightened, thumbs beginning to press her throat. Electric fear cleared her mind. He couldn't get away with this. She had to say something. "Ellie was always a melodramatic idiot. You ought to know that better than anyone." That wasn't what she meant to say.

"What?" His hot breath smelled of sour onions. "What did you say?"

Rhianna took in a thin breath and plowed on. "The day I met her, she was crying. She never stopped since. Maybe if you spent some time with her—"

"She knew what you were from the start!" Flecks of saliva landed in her eyes.

Her throat was crushed, bright sparks danced behind her eyes, and yet she wasn't afraid. She had made him crazed. It was a form of power over him, and she studied it from a distance. The pulse in his fingertips beat faster as hers slowed. The pressure in her head rose dangerously, and she stopped breathing in a dead calm. Maybe she could make him let go, she hoped with detachment.

Sudden slamming and shouting nearby brought a rush of air into her stinging lungs.

"Damn it, you weren't supposed to come in here yet!" someone said, but she couldn't see who it was.

The light bulb briefly floated back into view. Two men were shouting at Pulaski and a shorter person in white was coming forward. Rhianna couldn't hold herself up. She fell to the floor with a jolt, and a stranger's cool, thin fingers inspected her bruised throat. She couldn't muster indignation about her vulnerability before a soft voice asked, "Can you speak?"

Rhianna moaned, wondering if it was better strategy to appear more injured.

"I'm Dr. Liebowitz," the woman continued. "I've been assigned to your case. I'm very sorry I didn't get here sooner. He'll be punished, you can count on that."

Rhianna tried not to roll her closed eyes, knowing it would worsen her discomfort. The government's methods of punishing its own were surely not sufficient. She blinked and a freckled face appeared before her.

Dr. Liebowitz was a serious, pleasant-looking woman with reddish-blonde hair tied back at the neck. Rhianna suspected she wasn't much younger than this supposed doctor, but surely her gender was to her advantage. She understood women.

Now the doctor was smiling in a sickeningly maternal way, even worse than Rhianna's own mother did. Liebowitz helped her up and guided her to the freezing cold chair.

Rhianna gathered herself and bestowed her best simpering look on the doctor, who beamed.

A hulk of a man pushed his way forward. "We've just got to ask you some questions."

Liebowitz shot him a frown but stepped aside.

Rhianna studied him closely. His thick arms in his too-small shirt were nearly as big around as her head, but if he meant to hurt her, surely he wouldn't have stopped Pulaski. He was brusque but probably harmless. She hoped.

"Look," he began, "we know what you did, and if you confess, this will go a lot faster. Maybe we'll even let your brother out."

"No, you won't."

"How do you know that? You just got here."

Richard would know what to say, if she could only find him. She couldn't sense his presence, but she opened her mind and said the first thing that came to it. "It's simple. If you let me out, I'll tell everyone what Pulaski just did. Also, I'd have a lawyer, not a *therapist*."

The man's face twitched as he saw his pretense was worthless. Rhianna regretted that his demeanor became more unpleasant, but less time would be wasted.

"I know I'm right. Now, is it standard procedure to incarcerate people because of suicides?"

"I can see you're a smart girl. Good, I didn't want to stay late today. Just tell me what happened, and we can get on with this."

She'd already pushed the limits of sounding her age. How could she say this simply? "Ellie's parents got divorced. She was upset. I tried to make her feel better, but I guess she slit her wrists." She did her best to look sad.

"Who told you the way she died?" the agent asked immediately.

Rhianna thought fast. She could say it was Pulaski, but he could refute it later. "She always said she'd do it that way. She used to cut herself sometimes."

"Why didn't you tell someone?"

Should she risk a verifiable lie? "My mother tried to talk to her father, but he said it wasn't her business." Victoria probably talked to him about a lot of things during their rides to the library. Would they bring her here to question as well? It didn't matter, since the woman knew nothing. Now Sarintha, on the other hand... She might suspect.

"Can you tell me exactly what happened today?"

She knew she had to be specific to avoid repeated questioning. She explained with feigned patience, "Rhianna came over crying. Her father was working late, and she needed someone to make her feel better. She said he didn't love her because he was always gone at work. I told her that wasn't true, and I gave her a hug. I said he'd probably be home soon. She seemed like she felt better, and she rode her bike back home. I didn't hear anything after that."

He scribbled furiously in his notebook. "Then what?"

"Nothing. I went to bed, then Mr. Pulaski came over, then I was here."

He stared her down for what seemed like a long time, and she tried to blink normally. Finally, he rose without a word and left.

Strangely, Rhianna didn't feel triumphant.

* * *

"Where's Agent Pulaski?" Sam asked, surprised to see the young Asian man from his last visit.

The man, who had been stifling a yawn, looked surprised in turn. "I'm Agent Liang. Agent Pulaski's... busy."

"Probably talking to Rhianna then," he muttered.

Liang folded his hands. "I'm not at liberty to say. Do you understand why you're here?"

Because Rhianna's an idiot, and she dragged me into her problems as always, he was tempted to say. "Not really." It didn't come out as dull as he'd hoped, with a twinge of nervousness instead.

"You mentioned Agent Pulaski," Liang prompted. "I assume you think it has to do with him."

Shit. He couldn't think of a good answer for that. Obviously the police hadn't seen the whole scene at home with Pulaski's tirade and then his strange weakness. "He's the only policeman I know," he tried. "And he knows Mother."

Liang held up a finger and touched his small earpiece. He sat for a moment silently while Sam grew agitated. Something wasn't right. He knew it. Damn it, why didn't they just do whatever they were going to do to him?

"What's going on?" he finally asked, and Liang turned back to him.

"You said Pulaski knew your mother? How well?"

Sam was confused for a moment, but he took the opening. He had to think of something convincing, no matter how wrong it felt. "They worked together, sort of. I mean, he's been following us forever, and I think he liked her. He hates us because we're in the way." He forced himself to add, "I think he treated Ellie really bad. She was always crying." He cringed when he realized how nonsensical it all sounded. He was a terrible liar. Shades of everything were true, he reminded himself and steadied. He met Liang's eyes and tried to feel confident.

"You're saying Pulaski made advances on your mother?"

"I'm not sure," he admitted, "but he wanted something."

"Something," the agent repeated.

Sam tried not to squirm under his scrutiny. Finally he burst out, "How would I know? I didn't read his mind!"

The scrutiny intensified and Sam began to panic. Didn't or can't, which had he said? The agent made a note with his pen, and Sam felt he'd just unwittingly confessed to something awful. Then he understood why they were here.

Sarintha had warned him how the government felt about the Occult. She said that was why they had been under surveillance so long. She'd made him swear to act normal, to never mention unusual coincidences to anyone, even his mother. And now he knew why, and it was all Rhianna's fault. If only he'd never come back home.

There was no use taking it back. He looked up into Liang's eyes and his throat hardened. If this was the way it was, he couldn't fight it. If he were guilty of something, he'd face the consequences.

Liang's fingers tapped the table and he said carefully, "If you confess, we'll let your sister go."

Sam frowned. He still hadn't been accused of a crime. "I didn't do anything." Were they going to make him guess what he did wrong?

"Did your sister do it alone? If your sister says she did it, we'll let you go."

The sick feeling deepened. Sam tried not to laugh. Rhianna would never take responsibility for whatever she did to the girl. She was probably in her cell right now telling Pulaski how Sam killed Ellie, probably even adorning the tale with unrequited love or something else equally stupid. Rhianna had never done him a favor in her life.

He was tempted to blame it all on her. Maybe he would get to leave, and she did deserve anything that she'd get. But he had the feeling that they were still watching his whole family, and if he said anything suspicious, Sarintha and Mother would pay for it. The government had been waiting for his family to do something wrong since before he was born. They wouldn't give up now.

He took a good look at Liang. He was very well groomed and relatively polite, yet unprofessional enough to yawn during an interrogation. Last time, he seemed to have a slight soft spot for him. Sam was probably best off playing stupid. It might not be too late.

Sam smoothed his own hair. "Look, I still don't know what's going on. Could you tell me?"

Liang looked at his own folded hands in consideration.

"Don't you have to tell me what you think I did?" he asked.

"Not when it comes to matters of national security."

It made so little sense that he wasn't sure he understood it properly. "What? What could I do to the whole country?"

"Just confess, and this will be over sooner." Liang stifled another yawn.

"Confess? Because you're tired? Aren't you supposed to care if someone's guilty? Or do you just pick up random people and accuse them of things?"

"This isn't random, and you know it. This is about Ellie Pulaski's death. She was seen with your sister shortly before she was found dead."

Sam's heart sank as his suspicions were confirmed. He'd been foolish enough to hope Pulaski was wrong, that the officer had been confused with grief. "Well," he stuttered, "I heard she died, but how?"

"That's what we want to know, and you're going to tell us." Now the young man looked fully awake and furious.

What was Sam supposed to say if they wouldn't accept the truth or a lie? "I didn't know her very well. She was Rhianna's friend, not mine." Not that Rhianna spoke highly of her at all. "I wasn't with them, and I just don't know. I only heard when Mr. Pulaski came to the house. You can ask me all night, but I can't tell you more than that."

"Rhianna's friend," Liang repeated. "That's all we needed to know." He stood up swiftly, gathered his notebook under his arm and headed toward the door. His other hand hovered over a dark pistol at his belt as he reached for the door knob.

God, what was Liang going to do to Rhianna?

Chapter Nineteen

"I think we should put them together," Amber Liebowitz suggested.

Pulaski snarled. "What, so they can get their stories straight? I don't think so."

"They're twins. Surely they already have a story planned."

"No one has confessed to anything," Liang pointed out. "If we listened to them speaking privately, we may learn something."

Pulaski rolled his eyes.

Amber drummed her fingers on the table. "What would it hurt? You want to know if they're innocent, right?"

"Innocent?" Pulaski burst out. "Of course they're guilty. They're terrorists, and my Ellie was only the beginning."

Liebowitz tried not to scowl. She truly hoped someone would ask her to evaluate that man: he wasn't entirely stable. It wasn't her place to criticize, though.

"You do realize, Doctor," Liang said slowly, "we're not going to let them go. There's too much suspicion against them."

They had already decided? "Suspicion? They're children, as far as I can tell. Well, teenagers, but sheltered ones, and I can hardly see how you can detain minors without—"

"That's enough!" Pulaski shouted. "Do you want to be next?"

Amber quailed. Surely he was speaking in the heat of the moment. She glanced at Liang for confirmation. He was scowling, and he had clasped his hands together tightly. She had the feeling she had one foot over the edge of a cliff. "Okay," she began slowly. "What are we looking for, then?"

"The extent of their guilt," Liang explained, as if she were a child. "They've attacked the family of an agent, and we need to know if they've plotted against anyone else. We need to know if they have outside connections, and if we should arrest their guardians."

"Not Ms. Wight," Pulaski interjected.

Her curiosity was roused. This was looking more and more like a conflict of interest. "Let's should put them together. See how they act, and what they say."

"It's too dangerous."

"They would be closely monitored," Liang said. "I'm tending to agree with Dr. Liebowitz. They aren't going to confess on their own. No one ever does."

Then why put them through this, she wondered. Why isolate and interrogate when it does no good?

It must have shown on her face, because Liang gave her a look that said, *We are professionals.*

After a moment, Pulaski decided, "Fine, throw them in together. Then you'll see what they are."

Liang nodded. "I'll prepare Conference Room Three."

The room was already barred and electrically reinforced. Amber wondered what else they had in mind.

* * *

Sam stalked up to Rhianna and grabbed her by the shoulders. He didn't fail to notice her slight flinch. "What the hell did you do, Rhianna? Do you know what they're going to do to us? Didn't you listen to me at all? I'm not going to burn for you."

"Stop being so melodramatic."

"They used to burn witches alive, Rhianna," he hissed.

To his surprise, she clapped her hand over his mouth and looked toward the door. "I bet we'll be out by tomorrow."

He thought his head was going to explode. He pulled away from her. "Tomorrow? And who's going to get us out? This isn't a game. We're *stuck here.*"

"Sarintha will come." She seemed so self-assured.

"I swear to God, if I thought it would help, I'd kill you now."

She tossed her hair. "Why didn't you turn me in then?"

"Because I still don't know what you did!"

Rhianna looked over her shoulder again and spoke very evenly. "I did not do anything. Ellie came over yesterday, sobbing about how *her father* doesn't love her, and I tried to make her feel better."

"Yeah, sure. How?"

"I gave her a hug and told her everything would be fine. I told her she should just talk to him. She said he wouldn't listen, that he was *too busy.*"

Sam got the impression she thought Pulaski was listening to her. If that was the case, she was an even bigger idiot for baiting the man. "So that's all?"

"No. She said she had a box cutter and that she couldn't take it anymore. I tried to tell her no, but she ran off."

"Then why didn't you tell someone?" Sam asked, feeling like his mother.

"Oh, she didn't look serious. She's always saying these things," she answered flippantly.

Sam closed his eyes and gritted out, "You're losing your touch."

She looked as if she were going to spit on him.

"Look, Rhianna, they think you did something to her."

"I did not! She was home right on time. Mr. Pulaski should know that. Whatever she did, I wasn't with her. You know I was home."

"Did you tell them that?"

"I tried. Did you know they let him attack me? Look at my neck!" She shoved aside her collar to reveal fresh livid red bruises. "They can't do that!"

Sam found it hard to feel for her. She'd gotten him into this impossible situation, so she deserved some sort of punishment for it, and some bruises were hardly enough. "Didn't kill you, huh?" he noted sarcastically.

She whirled away from him to face the door. "You people can't do this. Do you think you can get away with this? I didn't do anything!"

He'd heard that before. Finally the unfairness of the world was reaching Rhianna, but he was dragged into it too. It figured. "Do you know what they're going to do to us, Rhianna?"

"No, but you don't either."

He had a good imagination.

She scoffed. "They let you out before. They'll let us out again."

"Rhianna, last time they locked me up for being in *lost*. They think you've *killed* someone. They're probably going to execute you."

"No, they're not."

"You know, I think I'll ask if I can watch." For once, he meant it.

"You're my brother, and you have a record. They'll get you too."

"This has nothing to do with me. Grow up, Rhianna. You've gone too far this time, and now you'll pay. They don't even care if you did something. You're too suspicious to let go."

A sudden change came over her, and Sam drew back in surprise. Rhianna's chest heaved, and she smashed her fist against the table, screaming, "She deserved it!"

Sam's eyes widened. What was she saying?

"She was a spoiled little whiny bitch who thought her petty life was so hard. She deserved to die. I only regret that she was such a waste that she wasn't even *worth* killing."

He sputtered. Of all the things she could have said, he didn't expect that. She couldn't be lying, not looking so inflamed like that. "But how?"

"I *encouraged* her to do it. I wish I could have been there. I should have done it myself. I could barely even feel it from that far away."

"Wait, you *told* her..." He'd suspected, but to hear her say it! Pulaski was right?

"You're so dense." The unrecognizable aura had vanished from her face, and she was Rhianna again, small and arrogant. "I expect you're just as worthless."

He took a moment to pull himself together. He still wasn't exactly sure what she had admitted, but he had a strong suspicion what it meant. She was guilty. His sister had killed another person, psychically or not, and she didn't feel a hint of remorse. He'd lost all hope for her.

After a moment, it occurred to him that he should be afraid of her. She could easily do it again. Maybe she did belong here, but he was certain he didn't. Somehow he always knew she'd screw him like this.

She laughed at him, and he withdrew into himself a little, afraid she could tell what he was thinking.

"Did you really think you could get away with this?" Sam spat out. "Her father's a federal agent, and you're lucky he didn't *kill you!*"

"He tried," she grumbled, as if she hadn't expected it to happen. She never thought anything had a consequence.

"All my life, I've sat by while you got away with... with murder, and now it's over!"

She looked disgusted, asking sarcastically, "What do you mean it's over?"

"No, Rhianna! I've had it! I'm turning you in, and this will be over for good!" With a flash, he saw himself standing over her, the silver knife shining in the moonlight, and he shook his head in a futile attempt to clear away the vision.

She didn't deserve to get out, and he'd make sure of it. "You ruined my life, and I'm not going to take it anymore!"

A low snarl cut through the haze of his anger. In a blur, he was knocked to the ground with feral hands clawing at his face. He coughed and flailed until he found his breath. He centered himself and shoved against Rhianna. She fell off him immediately, dazed for a moment.

Sam rubbed his stinging face and found his fingertips covered with blood. Strange laughter was coming from his mouth, high and unhinged, and he goaded her, "Do you want to kill me, Rhianna? Do you? Go on."

She charged at him again, and he pushed her back with ease.

"What's the matter? Can't you do it?" He felt like the ground was unstable, and he couldn't sense his feet, as if they were far away.

An incoherent noise came from her mouth, and she abandoned physical attack.

She smiled down half-lidded at the blood under her fingernails, and Sam's world tilted wildly. He pressed against the wall to stabilize himself.

Sam fought against the surreal dimness that was overwhelming his mind. His adrenaline abandoned him. With a distant hysteria, he wondered if he was losing his mind. Then his eyes lit on her: Rhianna's eyes closed beneath wild hair, vehemence on her flushed face and white legs splayed like some sort of discarded demon, and he could almost feel the pressure of her hands crushing his temples.

Vaguely, he waved his heavy arms out at the fog enveloping him before he realized it wasn't contacting anything physical. It was part of Rhianna. This is what she had done to Ellie, and now he was tearing at the skin of his own burning wrist with bitten-off fingernails, agonizing at his own knifeless inefficiency.

Submerging his panic, he ignored his own actions and tried to think. This command must be coming from some connection between them. The pain pulled him back down, threatening to drown him if he accepted that he had lost control over himself. He knew that would mean permanent madness. He reached out again and found her, clamping down on the red aura that was Rhianna, slicing her out of him, and filling up the holes she left in his soul as best as he could.

He could see again, and he found her cowering in the corner with his hand crushing her wrist so hard that his fingers had locked up. He took a strained breath and gritted out, "You've lost. Try that again, and you die."

Something was still swimming in his head, a sort of murky dark euphoria that almost terrified him. Rhianna was incapacitated, beaten down and blank, but a flash in her eye showed that she sensed it as well.

He shot to his feet, swallowed hard and backed away. She tipped her head slightly so their eyes still met and a ghost of a smile crossed her pale lips. He wanted to hit her so badly, but she looked sick and weak, trembling all over.

He eased himself into a padded chair. He crossed his arms and rested his head on the cool wood table. The darkness between his arms soothed him as he urged his racing heart to slow. The buzzing in his forehead faded, and he took a deep breath. Like a soft nudge in his mind, he realized they'd been watched the whole time. "Shit," he murmured, and then he blacked out.

* * *

"I told you they're dangerous," was all Pulaski whispered behind his sobs, knowing he'd just witnessed how his daughter had died. He didn't protest as they pulled him away.

Chapter Twenty

Despite the chaos seeping into society, Victoria's office at the library was a source of calm. Most people would be daunted by the sheer volume of papers and files lining the walls and piled on her desk, but Victoria viewed them as protective walls to be lost in.

She didn't look up at his presence, didn't even notice the head of brown curly hair poking in the doorway until she heard his breath. The man was average in every way but with the strong muscles and calloused hands of someone used to outdoor work.

"Pardon me, isn't this the library?" he asked in polite confusion.

She smiled. "Have you been away for a while? It's mainly a records office now."

"What sort of records?"

Victoria knew that however innocent the question, it would alert Jackson. She put her hand over her lips and rose to shut the door. She was never certain her office was entirely private, but she doubted most electronic surveillance still worked. She gestured toward a chair, and he sat down, folding his hands in his lap. "How may I help you?"

"Well," he fidgeted, "I'm just trying to figure out what's going on. I've been out of the loop a while, but lately I can't even get the news."

She tipped her head curiously. Where did this man live that he was just learning about the events of the last sixteen years?

He looked embarrassed and began to stand. "I can see you're busy. I won't bother you."

"No, no. I was just wondering why you were 'out of the loop.'"

"I live up in the foothills, on Elk Springs Hill. I never needed technology much, but now my stuff's breaking. It's been hard to get by, not like it used to be. My windmill used to cut it for most of my needs, but the output's really bad lately."

She knew she was giving him a bizarre look, so she blinked back into focus. "Are you Amish, or a Simplist?" she guessed.

"Nah. I'm just a farmer. You remember about fifteen years ago when the economy started going down the tubes? My brothers lost their jobs, so I didn't even try. We all stayed on the farm. We had almost everything we needed, so we were fine."

She was still a little confused. Something about him seemed odder than that explanation allowed for. "Oh. Where to start... You did hear about the Accident?"

"Oh, the one that blew up a big chunk of town? Sure. I'm not that out of it."

She wasn't sure if she should laugh. He looked so earnest that she decided against it. "A lot of computers started breaking around then, and... some other strange things happened."

"Heard about that too. I was getting paper news for a while after that. Took my tablet into town for fixing, but I had to throw it out. Don't look at me that way. I miss my microwave too."

She did laugh, and he smirked back. Odd or not, she was starting to like the man.

"But can't they fix all this?"

"No one knows what's wrong, even the government." She lowered her voice. "That's why you have to be careful what you ask. They're looking for any explanation they can find, and you don't want to seem suspicious."

He nodded slowly. "Well, how's your power? If my windmill generator stops working, I'm out of luck."

"It usually works, but there were a lot of blackouts over the summer. We didn't have air conditioning. I'm not looking forward to that again."

He looked disappointed and confused. It reminded her of Sam's expression when he was punished, she thought with a pang and tried to push the memory away.

Jackson glanced in inquisitively as he passed by her door. Victoria felt as though she was doing something terribly illegal, although really, how much more could they punish her after taking her children away? Suddenly she needed some fresh air. "Are you hungry? Why don't we go somewhere else to talk about this? This isn't… the best place."

He smiled in surprise. "I don't have much money—"

"Don't worry about that. Let's get out of here."

They walked in an awkward silence across the wet street, Victoria feeling thankful that he didn't comment on her cane. She turned her head as they passed the park that always gave Victoria the shivers, until they reached the little cafe on the corner. Victoria didn't particularly like the food, but there wasn't any other choice in this part of town.

She gestured at the menu and asked, "Have anything you'd like. I'm sorry, I don't think I caught your name."

"Caleb Kepler," he murmured and rubbed his nose to obscure his face.

"Victoria Wight," she replied. "I think I've forgotten to introduce myself as well."

He muttered something to himself. Listening closer, she couldn't understand it. "Excuse me?" she prompted.

He looked up with effort. "I can't have normal conversations. I have to rehearse."

She knew she was staring in disbelief, but he cracked a smile.

"You're joking," she finally laughed.

"Not really. I don't get out much. I really do practice. I didn't know what to expect this time, and that's why I'm doing so bad."

"You're fine," she reassured him.

The waitress came shortly with their food. Victoria poked at her burned hamburger with distaste, but Kepler seemed very appreciative.

"Nice to not have to cook. Thanks again. So why did we leave the library anyway?"

Victoria glanced up at the cash register to see the waitress swearing at it.

She'd be busy with that for a few minutes.

"The government runs the library now. It's best not to ask too many questions, or they get suspicious."

He looked surprised. "Don't they have better things to worry about than people talking?"

She twisted her lips. "You'd think so, but no. It's probably not good for you to be seen with me. My children have been arrested."

He leaned close. "For what? What the hell's going on down here?"

"A policeman's daughter killed herself, and she was my daughter's friend. I... I haven't seen Rhianna and Sam for four weeks." She had thought that Ellie was sweet, and she knew she'd be torn apart if it had happened to her own daughter, but nothing could excuse Pulaski's actions. Now it felt as if their years of tenuous friendship were all a trap.

"Don't they have to have evidence? Can't you get them out?"

It all came back to her: how she let them rip her children away without fighting back. Kepler looked like he would have charged into the facility to break them out. She blinked away tears. "They're held as terrorists, so there's nothing I can do. They've been after my family for years, just looking for a suspicious event. Things aren't the same anymore. There isn't any justice, and I shouldn't even be trusting you." Dear god, how much had she said? Why had she believed this man so readily?

"Why not?" he asked, slightly offended.

She sighed. "If you're working for them, just go and tell them whatever you want. I know I can't fight it. If you're only being honest, well, you're just not going to last long out here. I'm sure half the town already noticed you."

He scowled and stood up, digging a crumpled bill out of his pocket. "I'll just go then." He threw down the money and walked out.

She found herself staring down at the old twenty dollar bill that couldn't have paid for his food, realizing this truly was a man who didn't know how bad inflation was. She looked after him out the window, but he was already gone.

The human contact was gone; the chair across from her was empty. She closed her eyes and let the pain sink in before gathering herself enough to pay for their half-finished meals and then return to work.

* * *

Sam felt as if they'd been questioning him forever. First the policemen had threatened him, demanding that he tell them what had happened in the conference room, where the microphones had apparently failed a few minutes in. It seemed that only Pulaski had seen clearly, and he wasn't in a fit state to tell them anything right now.

Sam wasn't in the proper state either. He ranted and screamed and demanded legal council until they finally brought him to a cell, where a nurse with a hateful smile bandaged his wrist with unnecessary tightness and demanded that he take off his clothes.

He refused, and she sent in a large man in a military uniform to hold him in place as she gave him a sedating shot. He had no choice then, and they made him wear a gray pajama outfit. They even took his shoes, for some unfathomable reason. It was obvious he'd be staying for a while.

Then came the psychiatrist with the fake smile, who tried to imply that Rhianna was manipulative and abusive, which in fact Rhianna actually was. Sam was shocked that the incident in the conference room had even happened at all, as Rhianna was quite good at hiding her true colors. He was very tempted to beat her at her own game, simply by telling the truth, but he knew it wouldn't be over with that. They'd probably ask even more questions, and he had shown himself to be guilty by fighting back.

So he refused to speak, and they refused to feed him, and the clever little psychiatrist came back later to make sure he didn't want to exchange information for food, before they left him alone with no clock or window to track the days.

Sam would never, ever forgive Rhianna for this. He lay stiffly on the saggy mattress and lumpy pillow, imagining a thousand ways to kill her. If he was lucky, this institution would do it for him, and then maybe he'd be sent home. He had said he wanted to see her executed, and he meant it. He wanted to be calm and uninvolved, untouched by rage, so that he could see every moment clearly. He would relish the look of shock on her face when she realized she was actually about to die, and when they electrocuted her, or hung her, or whatever they did, he would stare into her eyes the entire time, and she would know that he had won.

For now, that was little consolation when faced with the enormity of the situation. No one was coming to help them. Sam suspected that his mother and aunt didn't even know where they'd been taken. Victoria would try of course, but Pulaski was the only person she could ask, and Sam didn't want to think what he would say to that.

Why hadn't Rhianna fought back when Pulaski attacked her in the interrogation room, as she seemed to do when they were being arrested? Sam had to admit that she was powerful; she had a decent chance of escape if she turned her powers against the guards. He recalled how alien she had looked, as if someone else were behind her eyes. Did it only take hold at certain times, or was she still trying to play the good girl for the police?

It wouldn't last long, he reassured himself. She'd slip up as she did in front of him, and maybe they'd just have to shoot her to subdue her. No, that was too quick for her. If he ever got out of here, he would make her pay.

The feral pleasure from his old dream resurfaced, and he swallowed it down like acid. As strong as his convictions were now, the feeling had terrified him. It was a lack of control, an unbidden compulsion. He didn't want to let that manic heat lead his decisions. Even with everything else stripped away, he had to be master of his own thoughts.

He squeezed his eyes shut and tried to block out his panic. He would get out. He had to find a way.

Chapter Twenty-One

Rhianna realized she'd have to make allies, something she had little experience with. Sadly, everyone here seemed as bad as Pulaski, some worse. She hoped in the midst of this militaristic order, she could find a bleeding heart young man to sway with her innocence and looks. She would do whatever it took to get the leverage to release herself.

It wasn't until the psychiatrist from her interrogation entered that she realized she had been waiting for days for Sarintha to free her. She recovered quickly, however and examined the intruder closer.

Doctor Amber Liebowitz was in her early twenties, perhaps, very fresh-faced beneath her strawberry blonde hair. The woman lacked the stiff fatigue and exaggerated weariness of the other administrators, and Rhianna expected she was new at the job. It was a tossup if the therapist would play maternal figure or concerned peer, until Liebowitz aimed a condescending smile at the younger girl.

Maternal figure it was, then.

"How are you feeling, Rhianna? My name is Doctor Liebowitz, and I'm here to help you. You may call me Amber if you like."

Rhianna found herself speculating darkly about what the facility considered helpful while she put on a weak smile. "I want to go home," she said pitifully.

The woman's levels of female hormones visibly leapt, and she grasped Rhianna's hand. "I promise you, I'm doing everything I can so that you can go home."

Even if that were true, Rhianna doubted the woman had much influence. "Is my brother all right?"

"Your brother is just fine. I just spoke with him this morning."

Sam was probably still sulking, rather than trying to learn useful information. Rhianna couldn't count on his help. "Will I see him soon?"

Amber's smile faltered. "I don't know. I'll see what I can do."

"What about Mother? Does she know where we are? Why hasn't she come?"

"I don't know what they told your mother, dear, but visitors aren't allowed."

Rhianna had known, of course, but hearing it from this saccharine-lipped hypocrite infuriated her. She changed her sigh to a sniffle. "How long will I have to stay here? What will they do to me?"

"We have some questions to ask and some testing planned."

"What sort of tests?" she asked suspiciously.

"Oh, just intelligence tests, psychological tests. Don't worry, they're easy. I'll be administering them."

"I don't understand why I have to take a test." Was this some cute way of determining how patient she was? If so, they were going to be sorely disappointed.

"We just want to learn more about you."

"Can't you learn more about me by watching me at home?"

Amber cleared her throat. "My records say we already tried that."

Rhianna scowled. This was ridiculous. They couldn't just keep her here forever. Cooperating had done her no good so far. "What if I won't do it? You can't force me."

The doctor sighed and stood up, indecision twitching on her face. "You've been arrested, Rhianna. I won't make you, but the guards can."

Rhianna examined her face closely. The woman couldn't be so new on the job that she'd never faced resistance before, yet she looked very uncomfortable. "Tell me, Amber, what would you do if you were innocent and being held against your will? I did nothing wrong, and you won't let me go."

Liebowitz's face twisted. "It's not up to me to decide if you're released."

"You have to have some influence. I lost my best friend, and you've kept me away from my family. I have no one. Have you ever lost your family, Amber?"

The woman shifted, and Rhianna knew she was right. Sarintha had said that much of the town had been deeply affected by the Accident explosion. Amber would have been a young girl when it happened.

"Um, why don't I come back later?"

Rhianna thrilled at being able to make the woman leave, but she needed to understand her better. She reverted to her original tactic. "Please don't leave me here alone."

"I've got other people to talk to."

"Are there other people my age here? Can I talk to them?"

"No, there aren't," Amber admitted.

"Do you usually work with children, then?"

"Yes, I do. There's not much need for that here, though." They must have called her in special. Then Rhianna remembered Ellie's classmate with the pentacle and wondered whether Amber was lying or simply naive. "Then why are Sam and I still here? Why can't we go home?"

Amber sat down on the bed beside her. "I'm afraid the prosecutor insists."

"Do you mean Mr. Pulaski? If you ask me, someone should test him."

The doctor's mouth quirked slightly. "Frankly, I did ask for that to be done. I was overruled."

"Is he still coming to my house?" She knew Pulaski would return to harass her mother.

"No, another agent has been assigned to escort your mother."

Had he been demoted? Pulaski had considered his career higher than his own family. She hadn't thought he'd waste it pursuing his fruitless revenge. Surely he'd get over it.

Rhianna imbued her voice with absolute innocence. "If he hates us so much, why did he let Ellie come over all the time?"

"I really don't know, Rhianna. There's no rule against it."

It showed how little he valued Ellie if he were to put her at apparent risk. Ellie had never said he questioned her outright, but she also knew better than to reveal their more private conversations. If Rhianna thought she couldn't control the girl, she would have sent her away long ago.

"If you pass the testing, I'll do everything I can to get you released."

Rhianna thought she said she was already doing that. "I'll do the testing then. What will it be like?"

Amber brightened, apparently convinced of her victory. "There are some pictures, and some questions, and a few games."

"Games?" Rhianna feigned interest.

"Card games. Guess the picture, things like that."

"Oh, card games." That was the same way the Occult woman she met long ago had described tarot. And guess the picture… Now it was clear what they had in mind. Well, it wasn't hard to lie. She put on her most earnest look. "Could we start soon? I've been really bored."

Dr. Liebowitz looked thrilled. "Sure. Just a moment. My briefcase is outside."

Rhianna rolled her eyes as the woman left. A briefcase was too dangerous to bring into the room? Amber did return with it though, opening it to reveal a disgustingly neat pile of file folders.

What Rhianna didn't expect, though, was for a stocky nurse to wheel in a large machine.

"If it's too cramped, we can use another room," Amber suggested, sitting next to her.

Rhianna stared as the man began to attach wires to the device. "Uh, no, this is fine." How was she supposed to lie now, if she was being monitored like this?

The man stuck electrodes to her chest and forehead and snapped the wires in place. Tethered to the machine, she never wanted more to be able to run.

The nurse pulled out a needle, and Amber gestured negatively to him. "We don't need that just yet."

Oh god, what were they going to do to her?

He pressed a few buttons on the machine and slid behind it to squeeze out the door, leaving the women alone.

Amber saw the look of horror on Rhianna's face and said kindly, "Don't worry. It just checks your heart and breathing. Like two tests in one to save time."

Damned if she'd believe that obvious lie. Rhianna fought to keep the skeptical look off her face. She had to do her best to stay relaxed and to believe her own answers.

To make matters worse, Amber pulled out a video recorder.

She started with stupid questions like Rhianna's name and address before she produced a deck of cards with childish shapes on them. "Just guess which one I'm holding up."

Rhianna desperately wanted to tell the doctor not to treat her like a baby, and the machine beeped softly. Amber blinked and scribbled on a piece of paper.

Rhianna didn't try at all, several times guessing shapes that weren't even in the deck. She did it with such empty boredom that the machine had to believe her. But it wasn't reassuring when Amber remarked to her recorder that the results were statistically *too* low.

Rhianna sighed in frustration, and Amber folded her hands together.

"How do you feel?"

As if the woman cared. "I'm annoyed. I'm scared of this stupid machine. I'm bored."

"Are you angry?"

Great. What could she say to that? "I suppose. A little."

She was preparing an explanation when Amber asked, "What do you do when you're angry?"

Rhianna stopped fidgeting. "What do you mean?"

"What do you think about?"

"I… think about how it's not fair." That had to be a safe answer.

"Do you ever want to hurt someone?"

Just Sam, she thought, and realized she was taking too long to answer. "Doesn't everyone sometimes?"

"We all get angry," Amber said condescendingly, "but we handle it in different ways."

"Sometimes I want to smack my brother, but I never do it."

"You've never hurt him?" she asked lightly.

Rhianna's stomach froze. If they knew something, why didn't they just say it? "All kids fight," she insisted. The device emitted another beep, and she almost screamed in frustration.

Amber looked down briefly at the monitor. "We saw you and Sam fighting after you first came here."

Panic rose in her as she was trapped in her lie. How could she have let herself be tricked this way? They waited for days to mention it to see if she would act just like this. "We were both really scared," she began.

"You did something to him."

"Something?" she asked weakly.

"He scratched himself," Amber reminded her.

"He does that all the time," she said quickly.

"The doctors didn't see any other scars like that on him."

No doctors had looked at Rhianna, even after Pulaski had tried to crush her throat. It had only been Amber. She had to be lying. They must not have heard the words Rhianna had said to him. "They didn't look very hard then."

Amber leaned closer. "You said he did it all the time?"

"Yes."

"Just like Ellie?"

Rhianna nearly jumped. She was boxed in, with no safe way to answer the question. Carefully, she said, "I never saw Ellie do anything to hurt herself, but she was always talking about how she wanted to."

"Hmm," Amber responded noncommittally. "And what would you say when she told you that? Did you tell an adult?"

She had a brilliant idea. "I wanted to tell Mr. Pulaski, but I was afraid of him."

"Did he give you reason to be?"

"He watched our house for a long time. He never smiled." She paused dramatically. "Ellie said he had a very bad temper. She was always so happy to get away from him and come see me."

"What did he do to her?" Amber asked, sounding interested enough that Rhianna knew she was out of the fire for the moment.

146

"He hit her. She only told me once, but I know he did it more than that. She didn't want to live with him after the divorce. He wouldn't let her mother talk to her though."

"We have no records of that."

Of course not. He was too important to let himself get caught. Rhianna sighed. "Look at what he did to me when I came here. You saw him choke me. Could you honestly say he wouldn't do it to someone else?"

Amber considered her words carefully but didn't respond.

Rhianna poked at the adhesive on her forehead. "May I please take these things off? They itch."

Amber rubbed her own forehead in thought. "Uh, yes. I think we're done with that."

As the doctor rose to squeeze around it, her back turned away, Rhianna kicked at the electrical cord. The machine died with a quiet whine.

Amber swore. Rhianna made an upset face to indicate that she didn't want to do it over again. The therapist looked pained. "It's supposed to transfer automatically to my computer. I bet we have most of it."

Rhianna fervently hoped the last few minutes were deleted.

"I'll tell you what. Why don't we be done for today? I've got to write up a report. You get some rest."

As if there were anything else to do around here. "Could I get some books?"

Amber paused. "All I have are reference books, but I can ask around."

"I'd really appreciate it."

Amber put on her fake smile again. "Okay, Rhianna, I'll see you tomorrow."

Rhianna smirked as the door swung hard into the machine as Amber lugged it out, before stretching out on the bed to consider ways to defeat it next time.

* * *

Next time came far too quickly. In a few days, a group of nurses shoved her down the hallway into a surgery room and strapped her chest and legs to a bed with thick leather belts. Rhianna was too surprised to protest, and

147

somehow it didn't seem she was in any immediate danger.

Amber Liebowitz came, murmuring a weak apology, and sat in the chair next to the bed with a clipboard.

Rhianna shot a furious glance that Amber didn't even notice.

"I have a few questions about your medical history."

"I can't believe you would tie me down just to ask me questions."

"Do you have any heart defects?" Amber asked, as the nurses put the electrodes on Rhianna's head again.

"There's nothing at all wrong with me," Rhianna spat. "You owe me an explanation for this."

"It's just a little examination," Amber said, but she wouldn't meet Rhianna's eyes.

"You're a bad liar." *Really?* Rhianna thought angrily.

"We aren't going to hurt you." Amber's voice was getting agitated.

"Then why," Rhianna demanded again, "did you tie me down?"

No one said a word. The nurses acted as if she didn't exist. "Look at me, damn it! All of you, look at me!"

A young nurse with short curly hair nervously met her gaze, turning away quickly.

"I haven't done a thing to you people. Do you ever think for a moment how it would feel for you to be strapped down?"

An older nurse moved forward with a large needle, but Amber stretched out her hand to stop her. "Rhianna, if you cooperated, this would not be necessary."

It was all Rhianna could do to stop herself from shouting, "Do you know what I could do to you?" but she kept silent. In fact, she could do nothing useful right now in her paralyzed panic, and it wouldn't do to be gagged, as speech was her only way of gaining any persuasion over them. A bad liar, indeed.

"What do you want then?" she asked coldly.

Amber rubbed Rhianna's shoulder soothingly, and Rhianna did her best to jerk away. "Just finish answering my medical questions, then you can close your eyes and rest if you like,"

This seemed even more suspicious. They *weren't* going to hurt her? "I don't have any medical conditions," Rhianna said again. And if she did, she certainly wasn't going to tell these people her weaknesses.

"Okay," Amber allowed. "Then I have a few questions about the rest of your family."

"I don't *know* about them. They never go to the doctor."

"But your mother walks with a cane. Do you know why? Does she take any medicine for her problem?"

"She says medicine doesn't work," Rhianna said before she could stop herself. Hastily, she added, "But she doesn't like doctors. I've only gone a couple of times ever."

"What did you go for?" Amber persisted.

"Shots, the kind everybody has to have." What kind of stupid question was that?

"What about your father?" she continued.

Rhianna thought of Richard with a sinking feeling. Why the hell wasn't he helping her? She began to suspect that she was so nervous that she couldn't hear him lately. "I don't know anything about him," she said with forced sadness. "I wish I did."

"We have limited records," the gray-haired nurse offered to Amber. "I can clear her based on those."

Without thinking, Rhianna tried to sit up. "You know who he is? Tell me about him! What happened to him?" This was her chance to find out why Richard wouldn't say anything.

A sudden calm came over her, with a pinprick in her mind, yet none of the nurses had moved to inject her. It must have been Richard, she realized, and she thrilled in the fact that she was no longer alone.

"Never mind that," said the older nurse. "We'll tell you everything you want to know later."

Like hell they would, Rhianna thought numbly.

"We're ready to start in room 10B," a man announced from the doorway, and for some reason, Amber looked furious about it.

"Okay, Rhianna, why don't you tell us about school? Didn't you want to go to school with Ellie and the other children?"

They were deliberately distracting her. How could they possibly think she was that stupid?

"There's no bus to our neighborhood, plus Ellie said they were mean," Rhianna tried. "She said the nice girls already moved away."

"After the Accident?" Amber prompted. "What do you know about that?"

I know that they all deserved it, and that I wish I could do it again, came a jumbled thought, and that damn machine beeped.

"Look at these brainwaves," the curly-haired nurse said enthusiastically.

The older nurse made a clicking sound of warning and moved forward with her hypodermic needle. The coldness of the chemical moved into her veins, and soon Rhianna was feeling very drowsy and a little dizzy. Amber leaned over her, looking blurry.

"Tell me, do you ever know what your brother is thinking?"

No, she couldn't answer that. It was a trick. But she said, "No," anyway. It was a safe answer, but she had to try harder.

"Do you know what anyone else is thinking?" Anyone? Richard was someone, and Ellie was someone, but they were dead and not anyone anymore. The muddled thought made her giggle.

Amber repeated the question, and Rhianna managed a "no."

"What do you think your brother is doing right now?"

"Why should I care?" she snorted, with effort.

Amber's eyes widened and she shook her head at the nurses.

"Maybe the injection is interfering," the gray-haired nurse wondered.

"That's significant too." Amber was scribbling something down.

"And I thought twins were such an opportunity for study. Perhaps it would be better if they were identical."

I'm not all used up, Rhianna thought, you can try again, and she wondered why she would think such a ridiculous thing.

"How do you feel, Rhianna?" Amber asked.

"Confused." That was okay, wasn't it? Why wasn't she supposed to tell the truth?

"Confused why?"

CHAPTER TWENTY-ONE

She giggled a bit. "I forget."

"I think it was too much," Doctor Liebowitz said irritably. "Did you adjust for her weight?"

The nurse said something defensive, and Rhianna began to fall asleep.

Someone was tapping her shoulder repeatedly, and the spot was starting to hurt. "What do you want?" she groaned.

"Tell us everything you know about the Occult."

The question was too big; she didn't understand how to answer it.

"We're getting that odd reading again," someone said.

Amber sighed and started again. "Do you know what the Occult is?"

"Sure, like magic and ghosts," she found herself saying.

"That's right, but it's also a name for a group of people. Have you ever met them?"

An alarm went off in her brain. People who knew about magic. Maybe they meant the people in the Accident Zone. She had taken too long to answer, and they were poking her again.

"Have you met those people, Rhianna?"

"I don't think so," she said, because she wasn't sure. "What do they look like?"

Amber sounded angry. "We don't know what they look like. We want you to tell us."

"What ghosts look like?" she asked, very confused now.

"Tell us what the Occult members look like. Do you know their names?"

"She shouldn't be this confused," the nurse offered.

"Why do you want me confused?" Rhianna said.

"We don't," Amber gritted out. "We want you to tell us what you know about the Occult."

"I used to have my own ghost," Rhianna said suddenly.

"Wait. What did he look like?"

"Like a ghost. Just blurry and stuff. You look blurry too, Amber. Are you a ghost now?"

She slammed something down in annoyance.

"Do you want to be a ghost? I can help."

"She's not making any sense," said the nurse, but Amber looked astonished and vaguely fearful.

Rhianna growled something deep in her throat that sounded like, "Fucking doctors."

Chapter Twenty-Two

Victoria leaned her head on her hand in deep concentration, wishing it were much later in the day.

A man cleared his throat, and she jumped, cracking her knee on her filing cabinet.

"Hello." She hadn't expected to see Caleb Kepler again so soon.

"Sorry to startle you. You looked so interested in those papers."

She smiled, knowing she wasn't half as interested as she looked. "How can I help you, Caleb?"

He dusted his hands on his pants nervously. "I didn't mean to upset you yesterday. I've done some checking, and it looks like you're right."

"Checking can be dangerous," she felt obligated to point out.

He shook his head slightly. "I know. I just asked a couple of old friends. They want to get the hell out of here too, but Quentin's house is all paid off, and Chris in the army. He swears it's not much better anywhere else, so I'll believe him. I don't know anybody else around here anymore."

"You have a friend in the army?" Victoria asked, trying not to sound judgmental.

"Yeah, once you're in, you're kind of stuck, you know? At least they've got reliable electricity. That's what he said."

Maybe she should change the subject. "How's your windmill then?"

"Well, it turns." He waited with a blank face.

She gave in and smiled. "But not much else?"

"No, and the truck isn't working so great either. A fine time for that to

153

happen."

"Are you considering moving to town then?"

He shrugged. "Quentin said he might have me. He's lonely. That doesn't solve my money problem though. Got to eat, you know."

"I'm sorry I can't be of help. I'm lucky to have a job here."

Caleb lowered his voice. "If they're the enemy, why do you work here?"

"I get charity rides to work, and they were supposed to leave my family alone." It sounded feeble. "I do like what I do though. The files are very interesting, and I stop them from throwing out the books."

"Does anyone get to read them?"

She gazed at the ceiling, thinking of the books upstairs. "I'm working on it. I want them to reopen to the public, but no one comes in here."

Caleb smiled. "Why don't I be your first customer?"

She smiled back conspiratorially, rising to her feet. "Why don't you?"

Victoria marched out of the room, waving at Jackson, who looked up interestedly.

"Thank you, Miss Wight," Caleb said clearly as they both headed to the archives in the back. "What all have you got here?"

"We have some older print periodicals, maps, and textbooks. Everything else is restricted." It didn't look like much, but it was all that was left.

Caleb appraised the shelves. "Could we find out more about the Accident?" he asked more quietly.

"The digital records we have left are classified. That's too new. Most of this is thirty or more years old. There are a few newer newspapers here, but not many."

"What did they say about all this?"

She sat down at the table by the atlases. "Not very much. If someone knows what's going on, they aren't telling."

"What do you think is going on?" he asked.

It was an innocent question but one she was afraid to answer. Her experiences with Richard led her to believe the explanation was far from simple. Speculating could incriminate her. Cautiously, she began, "I think it's beyond science, or it would be solved by now. I've seen some unusual things lately."

He seemed surprised. "Like what?"

"Things are breaking down for no reason, but there's more to it than that. Some people are saying they can read minds or have seen ghosts."

"Really? Like the Occult?"

He did know about them. She took a deep breath. "Yes. Some of the Occult people took credit for the Accident."

"So we should look for more about that? It's as good a place to start as any."

His easy acceptance relieved her. "Yes, let's try that."

"Wouldn't they have blown up other things then?" he asked abruptly.

She thought she had long put it from her mind, but the memory of the old leather bound journal came back as clearly as the day she found it here. Olivia's husband and the steel works accident. All she knew came from Olivia's diary, but the woman had suspected Richard Aldon was involved.

Victoria closed her eyes. "I read once... that there was a factory accident over fifty years ago. Maybe some strange things happened then." Or maybe the only strange things were written in the diary Victoria had hidden somewhere at home.

"Do you believe in this Occult stuff? I haven't ever seen anything odd myself, but I can't say it's not real."

Victoria gripped the edge of the desk tightly. "I've seen more odd things than I care to have seen."

"Is that why the government doesn't like you?"

He'd put it together too quickly. She knew that fear was etched plain on her face, and she stood up quickly.

He reached out for her. "No, no, I didn't mean to upset you again. It was just a lucky guess."

"Are you going to tell your army friend?" she blurted out.

"Tell him what? That you believe in ghosts? So does he."

She steadied herself against the table, feeling her legs cramp up. What a fool she was to have been taken in by this man's apparent kindness. It was too late now, but maybe she could tell Sarintha to run...

"No, you don't understand. I believe you, Victoria. I'm on your side. I just want this to be over too."

"Why did you come here, Mr. Kepler? Why are you asking these questions? They've already taken my children. Are you going to turn me in too?"

"Turn you in for what? Look, I'm not trying to trick you. A lot's happened lately, and…" He raked his fingers through his hair. "I'm just trying to understand."

She stared at his pleading eyes and faded clothes and found it hard not to believe him. No one had tried to deceive her outright so far. She'd known Pulaski was a threat, and it was her own fault that she hadn't avoided him and his daughter. If this man planned to get her arrested, he had enough information already. It wasn't worth it for him to grovel.

"If you want, I'll forget everything you said, and I won't come back. I don't want to get you in more trouble."

"No, don't go," she murmured. She saw a reflection of Sam again in his hurt face and knew she couldn't turn him away. What harm had he caused?

"I could use some friends right now, and you look like you could too." He raised his hand. "Look, I don't want to fight. Tell me what you want me to do."

He wouldn't wait around forever. She didn't have to trust him completely, but if she ever wanted to see him again, she should say something now. Besides, it wouldn't hurt to have help with the research.

She turned to wipe her stinging eyes before facing him authoritatively. "The papers from last century are stored on film over here, Caleb."

His face softened, and he patted her shoulder lightly. "I'm sorry too."

"Don't be," she answered, but the words died in her throat. "Ahem. Jackson will be looking for me, so I'm going to go up front for a minute. He's going to wonder why you're here, so I have to think of something."

Caleb nodded. "I'll keep looking."

Victoria walked slowly to the front desk, a plan forming in her mind. The books should be available to the public. She wasn't sure how much convincing their superiors would need, but she thought she had a good place to start.

"Hey, Victoria, what's up?" Jackson asked pleasantly.

"Mr. Kepler has come to see me about donating some books. He'd like to help re-open the library to the public." Where she'd actually get the books from, she didn't know yet.

"Why would we need to do that? We have a few records they can access. Isn't that good enough?"

Victoria smoothed her hair and leaned on the desk, feigning flirtation. "If you haven't noticed, it's just been us in here lately. No one is using the public records."

"That's really not our job," he reminded her.

"We're scaring everyone away. Morale isn't very good out there. People don't trust the government. This could be a gesture of good faith."

He raised his eyebrows. "People don't trust us? Who said that?"

"Come on, Jackson. You know the whole city's upset about the power going out all the time. They need a distraction." She couldn't possibly get in trouble for pointing out the obvious.

"How are we going to get the money for this?"

Remembering the old registration policy, she suggested. "We'll charge them."

"Nobody'd come then. Everyone around here is broke."

He had a point. Why hadn't she thought this through better? How could they get anything done for free? Her eyes lit up. "I'll take care of it. I'll reorganize, coordinate the donations."

"Nice try. You can't do all that by yourself."

"Come on, Jackson. The important records are locked up, and we've got all those books upstairs that no one's using."

"Maybe we should sell them." He seemed to enjoy the look of shock on her face, and she realized he was joking.

"I could get other volunteers. Mr. Kepler said he would be willing to help us get started." At least, she thought he might.

His mouth quirked. "You thought this through, didn't you?"

She was pleased that it seemed that way. "I think I can make it work."

"I'll think about it, but you know it's not my decision."

If sheer hope could tip the balance, Victoria thought it could work. "Thanks, Jackson. I'll tell him to bring the books."

"Wait!" he said to the back of her head as she smirked and walked away.

In the back, Caleb was poring over some antique microfiche, a disappointingly blank notepad beside him. "I've got nothing," he grumbled.

She rushed up to him and burst out, "Do any of your friends have books?"

His bewildered look resembled her own first impression of him.

"I need books," she explained incoherently.

"Okay, what kind?"

"Any kind. Just anything that's not banned."

"How do I know what's banned?"

"I know. Can you think of anyone?"

He laughed. "My father had a big collection. I must have read them all a hundred times."

"Do you need them?"

"Well…" he considered.

Her eyes moved over the shelves in a flurry, reorganizing the stacks in her mind. Finally, she realized she hadn't explained her idea. "I think I can get the library reopened in here if I can get some donations. I told Jackson you wanted to be a patron."

"Sure, I could spare some, but what good would that do?"

Her eyes widened, and she realized she was talking faster. "I could get them to stay open late. We could go over all these records together, and no one would be watching. Maybe I could even get into some of Jackson's private records, the ones I can't see."

Caleb went from confused to enthralled instantly. "Are you kidding? Would you do that?"

She licked her lips and grinned. "I'm going to start without approval. By the time they make a decision, everything will be ready."

He gave her an admiring smile. "It sounds like a plan."

She took a deep breath. Once she decided to go through with it, the enormity of it settled into her. "There's no way I can move these bookcases myself." Some of them were well over ten feet long.

CHAPTER TWENTY-TWO

"Will you need some help?"

Caleb Kepler was a well-built man, but it wouldn't be good enough. "I don't think just the two of us could do it, even if I were stronger." Her legs abruptly reminded her of that fact, and she had to sit down.

He reflected a moment. "I've got a couple of friends who could help you with that."

"Do you mean those two you mentioned before? The army—"

He waved his hand. "Chris. You can trust him, believe me." He slammed his fist to the table suddenly. "Wait a minute. He said those boys out guarding the Accident Zone hated it out there. Do you suppose they could use a few books to keep themselves busy?"

That would garner her some goodwill. "It's perfect! Could you tell him my idea?" She could have thrown her arms around him.

"I sure as hell will. He can pull some strings."

The ideas came into Victoria's head so quickly she could hardly keep track of them. Finally, she grabbed Caleb's pen and started writing frantically.

Caleb glanced at his watch.

"It's getting late, isn't it?" she realized. "Damn, I still have work to do."

"I'd better get out of here then." The heavy book slapped shut.

Jackson would be suspicious soon, if he weren't already. "Yes, I'm sorry. How about if you come back after six? I'll get him to let me stay late to finish working. Try to get some books, and I'll figure out how to rearrange this place."

He inspected the room. "How much space are you going to need? It's already crowded in here."

"I'll figure something out," she mumbled, back to scribbling a messy diagram.

"I'll see you then."

She looked up at him absent-mindedly. "Oh. Yes. I'll walk you out."

It was all she could do to hide her excitement as she walked past Jackson to return to her office. Never in her life had she been so excited by her work. She couldn't wait for Kepler to return.

Chapter Twenty-Three

Before Victoria knew it, Jackson was stopping by to remind her of the time.

"I'm still busy," she answered, trying to look tired. "I'll be stuck here for a while."

"I've got to go. How will you get home?" he asked.

She'd forgotten to think about that. Jackson always drove her home, and he knew she didn't have another ride. "I'll sleep in my office."

He snorted and put her coat on the top of her filing cabinet, the only place in the room uncovered by papers.

"Don't worry, I'll think of something," she said. "Go on home. Tell Sarah happy birthday for me."

He smiled widely. "I sure will. You can call me after eight if you get stuck here, okay?"

She was growing genuinely fond of the man. Spy or not, he didn't have to go to half the effort he made to be nice. She resisted the urge to remind him of her request to officially reopen the library. With any luck, she wouldn't need his help. She watched him leave and quickly unlocked the front door before settling back into her office.

"There's a lot of crap here," an unfamiliar voice observed.

Victoria jumped to her feet.

"I don't think we can do all this," an older male voice agreed.

She stepped out of her office to see Caleb looking over the first floor with a gray-haired man who wore glasses and a young man with a dark complexion.

The latter must be Chris, as he was wearing fatigues. She hoped fervently she was doing the right thing and prepared herself to use extra caution.

"I haven't seen her plans yet," Caleb said enthusiastically. "We'll see."

The older man was rubbing his forehead when Victoria reached out to shake her hand. He took it uncertainly and introduced himself as Quentin Doyle.

The army officer nearly crushed her hand. "Chris Natchez. I want you to know I think you have a great idea. My people have nothing to do with their devices all broken. Not to mention, we'd like to see the community come together too."

Victoria sighed in relief. It really was going to work, and the man had quickly put her at ease. "People are nervous," she agreed. "They'd love to get to know the soldiers in person."

"I think we can do that. I'm just a normal guy, like everyone else. I grew up here, and it kills me to see how empty this town's gotten." Chris put his hand on a shelf. "So, what do you have in mind?"

She held out her notebook. "I think I can readjust some shelves to add in more rows, and if I stack these tall books horizontally, there should be plenty of space. Of course, I don't know how many donations we'll get."

Quentin's eyes crinkled. "The whole back of Caleb's truck is full."

She couldn't believe it. "Can I see? Do you need help carrying them in?"

Chris suggested, "Why don't we do that first? Then we can see how much of this we'll actually have to move."

"I want lots of extra space so everyone can see we're committed," she said right away.

"If the guys are interested, half of it'll be borrowed right away," Chris said optimistically as they walked out.

Victoria couldn't believe her eyes. Caleb's truck bed was as full as travel would allow, and the cabin was crammed full of books as well.

"A few of those are mine," Quentin pointed out.

She beamed. "Thank you all so much. I can't say how much I appreciate it."

"As long as you're willing to sort through it all, I need the space," the older man answered.

"I'm moving into the city," Caleb explained. "Quentin offered to take me in."

"That's wonderful," Victoria answered. "Please visit here often. If you like, we could use some volunteers."

Caleb caught her eye and winked. "You can count on it. I don't have much else going on."

Together, they carried in the books while Victoria sorted them into broad categories and by repair need. Most were in remarkably good shape, ready to be used as soon as she could organize them.

The men made less progress than she hoped for with the shelves, and it was getting late. She hadn't even begun work on the books upstairs.

"It's not all getting done tonight," Quentin realized.

"You can all go. I'll move these books out of the way and call it a night."

"I'll be back tomorrow," Chris promised. "We'll start moving the heavy stuff, if you can stand a few books being knocked on the floor."

She cringed automatically before she realized he was teasing. "I really appreciate it, Mr. Natchez. Thank you so much. You too, Mr. Doyle."

Quentin started to pat her shoulder but stopped short. "I'll come back when I can. I expect this place to be crowded."

That wouldn't be hard, given the mess she'd made tonight. "Oh, with people," she half-joked.

"Good night."

The two men drove off, but Caleb lingered behind. "How are you going to get home?" he asked. "The parking lot's empty."

She made an offhand gesture. "I'll figure something out."

"This late? Would you like a ride home?"

She regarded him fondly, reaching out to knock a dust ball out of his hair. "I'd like that very much, Caleb. Give me a minute to get my coat."

She leaned on her cane stiffly, realizing that she was exhausted. The pleasant whirlwind of her plans had calmed down, and she was left to ponder how much work lay ahead of her. She smiled to think what Jackson would say in the morning when he received the unexpected call from Natchez's superior about their generous donations.

She gave Caleb quick directions, and they were off. Out of the parking lot, only Caleb's dim headlights lit up the road. So many people had moved away that the long rows of houses were all empty. It reminded her too much of the Accident Zone, as if it were a plague that had escaped outside of quarantine.

Caleb followed her look. "The city used to be too bright for me. Look at it now."

It wasn't right. There should be cars on the street, porch lights welcoming guests, children sleeping in their beds. Her children should be sleeping in their beds at home. She cleared her throat to cover her involuntary sniffle.

"What do you suppose they'll do with all those empty houses?" Caleb had to share housing with a friend, and Victoria and Sarintha lived in such small rooms, when these large homes were abandoned. It didn't seem fair, either to them or the owners who couldn't sell.

"I don't know," she said. Recalling the office buildings in the Accident Zone, she guessed, "Someone might come in and gut them. They could resell some of the copper and the newer cabinets and things to another town."

He shook his head. "It seems like bad luck."

She tried to be optimistic. "If they can get the power working a little better, I'd bet a lot of people would move back because of the cheap prices."

He made a non-committal grunt as he turned the corner onto Meridian Street, disregarding the darkened stoplights. "I like the traffic better the way it is now."

She tried to laugh and found she felt more at ease. It was comforting to have someone new to talk to, a normal person who didn't judge or accuse her. Caleb had only ordinary concerns. What was the worst thing he'd ever seen, she wondered, up in the hills all alone?

"It's nice to get home quickly. It used to take forever to get across town. We're almost there. It's on the left."

He crossed the empty oncoming lane to park in front. "Well, I guess I'll see you tomorrow."

"You could probably come earlier. I really haven't had much work lately."

"I expect this will keep you busy, then."

It would ensure she'd keep her position for quite some time, she hoped. She stepped down from the truck carefully, disappointed that they had arrived quickly. She waved and watched him drive off.

Sarintha met her at the door with a quizzical look. "You're late."

"Did I worry you?" Her aunt didn't seem displeased.

"Who was that?" Sarintha asked curiously.

Victoria could feel herself blush. "Someone I met yesterday. He's going to help at the library. I have the best news!"

Her aunt raised her eyebrows.

Victoria clasped Sarintha's hands happily. "We're going to reopen the library. Caleb knows a man in the army, and we're collecting books for them to read."

Sarintha waited expectantly.

"Oh, Caleb. He's moving into town from the hills, and the two of us are trying to find out why the electronics have been breaking."

Sarintha seemed to piece together her confusing statements. "Do you trust this man?"

It was a valid question. "He seems quite honest."

"Perhaps I should meet him."

Victoria shrugged. Part of her was awaiting Sarintha's appraisal anyway. "Certainly, if you like. We could use more help at work."

She looked concerned. "Men from the army will be there?"

"Not yet. Just one for now. It's a good opportunity to hear what's going on in other places," she said eagerly.

Sarintha regarded her with a quirked mouth. "You're fond of this man."

Victoria's ears burned. She most certainly was not. Well, not in that way. "I'll wait until you meet him to reserve judgment," she said hastily.

To her surprise, her aunt patted her shoulder and smiled. "I like to see you happy again. Just be careful."

* * *

Victoria realized she hadn't worked out a way to contact Caleb since she hadn't had a working cell phone in years. She went to work alone with Jackson, pretending nothing odd was happening. The man probably assumed she'd forgotten her quickly conceived plan. She heard the phone call from the army base come in on the landline, but Jackson didn't press her for details when he gave her the good news.

In the afternoon, Caleb arrived, and Jackson treated him very respectfully. She suspected Jackson thought Caleb was involved with the military himself.

Victoria rushed up to him. "I hate to ask you another favor, but do you think you could stop by my house?"

He gave her a look that said he had little else to do. "Sure. Why?"

"My aunt wanted to help, and she needs a ride here. She lives the same place I do."

"You should get yourself a car instead of asking strange men for rides," he teased.

She gave him a look of fake exasperation. "I would if I thought I could keep one running." Sarintha's old car had broken down long before Victoria had moved in.

He shrugged. "Guess I've been lucky with my old truck. It doesn't hurt that I don't drive much either. No problem, I can get her. What's her name?"

"Sarintha Malik. She was eager to meet you." Victoria couldn't wait to hear what she'd say. She wished she could come, but it would be better for the two to be alone.

He waved amiably and left again.

Victoria grabbed her lunch and waited outside.

Soon, they had returned. Victoria watched her aunt closely for signs of her opinion. The woman looked perplexed and uncertain, but Caleb had done that to Victoria too. She tried not to laugh when she imagined the two conversing. She'd see it for herself soon enough.

Sarintha shook her head as if to clear it, but smiled slightly at Victoria to reassure her.

Victoria set Caleb to work rearranging the periodicals and gestured to Sarintha to follow her upstairs.

"There's something odd about that man," Sarintha whispered.

Victoria turned to her. "What's wrong?"

Sarintha shook her head again. "I'm not certain. It's as if… he isn't there."

Victoria was alarmed. "Should I send him away? Is he dangerous?"

She sighed. "I don't think so. He may be adept at covering his thoughts."

What did this mean? Caleb didn't interact socially often, so why should he know how to protect himself? Maybe something had happened in his past that made him move away from the city. She was concerned, but it wasn't a reason to discount the man entirely. "We'll just have to do it the old-fashioned way," she decided. "Maybe he'll tell us when he's ready."

Sarintha gathered the books into small stacks while Victoria carried them downstairs. She returned briskly to see Sarintha holding a book with a disturbed look on her face. "Where did this come from?" the older woman asked softly.

"I don't recall. What's wrong?"

She took a deep breath. "It's familiar."

Victoria examined the cover. It was a common, unremarkable collection of poetry. "Maybe we have a copy at home."

Sarintha shook her head firmly. "It *feels* wrong. I believe it was Richard's book."

Victoria shivered, even though it made perfect sense. "He donated books quite often, actually. It was how I decided to meet him."

Sarintha's hands quivered as she sat down the book. "Yes, I'd forgotten."

"Are you all right?" Surely it wouldn't upset her so much that she had to leave. Richard's things were all over this room, impossible to avoid.

"I'm fine. It just startled me." It seemed like she wanted to say more, but Sarintha turned back to work quickly.

Maybe this was too much for Sarintha. Since the children left, the woman had only left the house for groceries, and now she was in the domain of their enemies. It had bothered Victoria at first also, yet here she was making plans without official government permission and researching forbidden topics in public.

It pleased her to think how much she'd changed in the past few years. Much had been taken from her, but she wouldn't let it happen again. She thought of Rhianna and Sam, realizing the government had only gotten away with taking them because she hadn't fought. She would start fighting now, if it weren't too late, even if only for the other mothers.

"I'm not keeping silent anymore."

"Perhaps you're right," Sarintha said softly.

She hadn't realized she'd said it aloud. Maybe she hadn't, but Sarintha always knew. "I think this changes things," Victoria said. "Caleb has another friend who seems open to discussing the situation. Caleb will be staying with him from now on."

The look in Sarintha's usually cautious eyes dared to wonder if they didn't have to live this way anymore. "If I'm right about Caleb, it will be a significant advantage."

"What do you think about him?"

"He is either very talented, or he has a strong natural ability to block out others. Either way, he's unique."

"Could we really... influence them to let the children out?" She hadn't the first idea of where to start.

"Is this a safe place to talk?"

No one was within earshot. "I don't think electronic bugs work here. The computers have been broken for years. We're back to typewriters and microfiche."

Sarintha nodded, thinking a moment. "You recall what Richard was capable of."

Victoria had gone to great pains to close herself off to the Occult. It even frightened her when too strong a twinge of intuition came to her. But damned if she were to let her family be punished for a crime they didn't even commit. She had already been judged; she should use any method available to her. Her eyes widened with anticipation and fear.

"It may be time to contact Lori," Sarintha suggested.

"Who?"

"One of Richard's people. She was the one who brought Rhianna back when she was eight years old."

Victoria clenched her teeth automatically. She doubted she could forgive the woman, but she did trust Sarintha. "They've been very quiet lately."

Sarintha frowned. "Yes. Too quiet. Wellington no doubt has something in mind."

Something was odd about Sarintha's pensiveness. "Are you going to ask them to help us?" Surely not. It might be the worst idea Victoria had ever heard.

Sarintha met her eyes. "Wellington's the only one who concerns me, and he has shown himself to be a poor leader. I don't believe he would be difficult to deal with."

"Shouldn't he want you dead?" Victoria asked uncertainly. None of Richard's followers could be entirely sane.

Sarintha indicated that it wasn't Victoria's concern.

They abruptly went silent as a voice called, "Hello?"

Victoria got to her feet and climbed down the stairs. "Hi, Caleb." She was shaking inside from the significance of the conversation, and it was difficult to act normal.

"Are you coming back?" he asked pleasantly.

"Oh! Yes. Let me grab a pile." She rushed back upstairs, where Sarintha had resumed work.

Caleb stacked the books on the table in the back for her. "Is something wrong? You've been acting funny."

Damn. Either she was being very obvious, or he already knew. Looking down at the books, she said neutrally, "We were discussing how to handle… what's been going on."

"You've got some kind of plan?" He seemed honestly surprised. "To do what?"

Turning to him, she could feel the anger burning in her eyes. "They can't just arrest people for nothing. We have to stop them. We have to get my children back."

"Tall order," he murmured. "I don't think Chris has the rank to help with that."

"They're arresting people for being involved with the Occult." She kept her voice low. "But the people who actually are involved haven't been arrested at all. If they were, they could escape in a minute."

"Do you know someone then?" He shifted his feet and sat down.

"I think I do." She paused for a moment. "Do you?"

He shrugged. "I don't know anything about that at all."

"You don't?" she prodded.

"If I could tell the future, I would have moved the hell away from here years ago."

"Really."

Caleb turned to her, his mouth in a thin line of annoyance. "What are you saying?"

She straightened. "I'm not saying anything. I was seeing if you could help."

"It didn't seem like that," he grumbled. "Bit too pushy."

"I'm sorry. I didn't mean it that way." She put her hand on his reassuringly.

He shook his head. "Yeah, sorry. I guess I'm tense."

His hand was warm and rough and his fingernails needed filing. She wrenched hers away, flushing, and covered her mouth. She could smell a trace of Caleb's strong soap on her fingertips.

His mouth curved in suppressed laughter. He took her hand again, and a warm shiver went through her. "I don't mind."

She closed her eyes against the tumult of thoughts that had begun to overwhelm her. Finally, she gained the presence of mind to take advantage of the physical contact. She tried to remember how she had sensed Ethan long ago. She reached out with her mind... and it passed straight through him. It hadn't worked.

She gazed up at him appraisingly. He seemed nothing but honest, even if she couldn't read him. He didn't seem like the type to resort to subterfuge, and he appeared genuinely happy right now.

His contented expression faltered. "What's that about? Why do you keep looking at me like that? Your aunt did that too."

"I'm sorry. I didn't mean—" Was he aware of what she had tried to do? Had he tried to block her?

He jerked his hand back. "Look, I'm confused. I thought I said you could trust me, and you keep looking at me like I'm an alien or something."

"I was trying to figure something out," she tried.

"Okay, what?"

"Are you psychic?" she asked straight out.

"No. I just said I wasn't."

"And you don't know anyone who is?"

"I might. I don't know."

"Would you like to learn?" came another voice.

Victoria jumped. Sarintha had come up behind them.

"Well, I suppose," he asked, still flustered.

"She's asking," Sarintha explained, "because I cannot read you at all. And that is very unusual."

"I don't know why." Caleb stepped back defensively. "I've always been terrible at guessing games and things."

Sarintha's brow furrowed. "Really?"

"Guess I'm special then," he muttered.

"Please don't be upset." Victoria patted his arm, like she would for Sam. "We were just curious."

He sighed. "Okay, then."

Sarintha asked, "Would you mind if we looked into this further?"

His mouth twisted. "I suppose that would be fine. Is this going to hurt or anything?"

Victoria saw he was smiling again.

"No," Sarintha answered. "This evening at our house?"

"Sounds fine." He still looked like he wanted to escape.

They avoided mentioning it for the rest of the day.

Chris showed up at three, and Sarintha showed some fascination with him. Despite Victoria's initial suspicion, she grew fond of the soldier's straightforwardness and sense of order. Chris set himself to work on the books without being asked, and he alphabetized the fiction as quickly as Victoria could have.

"Did you tell the… soldiers about the books?"

His face brightened. "I sure did. They were thrilled, just like I thought."

Strategically, she asked, "They have been bored then?"

CHAPTER TWENTY-THREE

He laughed. "Not much to guard around here, really. Everyone's moved away."

A brash idea came to her. "Do you ever hear about the prison?"

He didn't seem phased. "You mean the institution? Sometimes."

Before she could reconsider, she charged ahead. "You probably know my children are there. Are they okay?"

He drew back. "There aren't any kids in there."

Was he ignorant or lying? Her stomach clenched. "My son and daughter are locked up there. They're only fifteen years old."

He looked shocked. "Well, they don't say much about what goes on inside. How long have they been in there?"

"Since August. Two months." Her voice cracked. This was so stupid, so risky. What had come over her?

"Hey, I'm sorry. I bet they'll be out soon. They don't usually hold people for long."

Victoria couldn't speak for the lump in her throat. She stared at her hands, trying to gather herself. That wasn't considered long?

"Do you want me to go?" he offered kindly.

That was the last thing she expected him to say. She cleared her throat. "Uh, no." Not yet, at any rate.

He managed a smile. "I really didn't know. They've never found anyone there who actually was Occult. I think we've gotten a bit paranoid."

She mumbled an agreement.

"Maybe I can find someone to check into it for you. You seem like a great lady to me. It's got to be a mistake."

Now she was sure he was lying. She tried to explain what had happened to her children, but she couldn't even meet his eyes. There was no way to cover this up now. Chris would look up her records, he would tell Caleb, and this would all be over. Her stupidity had ruined everything.

He fidgeted for a moment. "Hey, you still need those shelving units moved?"

"They're over here. Caleb brought down some extras from the attic. I've got a diagram of how I want them laid out." She was talking too fast. She showed them what she wanted and turned to go to her office. She had to be alone.

Chris took her by the arm and swallowed uncomfortably. "Look, I know they're doing some things that aren't right. Not all of us are the same, okay?"

Victoria turned away so he couldn't see her tears.

Chapter Twenty-Four

Victoria knew she was hiding behind her desk, but she couldn't compose herself. Her mind was racing and she couldn't stop thinking about how she'd probably given them away. What would Sarintha have said to Chris? She regretted leaving the other woman alone upstairs.

Victoria was putting them all at risk. How many more times could she annoy Caleb before he gave up on her? He was beginning to resent the constant questioning. He must have better things to do with his time than helping a nosy, self-conscious librarian. She was sure he was starting to like her yesterday.

Why was she even agonizing about Kepler? Chris Natchez was the bigger problem. She analyzed everything she said to him. Maybe none of it was worse than what any overanxious mother would have said. It was too late now to be upset about it. If Natchez meant to tell his superiors, she would find out quickly.

Shortly before five, she forced herself to leave the office. The building was closing, and she didn't want to stay late today. She wanted desperately to get the confrontations over with.

Jackson was grinning at her from the front desk. "You won't believe what those guys got done."

Her mood lifted, and she glanced toward the back, even though she couldn't see them from here.

Jackson leaned on the desk. "Great job on that grant. Best idea you've ever had. You're getting a raise."

"Really?" She supposed it didn't matter if she were about to be turned in to the police, but Jackson's earnest smile relaxed her slightly. "Thank you."

"Go see it," he ordered, pointing toward the back of the room.

It didn't look like the same place. The bookcases, which once had been in long, imposing rows, now lined the walls to leave room for a sitting area. They had taken care to cordon off one side of the front desk with a long row for privacy for official matters. The tables were still piled with books, but they were pushed together to invite friendly conversation.

"So?" Caleb asked enthusiastically.

"It's great!" Her mouth was hanging open. "It's a much better layout than mine."

"People might actually want to come in here," Chris grinned.

She found herself smiling back. "We might even need more room. Jackson said you got us a grant!"

He smirked. "Guess it went through then."

She disregarded her still-jangling nerves. "You two are the best. It's better than I ever could have hoped for. How about dinner?" She wanted Chris to leave, but it was only polite.

"Nah, I've got to get back to the base. I meant what I said, okay?"

Why wouldn't he just drop it? She felt the blood drain from her face as Sarintha looked at her expectantly. "Okay," she murmured.

He tipped his head sympathetically. "It looks like you might not need me tomorrow, if you like."

Caleb put in, "I've still got some long shelves to do."

Chris looked to Victoria for a reply. "Whatever is best for you. We can get by if you're busy," she said.

He shrugged. "I'm on nights the rest of the week. How about if I just stop by to see how it's going?"

Victoria rubbed her stiff neck. "Sure."

After Natchez left, Caleb asked, "What was that all about?"

I've just been alienating everyone today, Victoria thought. "I asked him about the prison," she said outright. "He said they don't keep kids there."

Sarintha considered a moment. "I expect that isn't common knowledge. I don't think he's lying."

"He said he'd look into it."

"Then why do you look so scared?" Caleb inquired.

"I shouldn't have said anything. I've been an absolute idiot all week. I'm going to get myself killed."

Sarintha regarded her placidly.

"You haven't been much of an idiot to me," Caleb said.

"Not much?" Victoria sat down. "I should just quit. This isn't worth it."

"But you were so excited."

Sarintha said evenly, "That may be hasty. You should wait to make such a decision."

"I can't control my mouth at all."

"Are you sure you're not just nervous? It's normal." Caleb knelt down in front of her.

Nervous didn't begin to describe it. Victoria covered her face.

"Hey, look at me. I hardly ever talk to people. Don't you think I'm nervous?"

He had a fair point, but then what was her excuse? She wasn't a recluse. Well, not recently.

"Let's just get out of here," he suggested. "You want a ride?"

At the front door, she could see Jackson exaggeratedly pointing at his watch. "Go on!" she shouted to him. "I'll close up."

"See you later!"

Caleb shifted his feet. "I'll go start the truck if you want. It's a little chilly."

She knew it wasn't cold tonight, but she gave him a grateful smile for the chance to be alone. "We'll just be a minute."

Sarintha stared at her again, and she lost her nerve.

"Oh god, I know. Please don't say anything."

"Perhaps we should move the pertinent information somewhere safe," was all she said.

Victoria nodded slowly. She could always put it back later. She grabbed an empty box and piled local newspapers from Olivia's time and the next few years into it. Looking around quickly, she grabbed some heavy hardbound books of old magazines. Sarintha helped her carry the items upstairs, hiding them in the far corner near the window.

Victoria closed up the building and caught up with Caleb outside.

"You still want me to come over?" he asked politely.

"How about tomorrow instead?" she suggested, letting her fatigue slip into her voice. This day couldn't be over soon enough.

The conversation during the drive was polite and pleasant, but she wasn't really paying attention.

At home, Victoria sank into the couch, feeling vaguely like she was drowning.

Sarintha sat stiffly next to her. "Would you like to talk?"

"How bad do you suppose it is?" she groaned, afraid to hear the answer.

"It's not bad at all yet. That's fortunate." Her tone reminded Victoria that it was only sheer luck.

"You think he's truthful then?" she asked hopefully.

"Perhaps. I can't guarantee the same for his compatriots."

Victoria hoped Chris didn't share her own lack of discretion. "I'll be more careful," she said uselessly. It was too late now.

Sarintha paused in consideration.

Victoria felt dread building up in her. She already knew the consequences, but she didn't want to hear them aloud from the person she respected most.

"Mr. Natchez could be useful."

Victoria hadn't expected that. "I doubt he'll be telling me government secrets," she murmured. Especially not now that he knew she was practically a criminal.

"Not directly," her aunt said slowly.

She laughed weakly. "Should I seduce him?"

Sarintha's face stayed stoic. "No."

"What do you have in mind?" This was unsettling her. Then she realized what Sarintha meant. "We'll just search his thoughts? Could you do that if he wasn't already thinking about it?"

Sarintha pursed her lips. "Possibly."

She felt a wave of fear toward her aunt. The woman had never suggested this sort of invasive tactic until today. Victoria was the one who declared war, but she hadn't meant to go this far. "It doesn't sound right," she murmured.

"I've already done it to him today to ensure our safety."

"So that's why you know he's telling the truth." She dropped her hands in her lap. "Couldn't we just… let things go their course? What would you have done if he was going to report me?"

"He seemed to know nothing at this point. There was nothing to report. You didn't say anything inappropriate. He was rather curious though."

"It seemed much worse than that. Besides, you didn't answer me."

"I would have made him forget," she said simply.

She'd always suspected, but to hear Sarintha say it aloud left her stunned. Why had the woman learned to do such an awful thing? Even worse, had she done it before?

Sarintha sighed. "It has been a long time, and I have never done it to you."

There they were, plotting to unleash these abilities, even to teach others, and Victoria didn't know the extent of how dangerous they could be.

Sarintha was following her thoughts. "If we taught others, we would be in control. We would choose what they could learn."

Shaken, Victoria cried, "I didn't give you permission to do that."

"It was important that I know what you were thinking."

It was simple and slightly condescending. Shades of Richard Aldon shone in Sarintha Malik's eyes and voice. How could Victoria forget who taught her aunt? Why did there have to be so much risk? Last time, Ethan ended up dead. Conflict tore at Victoria. Could Sarintha have saved Ethan? Why hadn't she tried harder?

She looked at Sarintha, knowing her fear was plain. She was too exhausted to take it all in right now.

"You do not understand," Sarintha began.

She didn't want to understand. She turned away and went to her bedroom.

* * *

How could her aunt regard people in this way? It was almost as if she considered them less than human, if it was permissible to alter their memories for her convenience. Sarintha had always been secretive, but how could Victoria have missed something this important?

What other secrets might she be keeping? Frantically, she thought of Rhianna and Sam locked away. Were they guilty of something, too innocent to know that it was illegal? Had Sarintha taught them to use the Occult when Victoria wasn't there? She imagined Sarintha explaining matter-of-factly how it was necessary, and if only she'd taught them more, they'd be here right now.

Victoria had forbidden it! She had done it to protect them, so that they would never be taken away or threatened. She had tried her best to give them a normal life. Rhianna meant everything to her, but Sam... Maybe she hadn't spent enough time with Sam.

The guilt spiraled in her mind until she was too exhausted to think. She fell asleep clenching her blanket tightly, dreaming of an entire army squadron surrounding her house, demanding her to surrender all her books. Sarintha would say she brought it all on herself.

* * *

Sarintha made her an apology breakfast and mercifully stayed out of sight until Jackson arrived. Once out of the house, the oppressive worry in Victoria's mind lifted.

"I guess you don't need me anymore, Victoria," Jackson said with mock sadness.

"You can tell your wife the affair's off," she joked.

"So, who is this new love of yours?"

"We met by pure destiny." That sounded much better than saying he was a farmer.

"You pick good ones. He's a hard worker," Jackson observed. "It's handy to have him around."

She nodded absently

"Will you be needing rides any more? I could drive Sarah to school if I didn't pick you up."

"I'm not sure yet. It would be so much easier to plan for if my phone still worked."

"Didn't you just get a new one?" he asked in surprise.

"I did. That one's broken too. I think I give up."

He shook his head. "And I thought I had bad luck."

She shrugged.

"You must be contagious. That would explain why my car has been working better this week."

Her smile froze. Hadn't once Ethan said the computers where he worked crashed less when he was gone? She managed, "I'm glad to hear that."

"With your new raise, you could give me a ride."

"I'd love to get a car," she lied. She hadn't even thought about the money yet. "I wonder if I still remember how to drive."

He laughed. "I don't mind bringing you to work when you need it."

Shortly after they arrived, Caleb came in with Quentin Doyle.

Quentin spread out his arms when he saw the progress they'd made. "I don't have to do anything!" he declared and proceeded to "test" the chairs, patting the seat next to him for Victoria to join him.

"How did you hurt your leg?" Quentin asked kindly.

Caleb pretended not to be listening.

Damn that obvious cane. How could she explain it? She'd killed part of herself healing a dying man. "It's just a muscle problem," she said, rising. "I'm fine."

"You look tired," he observed. "There's no harm in resting sometimes."

"I just got here." She tried to smile.

"You've been very worried about something."

For a moment, she feared his eyes were probing her thoughts. "Everyone's worried about something." She tried to sound offhanded.

He tipped his head, pursing his lips. "You're right about that." He exaggeratedly folded his hands behind his head. "Now get to work."

She snorted and pulled her book tape out of her pocket, assessing the most damaged items. "So, how long have you known Caleb?"

"I went to school with his father ages ago. I remember buying vegetables from Caleb when he was a little boy."

Victoria smiled, trying to imagine her Sam selling vegetables. "How sweet."

Caleb flushed, trying to change the subject. "And now he's stuck with me."

"It's a pleasure, Caleb." Quentin paused, his nostalgia fading. "The house has been much too quiet."

Caleb had the grateful air of someone who had been spared from an embarrassing story. "You should meet Victoria's aunt, Quentin. She's about your age, I think."

Quentin froze. "That... wouldn't be appropriate."

"As a *friend*, Quentin. Don't be paranoid."

What was this about? "Are you married?" she asked gently.

"Abigail died seventeen years ago."

"She was a good woman," said Caleb.

Quentin turned his head to rub his eyes behind his small glasses.

"I'm sorry," Victoria murmured. "I didn't mean—"

"You aren't married, are you?" Caleb asked as if he'd just wondered. "Your kids..."

"Their father died. About that long ago also, actually." She hadn't mentioned Ethan to anyone since he died. Awkwardly, she said, "I suppose we have something in common, then, Quentin."

He stared at her intensely, asking hoarsely, "Was it the Accident?"

His raw pain cut through her heart. It seemed he had never begun to heal. "Not exactly." She considered her words. "It was a little later. He was killed."

Caleb murmured an apology.

The two regarded each other in an understanding so acute that it felt like it could kill her. Her loss was nothing compared to his. She hadn't known Ethan long at all. Quentin had loved a woman for decades and lost her in a senseless tragedy. Despite that, she felt the connection of survivorship between them. Quentin wanted answers too.

Caleb dropped a book on the table, shattering the silence.

"Hey, Victoria!" Jackson was coming toward them, pointing toward the front desk phone. "You've got a call."

She went to answer it, and the men tried to look busy. "Hello?"

"This is Chris Natchez."

She took a deep breath.

"I was wondering if you needed me today."

She surveyed the shelves. "I think we could use a hand."

"I can't stay long, but a couple of guys wanted to see the place. Is that all right?"

"That's fine." She'd have to get used to new people, even if she was still afraid of the sight of a uniform.

"I'll put them to work for you. See you."

She handed the phone back to Jackson. "It looks like we'll have our first visitors."

"I'd better clean my desk."

"Why doesn't he help?" Quentin asked after Jackson left.

"He has too much administrative work, plus a bad back."

"What a fine lot we are," Quentin grinned.

"Speak for yourself," Caleb said. "I'm lifting plenty."

"Chris is sending some strong young men to help us," she said with feigned vacuousness.

"More brawn than brains," Quentin predicted. "Be prepared for falling books."

Chris had implied that earlier. "We'd better get to work clearing off shelves then."

The work was considerably more enjoyable when she wasn't alone. She had underestimated how well she had borne her isolation. When Chris arrived with three others, she took pleasure in touring them around the building, which they seemed to appreciate.

They made short work of adjusting the bookcases. Victoria left them to browse the collection as Chris pulled her aside.

Despite Sarintha's assurances, she was still afraid.

"I talked to some people," he started.

"You didn't have to," she assured him.

He held up his hand. "I wanted to. There's a problem though."

She thought her heart stopped.

"They won't tell me anything."

"Nothing? There have to be records. We don't have them here, but—"

He shook his head. "I did what I could."

Her head fell. "Thank you. It was good of you to try." She hadn't expected anything, and it had been foolish to even mention it. If Sarintha found a way to rescue them illegally, this would draw unwise attention on her anyway.

Chris sighed. "I hope you don't mind, but I told them I was investigating you for your grant. I didn't think you'd want them to know it was a favor."

It was far more than she had expected from him. "You lied to them?"

"Not exactly. I was supposed to do check up on you anyway."

She stood up straighter. "What did you decide about me, then?"

He grinned. "Stop worrying. I'm putting in a good word, and maybe they'll lay off you for a while."

That was probably too much to hope for. "I really appreciate it."

"No problem. I'll let you know if anything changes." He jostled her arm in a friendly way. "You're one of us. You shouldn't have to put up with this."

She swallowed hard, realizing he meant that her government job elevated her over the general public. She hated the idea, feeling like a traitor. Her records were helping the government track people like herself. Was her position the only reason she wasn't in jail already?

She allowed herself a dark glare at the back of Chris's head. So, her supposed status protected her. When he found out what they were planning to research, would he betray his own friends?

***

Sarintha wasn't particularly pleased at the prospect of studying Caleb that day. After Victoria's outburst, Sarintha was sure to do something to upset her niece further. She was foolish to assume that the younger woman would understand simply because of her fight to stay alive against Esser. Perhaps motherhood made her too sympathetic.

She thought of the children, and her anger softened. She was being too harsh on an overstrained woman. Victoria hadn't chosen this life, as Sarintha had. Perhaps it was too easy to forget enemies were everywhere when one was desperate for companionship.

She resolved to put on her best impression for Victoria's new friend. She couldn't deny that Caleb's enigma intrigued her, but she mustn't push too hard.

The power flickered and went out at five o'clock as usual, and she had already lit the candles. She removed dinner from the gas stove just as they arrived.

The voices sounded reserved, rather than jovial, so perhaps Victoria was still in a dispirited state. Two men stood with Victoria in the living room, the brown-haired Caleb and an older man with glasses and gray hair in need of trimming.

Victoria introduced them. "Quentin, this is my aunt Sarintha—"

"Dear god," he gasped and went absolutely still.

Chapter Twenty-Five

Sarintha knew Quentin Doyle seemed familiar but couldn't draw an immediate reason why. She'd crossed paths with so many people over the years. His expression was of deep horror.

"I know you, don't I?" Quentin rasped. "You were there."

Vague as he was, the memory came back to her. *This one's alive,* someone has said, as the smoke from the secondary explosions still hung in the air. Even in hiding, there was no escape from her sins. Sickened, she drew back. His face was twisted with the beginning of madness as he backed against the wall, pointing accusingly.

Victoria was in shock, no doubt guessing what was about to transpire, but Caleb intervened. "Hey, what's this?"

Quentin was shaking with fury, but she sensed his fear. He still could choose to fight, at this point, if the other man allowed it.

"After the fire, in the Accident. You were there, with that man."

She braced herself, closing Quentin's emotions from her and cordoning off her own before they endangered her.

"What are you talking about?" Victoria asked, her voice too high as she looked between them.

Sarintha clasped her hands together. "I believe this man has met Richard before."

"Richard?" Quentin spat. "Is that his name? That man killed my wife!"

Caleb held him by the shoulders. "Calm down. Let's just talk about this rationally. Are you sure about this?"

184

As Sarintha expected, the patronizing tone irritated him further. "Let go of me," he said with deadly coldness. "You don't understand."

Caleb didn't budge. "Tell me, and I will understand. You owe these ladies an explanation too."

Sarintha stayed silent as Victoria moved closer to her.

"I don't owe her anything." His voice was dangerously soft now.

Sarintha stepped forward to meet his piercing eyes. "I don't remember clearly," she lied. "Please do explain."

He let out a wild laugh. "There were so many that you don't remember?" He clenched his trembling hands together. "That man—Richard—pulled me out of the fire with my wife. She was still moving. She was *alive.* She was going to make it, and then he did something to her."

Sarintha closed her eyes, smelling the smoke, the swift, passing heat of the hydrogen fire—shimmering like psychic energy itself—burning her even now. She hadn't taken this one, had only watched, but it easily could have been her turn.

Victoria asked a question, and she came back to herself.

"He touched her, and she made an awful sigh, and then she was dead. He had this look on his face, kind of crazed. He stared at me, like he knew I knew, and like I was next, but I got away. I stood and ran, and I left her there with him."

"She was already gone," Sarintha murmured.

"That doesn't matter. I know she wasn't the only one. I should have stopped him. No one believed me." His distress had turned inward now.

Victoria reached out to console him, and he jerked away. "Richard's dead now. I saw him die."

"He is?" Quentin asked weakly. "When?"

Victoria answered with a steadiness Sarintha was proud of. "He killed Ethan, my… friend I told you about. Richard was shot, and he died. He's gone." It was a simplification, but the true story would take some time to tell.

A mad wail escaped from him as his anger welled up again. He was denied his revenge; Sarintha knew he was now more dangerous.

"What were you doing with him?" he screamed at Sarintha. "Why didn't you stop him?"

Her chest tightened. "I didn't understand what he was doing." No, you thought they wanted to be released. Never did she ask them, never did she question, too afraid to leave again. "He told us we were ending their suffering." It was a hateful thing to say to this man and a poor excuse.

"Their suffering," he said softly. "She would have lived. I lived. Damn it, I would have given my life for her. Would he have killed me instead, if he pulled me out first?"

She was on the verge of trembling, her control lapsing. He couldn't understand. No one could understand. She had never known that the pleasure she took in helping others was something so much darker. It had changed her forever, haunted her to this day, but it kept her alive during that time.

She had seen the man moving, heard his hysterical cries seventeen years ago. The woman had been losing consciousness, her condition less clear. Richard wouldn't have taken such a risk. "No," she answered. "He would not have killed you, because I was there to see that you were less injured."

"Should I thank you then?" Quentin shouted. Caleb pushed him to the couch.

Sarintha drew herself up and regarded Victoria, whose hand was clasped on her throat in shock. "Now you know why I refused to speak of this before," she said.

Quentin had crumpled in grief, and his friend had begun comforting him. "I should think these men would like to leave," she suggested evenly.

Caleb's eyes flashed. "I don't pretend to understand all this, but I intend to. Are you saying that you and some psychopath used to go around after the Accident sucking the life out of people or something?"

Victoria finally spoke. "It was a cult. She couldn't leave. She did as soon as she could."

"Really," he said skeptically. "So this is why you kept asking me odd questions, Victoria?"

Her niece clenched her teeth. "You have Sarintha to thank for killing

Richard. She helped us do it."

Sarintha drew back. She had done far too little, in fact, afraid to try to stop him by herself.

"She enjoys killing people does she?" Caleb retorted, but he flinched.

"She does not!" Victoria shouted. "She helped stop a murderer that the police couldn't be bothered to look for, and we've paid for it every day since."

"That doesn't bring Abigail back!" Quentin cried.

Victoria knelt before him shakily. "No, it doesn't. It doesn't bring back Abigail, or my Ethan, or anyone else Richard killed. And it doesn't bring back my children or anyone else the government tried to blame for the Accident. There's no punishment, no revenge that can undo what already happened. We just have to keep living."

Quentin let Victoria take his hand, and it was over. Sarintha sat down heavily.

Caleb scrutinized her from across the room. Normally, whenever anyone studied her in such a way, she could feel a connection. However, there was none, as if the man were devoid of intuition entirely. "Where do you come from, Caleb?" she found herself asking aloud.

"I lived on Elk Springs Hill, north of town." He sounded as tired as they all felt.

"Were you alone?"

"For a while." He shrugged. "I just moved into town."

Perhaps his isolation explained his uniqueness. "I can't sense anything from you," she explained again.

He gave her a look of tense relief. "I think I like it better that way."

He might be straightforward, even a bit simple, but he was not unintelligent. Perhaps what he felt was merely little different from what he said aloud. Or perhaps Sarintha and Caleb were merely at opposite ends of a spectrum. There were a great many dangers, completely unknown to him, which he would be naturally safe from. She wouldn't want to change that by teaching him. However, if he were able to at least understand the Occult, he would be a useful ally.

Quentin gathered himself from the couch and rose to leave. Sarintha radiated what peace she could to him. They would all have much to think about tonight.

* * *

They were all strangers. Victoria had just barely entered a new world, and it had already toppled. There was no one to turn to. She longed to fuss over her children, to simplify and give distance to the insurmountable problems that lie outside this door. But they were alone as well.

It frightened her to not be there for them. Were they supporting each other, or had they long been separated? She couldn't let herself imagine it again. She'd already spent too many nights wondering if her children were crying for her. She had to believe that they were strong.

Finally, she realized she was only distracting herself. The only person she could help right now was in the other room.

Sarintha was sitting stiffly on her bed, her fingers braced to rip the yellowed pages from an old book.

"No," Victoria said softly, before she could help herself.

Unsurprised, Sarintha indicated the cover of the maroon necromancy book. "It's caused too much trouble," she muttered.

Victoria sat next to her and took it from her. "You can't make the people who have already read it unlearn what it contains. The government already tried that with the banning."

"If I could make them all forget, I would." She was still looking down at the book.

"It wouldn't change what already happened."

"There may have been a great deal I could have done."

"It's over. Richard's gone now."

"With Wellington in command. There will always be another man waiting to take Richard's place."

"What about you?" Victoria asked softly. "You talk about what you could have done. Would you have taken his place?"

"I don't think I would have been chosen."

She was skirting the issue. "What if you had just taken it from him?"

She sighed. "The rest would have killed me."

"And if they didn't?"

Sarintha gazed at her sadly. "I would have been corrupted as well. You can't understand. It drives everyone mad eventually."

"You don't seem mad to me." Victoria put her arm around the woman.

Sarintha's eyes were haunted with guilt. Victoria had never seen such open pain on the woman's face before. It hurt her to think of Sarintha bearing it alone for so long.

"You're not," Victoria assured her.

Sarintha whispered, "Sometimes I think things… I have dreams. I can't stop them. It's as if Richard were still here."

"Sometimes I feel the same way." She had avoided mentioning it because she thought Sarintha would think less of her for it.

"He must be gone for good," she said, as if convincing herself.

"What he did was horrible. If we forget, it could happen again."

"I've been afraid," Sarintha whispered, "that he would find a way to come after the children."

"Sam? He would probably tell us." Sam had become very moody and secretive though. What if something had happened when he ran away with no one to protect him?

"No, not Sam. Richard wouldn't choose him."

Victoria had spent all her time worrying about Sam, fearing secretly that he was Richard or Esser's child. "Why not?" she couldn't help but ask.

Sarintha shook her head. "Sam doesn't have the ambition Richard would want. He is too passive."

"Rhianna?" The girl wasn't aggressive, but she was persuasive. No, she refused to believe it.

Sarintha pursed her lips for a moment. "I've been concerned sometimes. This book… it was moved before."

"Wasn't it hidden? I didn't know you had it."

"It was." She sighed. "I'm sure it's just paranoia. Goodness knows we've had enough to make us paranoid."

Victoria smiled slightly and opened the book. "I always wanted to read it. Ethan tried so hard to get it. Where did you find it?"

"I picked it up after Esser died," she said if it were the natural thing to do. "It was on his person. It wouldn't do to leave it lying there in the open."

Hadn't Victoria done that herself though? "I took the knife," Victoria confessed. "I still don't know why. I guess I wanted to know it couldn't hurt someone again."

"We should have burned these things long ago," Sarintha murmured. gun Victoria cringed.

"The book was locked in the bottom drawer." She indicated her nightstand.

Victoria gestured to her to follow her to the other room, remembering Olivia's journal. Kneeling in front of her closet, she murmured, "I could have sworn I put the whole bag in the back after I wrote in it."

Sarintha shined a flashlight helpfully.

"It's not here. I know it was here." She couldn't think of anywhere else it could be, and she hadn't touched it in years. "Did someone take it?"

Sarintha strode to Rhianna's room, opening her closet door quickly. Unlike Sam's mostly orderly room, it was piled high with the girl's discarded favorite possessions. Grimly, Sarintha pulled out a worn black duffel bag.

Victoria gasped, "What does this mean? Why would she take this?"

"Is everything there?"

The side zipper was jammed, but she could still feel the shape of the diary within the pocket. In the main pouch, she found Ethan Sullivan's tarot deck and Richard Aldon's gun. "What," Victoria asked between clenched teeth, "would Rhianna want with a gun?"

Sarintha cautiously opened it. "There are still two bullets."

"I didn't know it was loaded. I should have gotten rid of it. She could have been killed."

"But she wasn't," Sarintha reminded her.

Victoria continued to rummage though it. "The knife's gone. I know I put it in here."

Sarintha went pale. "I think we have to consider that she's read the book and used these objects."

"Used them for what?" Victoria asked, a hint of hysteria in her voice. Why would a little girl possibly want them?

"Perhaps she just wanted to know who her father was."

She sputtered, "Well, do you—have you sensed Ethan?" She couldn't bring herself to admit that she was now certain of her children's parentage.

Sarintha shook her head.

Victoria's mind was racing. "Those people took Rhianna when she was little. What did they tell her? Could they have taught her to—to talk to Richard?"

"I don't know," Sarintha murmured, "but they chose her and not Sam for a reason."

"When we get her back, we'll find out. If there's a way to get rid of him, we will find it."

Sarintha's face didn't show much hope. "I fear we missed the opportunity to banish him. I hadn't anticipated his tenacity."

Victoria knew there had to be a way, and she swore they would find it. But she hoped even more fervently that they were wrong entirely. It wasn't like Rhianna at all.

She forcibly turned her thoughts back to Quentin. "There's something that confuses me, Sarintha."

She looked up tiredly, the shadows under her eyes much deeper. "What is that?"

Victoria considered her words carefully. "Why did you go back to Richard? You said before that you'd left him before the Accident."

She covered her face in a swift gesture of guilt. "I'd forgotten. I'd made myself forget."

Victoria regarded her curiously, certain not to push the woman too hard. She was no stranger to the idea herself. Sometimes revisionist history was the only thing that kept her sane.

"I was hiding here that day. I was in the hallway, right out there." She pointed near the stairs. "I felt the explosion."

"The walls shook?" Victoria ventured.

Sarintha squeezed her eyes shut. "Yes, but it was more than that. I felt what Richard was feeling. It was… ecstasy."

Sarintha's head had tipped back, and her mouth was slightly open. For a moment, she mirrored Richard, and Victoria suddenly wanted her to stop speaking.

"In that instant, he was everywhere at once," the woman intoned. "Before that, we were evenly matched. But after…" Sarintha pulled her long sleeve over her wrist. Brushing her fingers down over it, she revealed a long, thick scar that Victoria had never seen before. It encircled her dark skin like a jagged pink bracelet.

As Victoria gaped, Sarintha moved her fingers upward over her skin, and it vanished. "I always conceal it," she said, smoothing out her sleeve.

How many other scars was the woman hiding? Victoria clasped her own arm nervously. "He made you do that?" she asked, remembering with sickness the power Richard once had over her. But she'd been able to break it in the end, when she found out the truth about him.

"Yes, he did, quite easily. He had the power to destroy the rest of the city that day, if he wanted."

Victoria shivered. "Why didn't he?"

Sarintha gave her a twisted smile. "He preferred to work face-to-face, when possible."

"So he went to each of the survivors," Victoria whispered. Thousands in one stroke weren't enough for him. He had to see each one slip away himself.

Sarintha swallowed. "He was alone. The other women… I didn't know then, but they'd had enough, and Wellington was off hunting them."

"Richard wasn't looking?" It didn't seem his way to relegate revenge to another person.

She raised her chin. "No. He wanted to teach me a lesson."

She should have known that trying to kill Sarintha wouldn't be enough for Richard. "What did he do?" she made herself ask.

Sarintha's fingertips traced the worn edges of the necromancy book, her eyes distant. "He met many of us at hospitals," she began. "He looked for people who were sensitive, with high intuition, and he took us when we were vulnerable. He promised each of us what we wanted most.

"He found me after your father died. That's why I was in such a state at his funeral."

"I thought I'd never forgive you," Victoria admitted. "I should have known something was wrong."

"Richard told me I had potential. He knew I already had experience."

Victoria remembered her mother's warnings that Sarintha was "loony." It was two years before her father died that Victoria had gone to her aunt with a ridiculous request to find her true love that backfired into rape. She'd never told her aunt what had happened, but she suspected Sarintha knew.

"We used to go back to the hospitals together. He would take only one of us and we'd comfort the sick. Sometimes we would heal them, but sometimes…"

"You'd let them die," Victoria said gently.

"We'd end their misery, he called it. We had to be careful. If we… took too much, we could take their illness as well."

"That's what happened to me." Victoria clenched her cane, the pain shooting from her fingertips up to her shoulder. "I didn't know."

"I tried to stop you," Sarintha said softly.

"I know. I'm sorry." She hadn't listened at all.

"Esser seemed to have done that as well," Sarintha mused. "His heart stopped before his wound killed him."

"But Richard should have known that."

"Esser was insane. We may have been fortunate that he made many mistakes. Richard rarely made mistakes." She paused.

"He'd called you to the Accident," she reminded her aunt gently.

"Yes. I could have gone simply for his help. I was bleeding badly, faster than I could stop it. Naturally, he healed it as soon as I encountered him, but then he wouldn't let me leave."

"He wanted you with him."

"He knew that I wouldn't leave the victims in pain. People were crushed, burned. I'm told that later he volunteered with the paramedics and won an award." She cleared her throat. "And once I started, he knew I wouldn't stop."

"I don't understand." She clasped Sarintha's hand reassuringly.

Sarintha didn't meet her eyes. "The feeling is very strong. It's…" She looked up, asking permission.

She nodded hesitantly.

"No." Sarintha said to herself firmly. "I can't do that to you. You see, even now, how I can't escape it?"

Still curious, Victoria couldn't hide her fearful fascination.

Her aunt continued, "Murder becomes a common need, stronger than the need for nourishment or sex. To have power over another person's life is a consuming pleasure."

"You overcame it, didn't you? You've lived here for sixteen years in peace."

A shadow came over her. "Not in peace, but I have resisted."

"You've hidden it well," Victoria pointed out.

"Of course I did," Sarintha snapped. "I shouldn't be thinking of this, even now. It's too dangerous."

"I trust you. I want to understand."

"I could murder you in an instant, Victoria. I wouldn't even have to touch you," Sarintha said sharply.

Victoria pushed back her instant fear. It wasn't a threat. Sarintha shouldn't have to be afraid of herself. "But you won't."

Sarintha gritted out, "A normal person wouldn't even consider it."

"We aren't living in normal times! I don't know why the world has gone to hell, but the best we can do is survive right now."

Sarintha sighed. "This is the most peace we will ever have. This is not as bad as survival yet. At its worst, every day will be as when Esser was following you."

It frightened her, but deep down, she knew it was true. This wasn't outright war.

"If they want Rhianna, we should be thankful for that. It has kept them dormant for these years, waiting for the right time."

Victoria couldn't think about it. She wouldn't let it be true. She should have known if Richard was pursuing Rhianna. But if even Sarintha didn't know, how could she? Her breath was sharp in her chest, and Sarintha still looked vaguely ill. "How did you get away from him?" she asked.

"Get away? He let me go. He was so sure of himself that I wouldn't be able to resist him. He knew I would come back again."

Victoria squeezed her hands. "But you didn't."

"He died. There was little chance."

"I know you wouldn't. You stayed with us. You fought Esser. You never tried to bring him back after."

"I didn't fight Esser," she said tightly. "I was afraid."

Victoria sighed. When would the woman stop blaming herself? "You didn't, because everything would be worse if he possessed you. You did the right thing." All the uncertainty Victoria had about Ethan's death finally resolved itself.

"I suspect it's time to fight again," Sarintha murmured. "Will I have to fight our daughter now?"

Victoria let the pain wash over her, chilling her skin. For once, she was thankful Rhianna was locked away, safe. But had Richard's spirit followed her there?

Victoria absently traced her own scars on her arm. "Ellie slit her wrists," she realized and began to sob.

Chapter Twenty-Six

Rhianna knew something was seriously wrong instantly. Amber took her hand like a little girl and told her to come quietly. Rhianna's head shot around, but there were guards at the entrance to her cell. No escape. Something was seriously wrong if Amber looked upset about it.

She entered the hallway reluctantly, dragging a little behind. Down the left side of the corridor, a boy was yelling, and she locked eyes with Sam. His face was pale, with a shadow of stubble, and he looked twice as old as he used to. A flare of passing concern made her wonder what had been happening to him.

He was mouthing something, before his guard wrenched his arm to force him to follow. Rhianna gazed down the empty corridor feeling more lonely than ever.

She turned to Amber and implored, "You won't let them hurt me, will you? I know you won't."

Amber stepped back and let the security guard grab Rhianna's arm.

A burning needle pierced Rhianna's back, spreading pain down to her feet as she struggled to get free. Her wild arm smacked against the nurse's face as she slid down the hall. She didn't know the way out of the institution, but the end of the hall was the place all the nurses went. With her next step, her ankle twisted sideways, and her back foot wouldn't move. She clawed at the wall as she sank to the floor with a heavy haze in her head. The injection was too strong to fight.

Still awake, she was carried to a cold metal bed in a room that vibrated with a low whirring. She pressed her bruised hands to the table to push herself up, but she was nearly paralyzed. Instantly the nurse noticed and strapped down her arms, then her stiff legs, before fitting her head in a sharp metal contraption to hold it still. The nurse slapped electrodes on her head and snapped the wires in place. The guard jammed a foam plate in her mouth that made her gag.

She didn't understand what the nurse and the doctor were saying to each other in such hushed, low voices, but she felt even more afraid when they left the room. The door opposite her swung silently shut, and she began to wonder what was so horrible that they wouldn't even stay in the room to witness.

Then she felt it. Her scalp began to tingle, as if her hair was standing on end. Then a twitch began at the base of her skull, intensified to a convulsion that shot all the way down her spine. Her back rose violently off the bed and crashed down against the metal again and again.

She squeezed her eyes shut against the blinding flashes that accompanied each jolt. It had to be over soon. She opened her mouth to scream for them to stop, but all that came out was a strangled sound.

She tried to concentrate, to think of anything but this, but she was soon reduced to animalistic instinct. She forced the sedation to wear off, and she crashed her fists against the restraints, ripping the leather strap slightly. It was enough. Her arm was out, and she shot up, twisting to release her other arm and legs. She spat the sponge out. She scanned the room for the source of the whirring and beat at it viciously with her bare hands until she spotted the keypad. She slammed her fist against it, as she noticed the shuffling outside the door.

Keys clattered to the floor as too many people tried to push through the doorway at once to stop her. She faced them furiously, vision dimming at the edges and a strange sound escaping her throat. They hung back for a moment before the largest man took a step toward her.

That was when it happened. Though her fogged mind, some dormant part burst to life. She reached out for his chest and the electricity in her burned again. The man turned a sickly color, a jolt shook him, his tongue began to bleed, and he fell to the floor. She prepared to charge the next nearest man when something cracked against her head and she sank to the floor.

* * *

Sam kicked and bit like a wild animal, knowing instinctively that they were about to do it again. They tried the electricity once before, experimenting to see if Rhianna had noticed, and he knew she was too self-absorbed to notice anything but herself.

He could barely recall it now, nothing but the sheer terror that made him rip his hair out afterwards and the thick fog of confusion so deep that he thought at first that he was buried alive.

This time, he could tell they wouldn't be as gentle; they wouldn't give him drugs to forget. He wouldn't let them do it again. He tried to lunge at the guard, praying he would shoot and spare Sam from this, but the nurses held him back.

And then he saw Rhianna, and she looked as if she had no idea what awaited her. He tried to tell her to fight, but they dragged her away, and he knew that no one, not even Rhianna, deserved this.

He was right. They left out an injection this time, and he was fully awake when they strapped him down. He screamed nonsense until they gagged him, and then it came. His body exploded into white-hot shards that knocked the breath from him and wiped all thought from his mind.

Fighting to keep control, the next breath an eternity away, it let released him as quickly as it came.

The pretty nurse leaned over him and whispered softly, "I want to help you. Please tell me, did you kill Ellie Pulaski?"

Who was Ellie Pulaski? The voice was growing farther away.

"We need to know about the Occult. What do you know about the Occult?"

Dazed, he stared at the pinpoint sparks in her eyes, fading away like the spark that was her soul. If he could, he would kill her, but—

"Another neural charge, please. Raise the amperage to 1.6." She gave him a last look with those dead eyes, her body flat, unreal, and so distant, and she said hatefully, "Talk to us. We don't want to do this," as the world went to hell again.

A scream ripped its way out of him. Somewhere deep within himself, he knew he wouldn't live. No one could live through this. The pain overtook him, and then there was nothing.

Sam awoke not knowing where the hell he was, his head throbbing like it had been crushed. He drew his knees tightly to his chest and rocked slightly, trying not to scream.

His mind seemed empty, as if he'd been stunned by a blow to the head, and his few thoughts felt so distant that they could not be his at all. Somehow, who he was had slipped away from him, and the world felt two dimensional, as if he were watching a movie. He tried to scream and found he couldn't summon the emotion to do so. He hoped this was dying.

* * *

Victoria hadn't expected Caleb to pick her up in the morning. He didn't say a word as she got in the truck, and she was glad of it. She wanted more than anything to pretend her life was normal.

"Quentin isn't coming," she managed as they arrived in the parking lot.

"You don't see him, do you?" Caleb replied, but the sarcasm came out flat.

"Is he okay?"

Caleb regarded her with a hint of coldness. "He looks about as bad as you do, although I can't say why you're so upset."

Victoria hadn't slept the whole night, but she wasn't about to tell him why. "We all have our demons," she said, trying not to flinch at her own words.

"I expect he'll be okay," Caleb said stiffly. "What did Chris say about your kids?" It sounded like a deliberate gouge.

"He said nothing, and I don't want to talk about them. Maybe you should leave," she said as she got out of the truck. "Thank you for driving me."

"Don't bother to thank me."

She slammed the truck door and headed toward the building. Damn it, he was following her. At least he had parked far enough away that Jackson wouldn't see the scene they were making. She stopped and closed her eyes. "What do you want?"

He looked a little regretful. "You forgot your cane." He held it out for her.

As she took it from him, her face crumpled and she began to cry. "I don't know what to do."

Awkwardly, he put his arms around her. "God, please don't cry. I'm sorry. I know this isn't your fault. You looked as shocked as I was about your aunt."

Her tears overcame her humiliation as she buried her face in his chest. "I don't know how much more of this I can take. Things are only going to get worse."

He patted her hair. "I wish there was something I could do."

"Why would you want to?" she mumbled.

"I'm starting to like you," he said barely audibly. "I wish you were happy."

She wiped her eyes roughly. "If you knew what was best for you, you'd get in that truck and drive as far away from this town as you could. It isn't safe here, and it's going to get a lot worse." She'd already gotten one man killed.

"If I'd wanted to do that, I wouldn't have moved into Quentin's house. I want to help you, Victoria."

She looked into his earnest eyes and turned away. "Even after you learned how dangerous I am?"

"You're dangerous?" he laughed. "Your aunt, maybe, but how's that your fault?"

She opened her mouth and closed it quickly. She wanted so badly to tell someone her fears. "But Quentin—"

"I'm not Quentin," he replied firmly. "He doesn't tell me what to do."

She started to speak, and he leaned towards her and pressed his mouth on hers. It was soft, gentle, and perfectly normal. No unbidden onslaught of emotions came from his mind, no hands crushed her too hard. Her lips moved against his slowly, and he drew back, blushing.

"I've wanted to do that for a long time. I hope you didn't mind."

Puzzled, she laughed. "A long time? A whole week even?"

He searched her face nervously.

CHAPTER TWENTY-SIX

She smiled, suddenly shy. "Thank you, Caleb."

Jackson's car pulled up, and she managed to wave before going inside.

Caleb grumbled, "My face is going to be red the whole day."

Casually, she said, "I hope that won't stop you from doing it again."

He flushed brighter and muttered something to himself.

The distraction didn't last for long.

She could hear Chris's friendly voice chatting with Jackson up front. She composed herself and prepared to walk up front, when she saw that a squad of at least ten men followed him in. Chris was leaning against the butt of a rifle like a cane.

Her breath caught in her chest. Esser in his uniform, the light glinting off his knife blade, the soldiers with their guns who took her children away... She had been able to hold it back until now. Chris was smiling at her, and now she couldn't even face him.

"What's wrong?" Caleb asked comfortingly.

She searched his eyes and felt more alone than before. "I'm afraid my daughter's guilty," she wanted to say, but the words died in her throat.

"It's a nice day," Chris was saying, "so we walked over."

Walked? They were close enough to walk, the whole lot of them with their— "I don't like guns," she managed to apologize.

"Oh!" Chris said jovially. "There have been some reports, so they said we had to be armed." He looked entirely too pleased about it.

"Reports?" she asked dully, feeling she was hearing him from far away.

"Nothing to worry about, just a few odd people around. We'll be watching here too, to make sure no one has plans to break in."

As far as Victoria knew, she was the only criminal with an interest in the records. Was the cult surveying the area? Wouldn't the military base be their likely target? The illusion of this place as her safe haven was shattered. Something was wrong; Natchez wasn't looking her straight in the eyes. Had he spoken to someone?

The lights flickered twice, and they all looked at the ceiling.

He was telling Jackson, "...Still working on the power situation. We just transferred here to be closer to the prison. They've got a few minutes before their shift…"

She jerked back to awareness. The prison. The prison was nearby? She thought of the old asylum on the other edge of the park, and her stomach clenched sickeningly with the knowledge that she was right. Her children had been this close all this time, and she hadn't known it.

The men were chattering to each other, laughing, and she clutched the front desk with white fingers. The lights went out for a moment, leaving only a tunnel of light from the glass main entrance.

"We've already got you on the backup grid. This time of day, sometimes even the backup gets overtaxed—" Chris turned to her just in time to catch her from falling. "Hey, are you okay?"

Caleb rushed up to her side as Chris eased her to the floor.

"Haven't slept," she mumbled over the pounding in her head. Rhianna was in that place, with those men and their guns, and the Occult was coming, coming to do god knew what. It was more important than ever to get her out.

"I shouldn't have mentioned the prison," Chris was chiding himself.

Her eyes gained a blurry lock on his, and a well of hate burned in her like acid. These men had taken her children away, and she knew they were being hurt at this very moment. Chris knew something. "Why do you need so much power?" she asked vaguely.

He shrugged. "The fence and some medical equipment."

"Medical! Medical…" She wiped her face weakly as her vision wavered. Bizarre laughter bubbled out of her lips. "They say a woman can feel when her child is in pain."

Chris's face went slack, and he grabbed her shoulders. "What are you saying?" he demanded.

Her head rolled backwards and she regarded him sideways. "You said you didn't know. You do, don't you? You know what they're doing right now. You talked to Pulaski."

"How do you know that?" he shouted, but it was so distant beyond the rush of blood in her ears.

Caleb looked sick, and he was entreating his friend to stop, but another soldier had pointed a rifle at him when he moved too close.

The world was crashing down around them, but it would be all over soon. Victoria's lips opened of their own accord, "Justice is coming," she said. *Retribution is coming,* she though, but she was too far away now to keep speaking. Someone was dying, they all would die, and she was too late.

Chapter Twenty-Seven

Rhianna awoke numb and cold on her bunk with her neck twisted at a painful angle. She turned her face toward the door with a crack. Her chest heaved, and she groaned silently. Then she realized that she couldn't speak. Whatever had caused the electrical burst that killed the guard also had rendered her mind useless of coherent thought or speech. Wordless fury rose in her. Her brain was sluggish and weak, as if part of it had been destroyed. She soaked up her anger, willing it to make her whole. Then she began to shake, as if with a fever sickness and lost consciousness again.

"How are you, Rhianna?" a quiet voice asked quite some time later.

Rhianna peeled her eyes open, her groan catching in her throat.

"Can you speak?"

She realized the woman wouldn't leave. She forced her heavy tongue to move. First came a grunt, then, "Yeah." Her voice sounded thick and garbled, and she feared it was damaged permanently.

"You broke the machine, Rhianna. Everyone's very angry."

Was she just supposed to let them torture her? She turned her head away.

"A guard died. Would you like to tell me what happened?"

Her face flushed with pleasure, and her thoughts came clearer. She had done it. She had fought back. If she could kill one, she could kill them all and finally escape.

"Rhianna, are you listening to me?"

She forced her stiff body to sit. Her head whirled, but she faced Amber evenly. Very slowly, she managed to say, "They electrocuted me. This isn't right, Amber."

Liebowitz paled, and Rhianna thought she saw a slight tremor in her hands. The woman didn't give up though. "So you don't deny that you attacked the guard somehow?"

What was the point of denying it? She'd do it again in an instant. "I won't let them hurt me anymore. Get me out of here, Amber."

"You know I can't do that."

"What will they do to me next?" she asked in a deadened tone.

Amber gazed on her sadly.

"You do know, don't you?"

"They recommend surgery. They say you're unmanageable."

"What kind of surgery?" Rhianna demanded, feeling sick. "Tell me!"

"Neurosurgery. They're going to alter your brain so that you are less aggressive. I... I shouldn't be telling you this." Amber rubbed her eyes tiredly.

What she was suggesting was no less than a lobotomy. They intended to strip away her will power and personality. Apparently they had decided she was no longer worth studying and was more valuable as a zombie.

Rhianna realized she had seen one of these emptied souls in the hallway before, huddling against the wall with a sickening blank expression. It had disgusted her. The man was unguarded, so close to freedom, but he was locked up by the chains of his own mind.

"They'll have to kill me first," she said decisively.

Amber's eyelids fluttered slightly. Rhianna sensed that she was coming around.

"I'm letting you go, Amber. You know what to do?" Rhianna asked deliberately.

"Yes," the doctor murmured, but Rhianna realized she didn't have the authority to do anything but make suggestions.

The woman turned away, shaking her head quickly before she left.

If Rhianna had the strength, she would have killed Amber too. The woman was completely useless. She couldn't believe she had wasted time cultivating a relationship with her.

She was left alone for hours to recover. Rhianna liked the feeling of the hunger burning her stomach. It helped anchor her to herself. As she regained her faculties, she knew she was irrevocably changed. She wasn't brain-damaged, as she feared; in fact, she had a greater awareness of the world around her. She now knew that somewhere in this building, Amber had protested the surgery suggestion but had been refused. She knew Sam was huddled alone on his bunk, his mind still weak and submerged from the treatment. She knew the terrified administrators were holding a meeting to find out what to do with her. And she knew that they should be very, very afraid.

She reveled in these shadowy sensations until she realized her reach didn't extend beyond the facility's walls. That didn't matter. All she needed to be aware of was near, and her skill would improve with time. Soon she would be free, and she would kill them all.

* * *

Victoria was jerked roughly to her feet as a distant voice threatened to deal with her later. The room rang a cacophony of angry voices and pounding. Her vision cleared, and she saw that a crowd had gathered outside the glass front doors.

"You did this," Chris Natchez accused, but the hate in his eyes couldn't touch her. Frankly, she had no idea what was going on, anyway.

She was dazed, disoriented, and she tried to focus on Caleb's soft whispering. He was saying he was sorry, but what she wanted to know was why the people were shouting.

"Do you think we can't see your lights are on?" a man screamed.

"Winter's coming. We won't sit here and freeze!"

"Goddamn it, why won't anyone help? We know you know why this is happening!"

"I pay my bills, and the power company won't do shit!"

"We don't have any fucking money left," someone growled and fell upon the last man, fighting for his wallet. Both shrieked as the mob surged in to step on his back and the fallen man's hand.

"Let us in and we'll talk," said a more sensible voice, a woman pressing close to the door.

Chris's men jumped to action. Four crammed around the doorway while the others began to shove the heavy bookcases nearer to the front in case a barricade was necessary.

Caleb scrambled onto the reception desk to see clearer.

Jackson looked sick. "I knew they'd come. They'll burn everything for firewood if they get in." He crawled along the floor to hide in the enclosed glass offices.

"Can't we talk to them?" Caleb asked. "They're just scared and cold."

Victoria doubted that was what they were feeling, sickened by the crunching as someone else stepped on the two men. Looking between the soldier's legs, she caught a glimpse of the discarded wallet kicked by someone's feet into the bushes.

She gasped in disbelief as the soldiers raised their rifles. Were they going to shoot through the glass?

"No!" Victoria cried, shoving her way to the entryway. A soldier jabbed her in the shoulder blades with his rifle and she couldn't even feel the pain over her shock. She couldn't let them do this. These were innocent people!

"I'll go out!" she offered. "Let me talk to them."

"We know you've got heat!" someone screamed.

"Door's blocked," one of the military men muttered.

The glass door only opened outward, and the crowd was jammed in close. Could she get them to step back? "We'll help you!" she shouted through the glass. "What do you need?"

As a soldier shoved her away, a woman shouted, "We want our power back! We want this fixed."

"What about jobs? I've gone to every office—"

"We want a goddamned explanation!" a man screamed, his face bright red and livid.

Guiltily, she glanced back at the fluorescent lights now glowing steadily and heard the hum of the furnace turning on.

"If any came up to the base, they'd be shot by now," Chris growled. "We just weren't ready here yet."

"They haven't hurt anyone," she insisted, and he rounded on her.

In a swift movement, he raised his gun and pointed the barrel against her forehead.

Her head swam, but she stifled her cry.

"What the hell are you doing, Chris?" Caleb screamed, jumping down from the desk.

"Stay where you are, Kepler," Natchez ordered. "Don't interfere. We have a situation here."

"The situation's outside!" Caleb exploded. "Am I supposed to believe you're going to shoot us all?"

Chris's aim held steady. Victoria resisted closing her eyes; she had to know what was happening around her.

The other men all stood still, as if waiting for orders. Chris could do anything he wanted, and they wouldn't question him. He'd probably get a commendation, she thought vaguely.

"I know all about you now, Victoria," Chris hissed. "You thought you could fool me, didn't you? You should be in prison! Do you think if I pull this trigger, anyone's going to care?"

"Chris, you're confused," Caleb called out, and two men stepped forward to restrain him.

"I know you called them here. Did you really think it would work?"

She hadn't called anyone here. Didn't he know the people were desperate because their electricity kept shutting off and they had no jobs? They'd probably gone to every government building in town demanding answers and compensation. Chris sounded half-insane, and she knew he wouldn't listen.

"I don't know what you're talking about," she mumbled. The shouting outside sounded as if it were moving inside her head, and Chris's face was flickering dark before her.

"Look at them out there! You're destroying society. I can't let this happen."

Victoria's eyes fluttered to the door behind him, and dimly, she saw a man outside raise an axe.

Fear wrenched her to focus. She stared at Chris in hatred, willing with every ounce of her being for him to hesitate. If she was to be condemned, she should deserve it. She felt something stiffen within him, growing sluggish and weak. She sensed movement and ducked, flattening herself to the floor.

The glass shattered in a sharp explosion that cut her in a thousand places, and the bullets began to fire. She felt herself being dragged away through the crunching shards.

Distantly, she heard the screeching of heavy objects being moved, and she knew the soldiers had blocked off the door with the smaller bookcases. The screaming grew more intense and she felt herself swept up and carried up the stairs.

When she opened her eyes, Caleb was staring at her fearfully. "They locked us up here. The mob didn't leave when they started shooting."

Victoria sat up painfully and shook glass out of her hair. "What about Chris?" she started.

Caleb shook his head. "The axe hit him. He's in bad shape, and we're under arrest."

"What?" Victoria burst out. "That wasn't my fault." She hadn't seen it happen, but she couldn't deny a slight satisfaction. He was ready to murder her in her irrational rage, and he had betrayed them all.

"They saw you duck," he said softly.

That was true, and she'd deliberately made Chris freeze so that she could get away from his gun. No, she hadn't intended to get him killed. She hadn't wanted anyone to get hurt. "Is he still your friend now?" she asked bitterly, before she could stop herself.

Caleb swallowed hard and ignored her. "We have to get out of here."

Victoria sighed. "The front door is the only way out." Here she was, trapped again in this room sixteen years after she had first met Michael Esser. And she had thought Esser was the worst threat she could imagine!

Caleb was staring up at the high window near the ceiling. "Do you think we could fit through that?"

It did have a latch, but she didn't know how far it tipped out. "I could get through, but we're on the second floor!"

He bit his lip. "It's a partial attic, right? Maybe there's an overhang out there we can step onto."

Victoria thought quickly and decided they were better off dead out there than dead inside at the hands of the armed soldiers. They would want revenge for Natchez. Caleb started to move the wooden shelving unit, and then Victoria remembered the newspapers she'd hidden here. "Think we can get these out?" she asked, pointing to a three-foot stack of books and microfiche.

He nodded, and her heart thrilled that he understood the need to save them. "We'll throw them down."

Victoria didn't think the bookcase was steady enough, so she jammed more items on the bottom to counterbalance it. "I'll go first," he offered, carrying a heavy book in case he had to break the glass.

The bookcase wobbled dangerously as he forced the old window, but he did manage to open it.

"We have to take everything we can carry," she said, passing a heavy stack of bound magazines to toss out the window.

"That won't be much," he reminded her as he crammed a cardboard box of history texts out next. The thump followed comfortingly close behind, so she knew they wouldn't have to fall far.

She looked around the room desperately to choose the next items. They couldn't afford to lose anything, even the public records, but she settled on an unbound pile of newspapers to toss up to him.

"That's it," he announced. They already couldn't carry what she'd given him.

She started to climb the shelves and realized she didn't have her cane. Adrenaline had dampened most of her pain. If they made it, she could get another from home.

Was it safe to go home? She hoped Sarintha knew what was happening. The army was occupied, the phone lines glitchy at best, so maybe she was safe from arrest for the time being.

Victoria balanced precariously as she pulled herself through the window and crawled down onto the rough black shingles. Caleb was dropping the papers onto the ground below, the sound easily obscured by the sound of gunfire on the other side of the building. It seemed more soldiers had come to help, and the mob was being slaughtered swiftly.

Victoria crawled to the edge, and hung from the gutter, slicing thick lines in her fingers, and then she dropped down. "Can we get to your truck?" she realized abruptly. The front of the building seemed so far away, and it was surrounded by the army and dwindling rioters.

Caleb hauled a large pile of newspapers from the dry grass and left the lighter box for her. "We're parked at the edge of the lot. There's a lot of people out there though."

Victoria bit her lip as her legs twinged in pain.

Caleb put his pile back down and walked out toward the side road cautiously. "I can see it from here," he reported. "Nobody's nearby, but that doesn't mean they won't see us." He took a deep breath. "Why don't you stay here and guard the books? I'll come around back to get you."

As afraid as she was, she couldn't let him go alone. "No, I'll help. What if they see you?" What if they shot him?

He patted her arm awkwardly. "If that happens, I'll try to keep them busy, and you can run away somewhere else. Damn, your aunt doesn't have a car, does she?"

Victoria felt herself on the verge of tears. They were almost free. He wouldn't leave her now, would he? She grasped his sleeve as he turned to go. "Please come back for me."

He looked at her imploring eyes. "I don't like this either. If you think you can do something to help…"

Oh god, she had to get them past the army out front without being seen. She knew that Caleb may have some protection from the Occult, but she wouldn't bet it would help against well-trained military officers who depended on more conventional methods of detection. She had to try.

"I think I know a way," she found herself saying, "but you have to stay here."

He wavered, but she squeezed his hand reassuringly. He held out his keys and she took them shakily. "You wait here," she said, without even knowing what she intended to do.

Chapter Twenty-Eight

Victoria walked with a tight, measured pace, as if she could somehow make herself smaller by taking smaller steps. Ethan had done this once at the airport. She could do it too.

"Don't see me," she muttered aloud. "You're too busy to see me."

Caleb's truck was now in sight, but the exit was blocked by the military jeeps that had recently arrived. She took a quick glance toward the front door and dropped to her knees.

The shooting had stopped, and now the men were busying themselves with checking over the bodies of the dead. She saw one reach into a woman's pocket, checking her identification and writing her name on a long list. When he finished with the body, he dragged it to a pile near the gutter, where a dark puddle had begun to collect, grayed by the overcast sky. It hadn't rained in weeks.

Victoria gritted her teeth and stood painfully, fixing her eyes on her target. She ran in a wide arc, smacking her hands with relief against the dirty truck door, as if looking for physical reassurance that it was real. She hunched over, hidden from the soldiers, and unlocked the door.

She let out a deep sigh and rubbed her sweaty hands on her pants before grasping the steering wheel with an iron grip. She was in, but how could she drive away unnoticed with a gasoline engine? She watched the soldiers by the door. Several were heading this way to their jeeps. She considered ducking down until they left, but what about Caleb in the back?

If they were inventorying the dead, they intended to take working vehicles, in very short supply, as well. She had to hurry. She closed her eyes. "Just please don't notice me," she thought with all her being as she turned the key.

The truck started with a growl, and she forced her eyes away from the parking lot. She pushed down the accelerator with both shaking feet and drove over the curb and through the bumpy lawn. Caleb ran up to her, carrying the large box. His tanned face was drained of color.

Immediately, she slid aside to let him in to drive, and he piled the heavy periodicals on the seat between them. She tensed every muscle as she listened for sounds of pounding feet and cocking guns, but none followed. They had done it.

Caleb dropped the last stack on her lap as they sped off east to find Sarintha.

* * *

"What is so important, Sarintha?" Lori asked quickly, ducking inside the townhouse. "It was a great risk for me to come here."

Sarintha raised her eyebrows. "Do you think that risk doesn't extend to me?"

"Fine," she answered nervously. "Please hurry. I don't have much time."

"Rhianna and her brother have been incarcerated and are being tortured for information."

Finally, a blunt answer.

"Could you help us secure their release?"

Sarintha was encouraging the Occult's plans? "Do you mean *persuade* them to release them or—"

Sarintha looked down almost shamefully. "I don't believe even extreme persuasion would work. They are too organized."

"I think I could easily convince Wellington to try." He would do it in an instant. It was a full time job to stop his warmongering. "But how would you get the children from us?"

The older woman pursed her lips. "I plan to wait in the area."

"Wellington will probably take them first, even if the situation is chaotic," Lori pointed out.

"That is why I depend on you," Sarintha said sharply.

"I can only try," Lori responded. "I can't control everything."

"Make sure the children aren't hurt. That is what I want most."

Lori couldn't believe Sarintha would even say such a hateful thing to her. The old anger flared in her, but she pushed it aside as counterproductive. Sarintha's eyes held no cruelty. "I expect even he could manage that," Lori said.

"He will, or I will find him," she said simply. "What has he been thinking lately?"

Lori shifted. "He is very difficult. He plans things that are impossible or foolish, and I dissuade him. I tell him we need more people."

"How many are there now?" Sarintha asked, deceptively casually.

Lori's loyalties warred within her. "Three more, who were homeless and weak. There are only six."

"Six!" Sarintha laughed. "What does he think he can do with six?"

You mean six who are weaker than you, Lori thought bitterly. Richard had seemed to think many times that only he and Sarintha were necessary, and he treated the rest of them worse for it. "He wants to destroy the military's electricity."

Sarintha gazed suddenly at the candles around the dim living room. "Really." She almost seemed to approve. She removed a paper map from a drawer. "Show me where." Lori pointed out the targets in the area.

"It isn't a poor idea," Lori agreed, "but the facility uses fusion."

"Fusion," Sarintha breathed. "They would dare use fusion again after what happened before?"

Lori shifted uncomfortably. She sounded just like Richard in that moment. "That's what our information says."

"We can't let that happen. Wellington would go mad if it worked, and god knows how many people might be killed."

Lori had been hoping the man would miscalculate and destroy himself. He had been as unaware as the rest of them how great a reach the first explosion would have.

"Do you understand?" Sarintha gripped her shoulders. "He is only inept now. Ineptitude with actual power could be the end of us."

Lori found herself searching for excuses. "The area is mostly unpopulated."

"Except for the base itself, and the institution, and the government offices."

Surely it wouldn't hurt to damage the government further, but killing the prisoners wasn't worth the risk. Somewhere along the line, Lori had come to regard Rhianna as a sort of savior. If Sarintha wouldn't stop Wellington herself, perhaps the girl could. "No, we can't let it happen. I will try to distract him with this instead."

"Good. Send word when you're ready."

Lori felt a wave of defiance rise in her. "Why haven't you killed Wellington?" she finally asked.

Sarintha's eyes were deep and searching. The fire had drained from them. She was about to say something, but she only shook her head.

Was she afraid? She couldn't imagine Sarintha afraid, no matter how many times the woman had let her down.

Sarintha said coldly, "Where would you go if he were gone?"

Another illusion Lori didn't even know she had was broken. She supposed she had always hoped Sarintha would help her, hide her if necessary. Now the woman was refusing before even being asked.

"I didn't mean that," Sarintha said softly. "You need to look to the future instead of feeling trapped in the present."

She felt chagrined. The woman was right. There was no sense plotting to overthrow Wellington if Lori didn't even know what to do with herself if she won. She put a note of gratefulness into her weak smile. "I should leave soon."

"Stay away from the institution for a few hours. There's a riot nearby."

So that was what motivated Sarintha's sudden change of heart. She felt pressed to act soon, but if it went wrong, her enemies would all be captured. Security would be worse, but it was an opportunity to gather the military all in one area…

Sarintha gave her a last searching look, asking with difficulty, "Is Rhianna in contact with Richard?"

How could the woman not already know, with as much as she saw? The girl must be a blind spot for her. "I believe so," Lori answered and ducked away.

* * *

Amber was overwhelmed with the loss of the security guard. For the first time, the prospect of continuing her job filled her with terror. She had the sensation of being in the middle of an unearthly war, trapped between two forces that would surely crush her.

Deep down, she knew who would win.

Rhianna fascinated her. How could the girl move from such vulnerability to complete self-possession so quickly? Was she exceptionally courageous, or had she been lying all along?

Guilty or not, the girl was very self-assured. Would Amber be able to act the same in her place, or would she just sink into misery? Would she just lie down and die?

One thing was certain: the military was wrong. Neural charges were reserved for the most violent of criminals, and even full-grown men were known to break down into hysteria afterwards. Amber had told them she'd recommended against it, but no one listened to her.

She'd been under the mistaken impression that they'd hired her for her opinion, but now she found she was at their mercy. Now they spoke of surgery, quite probably rendering the girl helpless. Even then, they still wouldn't release Rhianna. What would they do to Amber if she finally just refused to assist?

At any rate, tomorrow was her day off, and whatever happened that day was not her responsibility. She resented being stuck here for now: they said there was some sort of situation in the area, and she had to stay late. She put her head on her desk and waited for the end of the day to come.

* * *

It didn't take long for Rhianna to find Amber Liebowitz's mind. The woman

217

was wallowing in self-pity nearly as much as the prisoners in the place. Rhianna couldn't understand what she had to be upset about. No one had tried to torture her.

Amber was asleep, the most vulnerable state anyone could be in. Rhianna reached out to the warmth that signified her presence and searched her knowledge. Unsurprisingly, the woman knew very little. It was a wonder no one had managed to kill her yet.

Of course it seemed the government had never managed to capture anyone with real Occult talent, so it would explain their lack of preparation. For all their ambitious experiments, they had learned very little. Now they felt the need to dissect Rhianna's brain.

As Rhianna's fingers reached out and tangled themselves into the mist of Amber's pliable mind, Rhianna's skin grew hot and electric with the contact. All she had to do was clench down to damage Amber the same way she tried to damage Rhianna.

Experimentally, she pulled on the connection between them, and bits of Amber's soul flaked away, drawn into Rhianna. Amber's sleep grew deeper as her light flooded into the girl.

She dared for a moment to follow that thread back to its source, lying within the body as it weakened, savoring the power she had over the therapist. Rhianna could even slow Amber's breath to feel her slip away faster.

A note of panic rang in her mind. Somehow this was dangerous, and she should stop. Rhianna jerked herself back into her own body and found that her own breath was coming too shallow. She coughed until her heart grew fast again, doing her best to keep her anchor on Amber.

A lingering darkness remained at the corner of her vision, and she felt an empty ache in her head, as if something were pushing her consciousness down. She reached out to Amber again, on the other side of the complex, unconscious on her desk, and pulled more energy toward herself. White tingling filled the gap in her aura, flashing brightly behind her eyelids, and Rhianna was more than whole again.

Amber's energy charged through her veins, making her breath come faster and sending a thrill in her heart. It filled her mind and expanded it, and soon

Rhianna was satiated, as if some invisible part of her had been starving all along.

She paused for a moment to consider what to do with the doctor. Amber's body didn't seem to want to let go of life. It held on, in a coma, the heart stubbornly still pumping, the brain insisting that the organs continue functioning. Short of killing her in person, there was nothing more Rhianna could do.

She cut the connection between them and left Amber as she was, knowing soon she would be found, and the others would see the future that awaited them.

* * *

"We've listened to you long enough, Lori," Wellington decided.

Lori flinched, knowing her last chance was over. She had presented the information in a careless way, as if she didn't think that entering the prison was a good idea, but Wellington had responded with immediate aggression. They had gathered three new members, and now he couldn't be stopped.

"We'll destroy the entire prison if we must. We don't know what they might be learning about us, and we have to put a stop to it."

"We don't have to kill everyone. It'll just bring more military here." Would he risk killing Rhianna as well?

Wellington turned on her, eyes flashing in reckless fury. "She's one of our own. We have to show them they can't get away with holding her."

He sounded so childish and contradictory that she knew she could no longer debate him rationally. He would probably do the exact opposite of what she suggested, but she must calm him. "We're not certain she's being mistreated," she pointed out.

"I had a vision," he explained tersely. "They're torturing her."

Strange how he hadn't claimed to have a vision until Lori gave him the news that Rhianna was being held prisoner. "Very well," Lori sighed. "Shall we rescue only her or everyone in captivity there?"

Wellington made a rude gesture. "Everyone. It's the perfect chance to increase our numbers."

They could never find the time for that. "And you intend to do this how? There are armed guards."

"We'll destroy the power plant. They'll be in the dark like the rest of us."

"I don't think—"

Wellington turned on her with a sneer. "I don't care what you think."

Lori glared back. "You would care, if you destroyed yourself in the process."

Wellington sighed. "Let's hear it then."

"Give me the map," she snapped. She laid it out neatly on the floor and seized Wellington's sharp compass as if she were to attack him with it. The thought had crossed her mind.

She stabbed a point in the southeast portion of town. "This was Calin Energy Labs." Peering closely at the map, she adjusted the width of the compass to stretch to the edge of the Accident Zone. "The destruction spread out this far, see? About five miles in diameter, but there was nothing built at the southeast edge of the desert." Holding the compass carefully at the same width, she located the military base at the north edge of town and drew a circle from the point. "Do you see the problem?"

Rebecca spat, "You were going to destroy the prison too, you idiot."

Just within the southern half of the circle fell the converted institution, much of Laylen Park, and the records and library building. Archly, Lori said, "I expect that since this power plant is working properly rather than experimental, this area will be completely within ground zero." She was exaggerating, but he wouldn't know better.

His mouth was open, but he was silent for once.

"I submit," she said, "that we rescue the incarcerated first, then destroy the plant later as retaliation." That might give her enough time to dissuade him or to warn someone about evacuating.

"It would be easier with Richard's help," he considered.

So he had a bit of sense after all. "How did you find this out?" he asked suddenly.

"I have contacts, of course."

He seized her arm, pulling her close to his stinking mouth. "Tell me."

She relaxed her muscles and slid from his grip. "No. It's bad enough that I have to do your work for you."

"You stupid bitch." His voice sounded unhinged. "I should kill you."

She stared into his face and let her hate slip through. "Without me, you would be dead, and you know it. If you like, I'll simply stop helping you, and we'll see where you end up."

Rebecca was still on Lori's side for the moment, and she shot him a haughty glare.

Lori waved her hand to show his insignificance. "Orchestrate this yourself, if you think you can accomplish it without my participation."

She knew his desire to succeed would win out over his rather inflated pride.

Chapter Twenty-Nine

"I called for help," Sarintha murmured as soon as Victoria and Caleb entered the door.

"The Occult is going to get Rhianna and Sam out?" Victoria sputtered.

Sarintha pushed her onto the couch. "Be still." She ran her hands over the worst of Victoria's cuts, easing her pain.

"You trust them?" Caleb asked.

"Not at all, but I can't do it alone." It wouldn't be difficult to enter the building or to put out the lights, but leaving was another matter. Wellington would surely plunge the place into bedlam, but panic could be to their advantage.

"I'm not going to let you go by yourself!" Victoria insisted. "What if they see you?"

"I can manage to remain unseen," Sarintha reassured her. "You need to rest."

She shot up. "I can't wait here. What if the army comes? I have to help."

"What do you expect to do?" Sarintha asked evenly.

"If there are two of us, we can find Rhianna and Sam faster. I can wait for them in the park and get them home."

She was still so innocent, even with all she had seen. "We can't come back here, Victoria." The older woman gestured to the black duffel bag she had placed near the door.

Her niece blinked back tears before saying, "All the more reason for me to be already gone."

"Where will you go?" Caleb asked. "How will you get there?"

"I'm not certain," Sarintha said.

"You'll need help," Caleb began confidently.

Sarintha had planned to return to the Accident Zone, but she doubted they could hide there for long. One of Wellington's inept people would eventually make a mistake and be followed by the military.

"I'll drive you," Caleb said quickly. "I'll take you to my old house. It's not even on the map. They won't look there."

Sarintha met his earnest smile and Victoria's look of fierce determination. Even if they escaped unseen, they couldn't hide forever.

"I can't let you go into this, Caleb," Victoria said. "The more of us there are, the more likely we are to be seen. You'll be hurt."

"I think I'm already in it!" He considered a moment. "What if I wait for you in the park, and I'll be ready to drive off."

"The Occult might find you! I don't want you anywhere near there!" Victoria exclaimed. "You don't know what they're capable of."

"There isn't enough room in your truck," Sarintha pointed out practically. Four people might be able to squeeze in but not five.

Caleb's mouth twisted. "I'll put the books in the back. I can't let you go alone."

Sarintha explained, "It's very dangerous. These are the same people who caused the Accident Zone explosion. You would be safest if you waited far away." The boy would only be in the way.

"What about the army?" he asked pointedly.

"I've done my best to diffuse the situation. I'm hoping to convince them to focus their efforts on guarding their own base tonight."

"You can do that?" he sputtered.

She nodded. It was easy enough to plant the suggestion in the mind of a superior officer. "Unfortunately, I expect they will still increase the security at the prison. It will be difficult."

"I don't like it," he said again.

"They won't be patrolling freely. I don't intend to change my mind,"

Sarintha said firmly.

Caleb glanced between them and saw that Victoria agreed. "Well, I'll wait for you up at home, if you insist. It's a slow drive, about twelve miles on the hill road, so let me make you a map."

Sarintha nodded in agreement. She could tell Victoria was fussing about her driving skills, so she volunteered to drive.

"Maybe we should go there with you first, and drop you off," Victoria suggested.

Caleb looked up abruptly. "Wait, how soon are you going to do this?"

Victoria looked to Sarintha to answer.

She sighed. "Tonight, if I know Wellington. He wouldn't wait long."

The two women gazed around the room, preparing their goodbyes.

Caleb was looking at Victoria expectantly.

"We don't have much time," Sarintha said.

Victoria signaled him to wait and rushed upstairs. Sarintha saw her jam the necromancy book into the battered black duffel bag, as if history were repeating itself. She handed it to Caleb. "Put this with the newspapers at your house. It's important."

Sarintha prepared a light bag of clothes for each member of the family, gazing sadly at the children's bedrooms, and they left their home behind.

* * *

The Occult members, along with three useless new recruits, assembled at the eastern edge of Laylen Park, south of the institution. The cover was better there and the escape easier. The northern side of the brick institution building was weakly guarded, but for good reason. It abutted the rocky foothills, at the bottom of a very high cliff, and it had no accessible entrances. Once it had been an asylum, and the people of the city preferred to keep the mentally ill as far away as possible.

Lori's eyes gazed up to rest on the army base above them in the west. High on the hill, tall power lines rose from behind a huge dilapidated building protected by a high barbed-wire fence. It had once been some sort of steel factory, and the military was still in the process of restoring it. Foolish of them to move everyone there before it was finished. Did they really put all their trust in fences?

The prison institution had its own high fence. Normally, it wouldn't be an issue, but the prisoners needed to be able to exit. Closer inspection showed that it was electrified, and the gate was magnetically sealed. A heavy lock would be better protection against the Occult. The military didn't even comprehend what they were dealing with!

She tempered the confidence that rose up within her. It wouldn't be wise to rush to conclusions. Wellington was already chuckling to himself about the soldiers' stupidity.

"I think I should go alone," Lori tried again.

Wellington snapped, "Why do you persist in telling me this?"

The others watched her expectantly.

"It would be considerably easier for only one of us to get in and out." There were many more guards tonight than their earlier reconnaissance had shown.

"You want her for yourself!" Nate accused.

The man was a bit erratic, and even Wellington didn't listen to him. This time, however, Wellington's eyes narrowed.

Lori did her best to ignore them. "I can tell them I'm a doctor and persuade them to let me in. There will be a minimum of difficulty, and if I don't succeed, one of you can make a second attempt."

"I don't trust her," said Nate.

"I don't trust you," Lori retorted. "The odds are bad. You'd have us all shot. Occasionally, strategy is in order."

Rosa, an older and very subdued woman, put in, "She has a point."

"I didn't ask for your opinions," Wellington said.

Emma, the youngest of the new members, hadn't said a word and looked a little taken aback.

"We can take out the power and climb the fence," said Wellington.

Lori frowned skeptically at the electrified barbed wire. It seemed an unnecessary danger to begin a mission with injuries. She had no intention of healing Wellington if he persisted in his foolishness.

"Listen to me," Lori said threateningly. "The girl trusted me. You do as I say, or she won't come with you."

"She'll be happy if anyone lets her out," Nate scoffed.

"That doesn't guarantee she'll come with us."

"We'll make her!"

Lori laughed. Who did he think he was? "This is Richard's daughter. We couldn't make her do anything."

Nate, who never knew Richard, merely scowled.

Wellington murmured, "She's right."

Perhaps he finally remembered how he had frightened Rhianna before.

"But I won't let you go alone," he insisted.

"Fine," Lori growled, "but you'll be silent and inconspicuous. I won't have you jeopardize the plan."

Wellington spat, "My plan, not yours!"

Let him think whatever he chose, but he wouldn't be in control much longer. She kept silent, lest he change his mind about rescuing Rhianna. She merely nodded her head, and he fell silent.

She listened to the guards as they waited.

"Look at that, the whole city's out," said a tenor voice.

"Was that what the riot was about, them getting screwed out of electricity?" The second guard's voice was deeper and anxious.

"Shit, they'd better not complain. You want screwed, you should go to Turkey. When I was there, not a damn thing worked, and the place was full of superstitious lunatics."

"How's this better?" the second joked.

"There's not a damn thing to do around here. Now, I'm just bored instead of freaked out about maybe glowing in the dark."

"You get assigned to all the nuclear shitholes, don't you?" the second said admiringly.

"No kidding. Have me guard something that's worth it for once. You get some accident a few years ago, and everyone goes paranoid and witch-hunty." The first guard laughed.

"You think they've got witches in there?"

"Wouldn't they have tricked their way out by now?" he snorted. "They're just wackos. We should let them all out and get transferred to a tropical island somewhere."

She jumped on the opportunity. *Let them all out. Let them all out.* She could sense the tension in his mind slacken as he grew susceptible to suggestion.

"Guarding naked babes," the second sighed and smacked the button that opened the gate before he drifted off into his own reverie.

Lori led the way as they slipped past the gate. Walking confidently up to the front doors, she waved a blank badge in front of the armed guards. "I'm Lauren Hutchford, and I'm here at the request of..." Quickly, she searched their minds for a name. "Amber Liebowitz, to start the new experiments."

The two men's faces went slack as she sent the sensation of extreme relaxation to them.

"Kindly step aside and let me in," she coaxed and the nearest guard entered a long password onto the security pad.

Then all hell broke loose.

Wellington sent out a jolt of energy that knocked out the video cameras and rendered the alarms silent, and as soon as they all entered, the entire facility went black.

Lori had known there were too many of them to avoid electrical interference, and they refused to listen. Now they would be detected much too quickly, and there was no time for the leisure of rescuing others.

She rushed down the corridor alone. She followed Richard's thread in her mind outward, to find the little girl. Not so little anymore, she reminded herself, and she was so lost in her mind that nearly slammed into the locked door before her.

She fumbled along the wall with her hand until she found a box at waist level. It was a magnetic lock, but the laser had gone dark. Placing both hands on it, she closed her eyes and drew in the energy around her. When her fingers began to tingle and glow slightly, she released it into the machine, and the door clicked quietly.

She didn't stop to hold the heavy steel door open for Wellington, who was crashing noisily behind her.

This was the right way, it had to be, but where were the guards?

She stopped dead as she felt a barrel point at the side of her head. She closed her eyes, reached out with her mind, but this was no bored man waiting for his shift to be over. She only found his name before his self-discipline blocked her out. "Pulaski," she snapped, "let me through." She tried to convince him she knew him.

"Dr. Liebowitz?" he asked Lori in confusion. "I thought you had gone home." He sounded nervous, as if he weren't supposed to be here either.

"Obviously not," she said, and she felt a pang of fear that the person she was impersonating wasn't very aggressive. She began again, softer. "This is an emergency. Let me through before someone shoots me by accident."

He clicked his tongue condescendingly. "I know you hate guns, but we've got to have them. Make more noise or something. I wouldn't want to shoot you." He didn't sound like he would regret it.

After he had relaxed, she found she could make him forget her presence and she touched in his mind a trace of another person she knew: Rhianna.

* * *

When the lights flickered, Rhianna knew they had arrived for her. She had gone willingly to the surgical room, pretending the neural charges had weakened her resistance. They had just begun to strap her down when she made her move. The doctors stared up at the flickering ceiling lights, and she lunged, sending the nearest crashing into the wall. She caught the next by the neck, jabbing her thumb into the hollow of his throat, before ducking from his flailing arms. Then the lights went out.

She could sense their indecision. Their hearts weren't in fighting her, she knew, and that was her advantage. They were simply overworked employees who wanted to go home. Unlike the military guards. They were still outside the door, unmoved from their posts.

She flipped the lock slowly and slipped out the door. The hallway was completely black, lacking even the usual dim emergency lights.

"State your name," demanded the guard on the left, and she placed his position exactly. In a swift movement, she lunged and ducked, and he pulled his trigger.

A groan came from behind her, and her lips curled. The second guard, jumping to action, had been shot by the other in the darkness. She knelt down, seizing his handgun from the holster and aimed for the tumult of emotions that was the first guard.

He sank to the floor and she screamed, "How many of you are there?"

He wouldn't answer. She grabbed his head in her hands, and he shifted beneath her. The blood seeped from his chest onto her shirt, sending a fresh charge of energy through her. He moaned as she pierced his mind, ripping through it to learn the layout of the place. It took little effort. Really, they hired such incompetent people to guard what they considered a chief danger. She brushed her lips along the skin of his forehead and slammed his head against the wall.

The other guard had managed to rise, and his eyes had adjusted to the darkness. She shot him easily in the head with his own gun.

Her feet froze in place. The exit wasn't far, but she knew she had to go back for Sam. Part of her resisted, telling her it was an unnecessary risk. But she couldn't just leave him!

He was hard to find. She suspected he was back in his cell at the hall in the opposite direction of her own, but his mind was in turmoil, as if he were very ill. She let her mind guide her to him in the darkness.

She stood in front of his door now, and it clicked open when she pulled on the handle. It had been unlocked the whole time, but Sam was still lying on the bed, his skin too white and his expression disoriented.

He sat up when he saw her and reached out his hand.

"We're leaving now," she whispered to him. "Get up. They've come to get us!"

"Who? Nanny?" Sam asked, struggling to his feet.

Rhianna's nerves clanged, and the part of her that was Richard demanded that they leave him behind. *He's valuable,* she told herself. *There's no one more valuable here. You see now how rare Occult ability is? We need him.*

He's damaged. Leave him. She decided to ignore Richard for a while.

With each shuffle toward the door, Sam grew steadier.

* * *

Someone was outside the door. Cracking it open, Rhianna peered through, aiming the gun at the silhouette and heard a soft voice cry, "No."

The children stepped outside to see the Occult waiting for them.

"Who are you?" Sam asked weakly as Lori put her hand on his forehead to heal him.

"We know your aunt," Lori said softly, and Rhianna detected a tremor of emotion in her.

"It's time to fight," Wellington said. "We're going to stop these people. We'll make them pay for what they've done."

Sam took a knife from Nate with hesitation, but he held it tightly.

Rhianna regarded Wellington appraisingly and frowned at Nate. "Who is this you've brought for me?" she asked with distaste. "He's worthless. We should leave him behind."

Nate lunged at her, and in a swift motion, she jabbed her gun against his throat.

"Disregard him, please. I have been loyal to you, Aldon," Wellington said, inclining his head.

Rhianna scoffed. "You haven't done a damned thing." She knew it wasn't the proper way to speak to an adult, but she didn't care.

Wellington looked taken aback. "There is a military base near here, on which lies their power plant. We are going now to destroy it."

Rhianna raised an eyebrow. "Good. I may let you live. Prove yourself to me."

Chapter Thirty

Rhianna's eyes were feverishly bright, and her bloody hands were trembling slightly. She carried the gun naturally and spoke to these men as if she were their leader, and it unnerved Sam. Had she called them here? Were these the people she'd met as a child?

He didn't trust the tall man, Wellington, and the younger one who had handed Sam the knife looked practically unhinged. Sam preferred to get away from him as soon as possible.

Rhianna was still speaking and moving out the door as casually as if this were her own home. He tiptoed down the dim corridor at a distance, wondering if she knew how to get out.

His heart was beating so loud he was sure someone could hear, and he screamed when someone seized him from behind. His upper arms were pinned down by a much taller figure. Propelled by adrenaline and fear, he struggled with all his might. The man swore, and Sam heard an ominous click.

Sam gritted his teeth and clenched his fist tightly in his sweaty hand and swung it around behind him, feeling his knife sink into the man's upper thigh.

With a moan, the man fell to his knees, his gun clattering to the floor. Now Sam was close enough to see his face. The dark eyes were full of fury as his hands swiped out at Sam. Sam wrenched his hand back as if to punch him, and pummeled the man in the stomach with his knife, gripping the wet handle so tightly his fingers went numb, until the guard no longer moved.

Sam's eyes focused as he recognized Andrew Pulaski's body. Gasping and shaking as a strange warmth pulsed through him, he turned to find the others.

Rhianna was watching him, unmoving, her gun not even raised, a look of satisfaction on her face. He knew it was not his sister looking at him through her eyes. She'd used him, tested him, against her enemy, and he'd won.

Shouting echoed down the maze of corridors, and they all began to run, the soldiers gaining on them.

Sam felt a manic scream rip from his own throat as he turned to face the guards. He fought in a vicious flurry that blurred in his memory. Each one came and he fought back, growing stronger and more powerful with each blow, words he hadn't really understood before, like retribution and justice, ringing in his head. When they were gone, he turned to challenge the empty corridor, desperate to prove that he couldn't be defeated.

With an enraptured look still on her face, Rhianna pulled him out of the building and then ran off on her own towards the fence.

* * *

Outside in the park, Victoria had convinced Sarintha that they had a better chance of finding the two children if they were to separate. Sarintha had protested of course, but Victoria refused to wait passively this close to rescuing them.

The records office and library in the south, with its shattered windows, drew her attention. She was too far away to tell how much damage it had taken. It hurt her, but she supposed it didn't really matter now: there was no time to rescue more books now, and she would be in hiding after she found her children.

It wasn't long before she saw a slim figure tossing something to the ground and running towards her. She was wearing stained nondescript gray clothes, with her unkempt hair flying behind her, but Victoria knew her from a great distance. "Rhianna!" Victoria shouted joyously and spread her arms wide, ready to hold her close forever.

The girl stood stiffly, and then a hideous change came over her. She seemed taller, more confident, and her eyes narrowed as she looked over Victoria.

"I've been waiting for you," Rhianna said coldly, but it was not Rhianna who said it.

Victoria's world tilted wildly. The past and the present seemed to collide, and she felt she must be dreaming. It wasn't Richard Aldon. It couldn't be, and dear God, what had he done to her daughter? "Leave her alone," she gasped, calling on all the courage she possessed.

"It's a bit too late for that."

Victoria jerked back as if she had been struck. "What do you want with Rhianna? She's just a little girl."

"Little girl? Mother, you haven't been paying attention. I'm far stronger than you."

It was then that she realized Rhianna was not being controlled; she and Richard were intertwined. "Take me instead," she said weakly, knowing in her heart it was too late.

"What would I want with you?" she laughed.

Victoria closed her eyes tightly against tears. "Don't hurt her."

"I don't plan to hurt myself at all. I rather like who I am."

"I came to get you," her mother said softly. "I know they were hurting you in there. I felt it. I'm here to help."

Rhianna's eyes probed hers with deep fascination, and she realized her error. Richard hadn't realized that there was already a connection between mother and daughter, which made Victoria more vulnerable.

Finally, Rhianna threw back her head and laughed. "Help me? You want to help me. How generous. What do you think you can do?"

Victoria clenched her fists and choked back a sob. Everyone had told her she could do nothing, but she wouldn't abandon her child to that demon. "I'll fight you," she swore.

"You're half dead already," she scoffed, and the pain in Victoria's body flared in response.

Rhianna was watching her with cruel amusement. "Oh my, did I *hurt* you,

Mother? Why don't you fight back?"

Victoria's eyes rolled back in her head as the pain was amplified. She had accepted the twinges that always accompanied her, learned to overcome them, but this agony bit deep into her core. She found herself gasping for air as her heart tried to fight its way out of her chest.

Her eyes had gone dark, but she turned to where Rhianna was and implored her silently, *Why are you doing this, my daughter? What have I done to you?*

The only response was a far-off laugh as she was ripped apart.

It swept through her like a wildfire, searing away her thoughts and leaving only an encompassing panic to cling to. Her body grew so heavy she could barely support it, yet it was drifting away even now. Her limbs jerked wildly and she began to fall backwards, floating like a feather, sudden lightness washing away her pain forever.

* * *

Wellington explained where they were going, but Sam hardly listened over the loud pounding of his blood. He was so elated, so free in this cold fall air, that nothing seemed to matter. Finally, Wellington grasped his arm.

"Come with us and fight, and there will be no more hiding. We'll drive them away."

Sam thought of the bloodied men, how easily he had killed them, and how many more he knew there must be. He wouldn't let them take him ever again.

"I'll come," Sam gasped.

The woman, Lori, looked vaguely sick, and he wondered what could possibly be wrong with her. Didn't she know they couldn't be defeated?

"Where's Rhianna?" Wellington asked.

Lori blinked, and Sam could tell she knew. "Go find her, Sam. We'll wait." Wellington gave her a sharp look.

"I'll go too," she offered hoarsely, but she rushed off in a different direction.

* * *

Sarintha looked much older than Sam remembered her. Her forehead was creased, and her eyes were swollen and bloodshot as if she hadn't slept in a long time. Suddenly she seemed very fragile and small.

"Hello," he said to her, coming to a halt. Somehow he couldn't accept her presence among all this bloodshed. Why was she standing there doing nothing?

"Come home with me and forget this," Sarintha begged.

"Come home?" Sam laughed hoarsely. "You want me to come home after what I've been through?"

"We'll go somewhere safe. I'll make sure they don't take you again."

"You want me to hide?" he screamed. "You'd dare to ask me to hide again?"

"I'll protect you—"

How could someone so pathetic protect him? She looked weak just standing there. "Fine job you've done so far."

"Come with me, and we can talk. There's still time left."

"I'm going to fight. I won't let you stop us, Sarintha." The fury rose up in Sam, coiling around his mind. Torture had stripped away any lingering tenderness that would have once weakened him. All he knew was that this woman had done a great injustice to him, and he wouldn't let her do it again.

"There are other ways," Sarintha began futilely.

"I tried living by your ways. I tried to make you proud, and what did it get me? I've had enough."

"I tried—" she started weakly.

"You didn't come to get me! They did. They're the ones who care about me." The words became true as they left his mouth. He finally had somewhere to go.

"Sam, listen."

"I'm through listening!"

"I understand how you feel." She was trying to send him soothing feelings, but he forced them away.

"Oh, you do?" His voice cracked. "Did you feel the pain too when they shocked me? Maybe you'd like to feel it now."

She seemed to reach deep within herself. "This was Rhianna's fault, not yours. I know that now."

"Rhianna!" he laughed. "You raised her, didn't you? Wouldn't it be your fault then?"

"I didn't know."

That was inexcusable. "There are many things you don't know, and even more you aren't willing to do. Rhianna is at least willing to fight." And if he chose to leave her later, now he had the strength to do it.

"I called them here," she said between clenched teeth. "It was my idea."

"But I don't see you lifting a finger!" he screamed, waving his knife. "You didn't even come inside. Do you know how many people I had to kill to get out?"

She grew even paler, so fragile he couldn't believe he ever believed in her.

"Do you?" He clenched her wrist with his bloodied hand. "I killed six men. Every one of them would have shot me without a second thought. That was six chances to die that I won against. I won't let them try again. *I* killed Pulaski, when *you* let him take us away!"

Sarintha's eyes had unfocused; she seemed not to recognize him.

He shook her until she looked at him. "Listen to me," he said, a strange rasping in his throat. "You are with us or against us."

"You don't know the truth," she tried.

"You're blind. You lie, and you're blind."

"I love you, Sam." Her face cracked with grief.

Something burned in his heart, and he hated her for it. How dare she, after she abandoned him. How dare she try to use him again, and how dare he let himself feel sympathy right now? "I shouldn't have even given you a second chance." He threw her to the ground and heard the snapping of bone. Sarintha did not move.

"You won't even fight me! You're completely worthless!"

Her eyes penetrated his, and some of the growing weakness within her slipped into his body. She was trying to tell him something, something vitally important to her and no doubt irrelevant to himself. He waved it away like smoke.

He knew she wouldn't beg.

His hands closed around her shoulders violently and he sent it to her: hundreds of volts of searing pain, confusion, and loss of identity, and the immeasurable hours spent hating and crying, too weak to even die. And she had stood by and let it happen, uncaring until it was Rhianna's turn.

She didn't even flinch.

He railed against her in his fury, incoherent statements about destiny and power and vendetta that she seemed to understand from within. When that sad compassion refused to crack from her face, it split something within him, and he jammed the knife into her gut with a primal scream until the tumult in his disordered mind was silenced.

She seeped into him like water into thirsty soil, and he was filled with her dreams and nightmares and no—he must be rid of her—and he fought until he was too tired, and then he *saw*.

He saw her in his entirety, the many-layered threads of life within her that she had taken before, and he felt her inhuman grief cut through him and knock him to the ground.

All was lost; all was lost.

And he felt her say, "I will fight, then," and he pulled himself back up and went to Rhianna, as someone more than Sam, more than human.

* * *

There was no time to wait. Rhianna found herself propelled to the western edge of the park, her eyes locked upward.

The military base lay high in the hills, resting upon a scarred section that had long ago been blasted flat into a plateau to make way for progress. Once there had been factories here, positioned imposingly above the city to spare it from their noxious smoke.

She knew that she had been here before, had done this same thing before, but her memories were vague. Then she recalled the name Olivia and smiled.

She sensed hundreds of soldiers, working or dreaming safe behind their tall electric fence in their high stronghold. They had no idea what was about to hit them.

Impatiently, she sent a last summons to the others and began.

Rhianna locked her mind around the throbbing source of power high above her, bidding it to throb in time with her. It was enormous, the largest source of energy she had ever encountered, and she revered it a moment for what it was, before it would become hers.

Then swiftly, she sliced at it with her mind, jerking her head roughly as she destabilized the reaction and overloaded every fragile computer in the complex.

It burst apart from its confinement, shining like the sun, and exploding even brighter. She expanded with it, her aura lighting up the night and touching a thousand places at once. It was so beautiful, so overpowering, that she hated to see it fade.

She felt the sensation of water pouring over her, passing through her, as hundreds of shattered souls fled into her welcoming body. She sank to the shaking ground in her bliss, daring the fire to come closer, to engulf her, and she was much too close, but she would be safe. Nothing would hurt her again.

* * *

Sam didn't remember what he thought as he helped raze the building. He only felt its heat blister his fingertips and scar its memory into his mind. Those men, their lives were his, little as they were and all blurred together and indistinct.

And Rhianna saw through him, and he saw back, and they knew each other completely in that moment, and her ugliness was open to him, bare and bloody and impossibly deep, and he found where his hate belonged.

God, he was wrong, so wrong: the blood of the only one who loved him on his hands and their mother's on hers. She had killed Victoria just for a laugh, to finally sever the connection that had remained open too long, and not a shred of the woman remained undevoured. Rhianna was no longer Rhianna, and Sam was no longer Sam.

And Sam did not know what he was.

238

Rhianna was calling to him, bidding him to follow her, and his heart was frozen in his chest, and he found he could not even hate her, lest he hate himself. She called again, and his feet were leaden, and he was rooted here, part of his soul etched in these flames forever.

She stood there, and he walked away.

CPSIA information can be obtained
at www.ICGtesting.com
Printed in the USA
BVHW041328160522
637117BV00005B/49